MEGIDDO'S RIDGE

Borgo Press Books by S. Fowler Wright

Arresting Delia: An Inspector Cleveland Classic Crime Novel
The Attic Murder: An Inspector Combridge & Mr. Jellipot Classic Crime Novel
The Bell Street Murders: An Inspector Combridge & Mr. Jellipot Classic Crime Novel
Beyond the Rim: A Lost Race Fantasy
Black Widow: A Classic Crime Novel
The British Colonies: No Surrender to Nazi Germany!
The Capone Caper: Mr. Jellipot vs. the King of Crime: A Classic Crime Novel
Crime & Co.: An Inspector Cleveland Classic Crime Novel
Dawn: A Novel of Global Warming
Dead by Saturday: An Inspector Cleveland Classic Crime Novel
Dream; or, The Simian Maid: A Fantasy of Prehistory (Marguerite Cranleigh #1)
Elfwin: An Historical Novel of Anglo-Saxon Times
The End of the Mildew Gang: An Inspector Cauldron Classic Crime Novel (Mildew Gang
    #3)
Four Callers in Razor Street: An Inspector Combridge & Mr. Jellipot Classic Crime Novel
Four Days' War: The Alternate World War II, Book Two
The Hanging of Constance Hillier: An Inspector Cleveland Classic Crime Novel
The Hidden Tribe: A Lost Race Fantasy
The Jordans Murder: An Inspector Combridge & Mr. Jellipot Classic Crime Novel
The King Against Anne Bickerton: A Classic Crime Novel
Megiddo's Ridge: The Alternate World War II, Book Three
The Mildew Gang: An Inspector Cauldron Classic Crime Novel (Mildew Gang #1)
Murder in Bethnal Square: An Inspector Combridge & Mr. Jellipot Classic Crime Novel
The Police and the Public: Some Thoughts on the British System of Justice
Post-Mortem Evidence: An Inspector Combridge & Mr. Jellipot Classic Crime Novel
Prelude in Prague: The Alternate World War II, Book One
The Return of the Mildew Gang: An Inspector Cauldron Classic Crime Novel (Mildew
    Gang #2)
The Rissole Mystery: An Inspector Combridge & Mr. Jellipot Classic Crime Novel
The Screaming Lake: A Lost Race Fantasy
The Secret of the Screen: An Inspector Combridge & Mr. Jellipot Classic Crime Novel
The Song of Songs and Other Poems
Spiders' War: A Novel of the Far Future (Marguerite Cranleigh #3)
Three Witnesses: A Classic Crime Novel
Too Much for Mr. Jellipot: An Inspector Combridge & Mr. Jellipot Classic Crime Novel
The Vengeance of Gwa: A Fantasy of Prehistory (Marguerite Cranleigh #2)
Was Murder Done? A Classic Crime Novel
Who Murdered Reynard? A Classic Crime Novel
The Wills of Jane Kanwhistle: An Inspector Combridge & Mr. Jellipot Classic Crime Novel
With Cause Enough?: An Inspector Combridge & Mr. Jellipot Classic Crime Novel

MEGIDDO'S RIDGE

THE ALTERNATE WORLD WAR II

Book Three

by

S. FOWLER WRIGHT

THE BORGO PRESS

An Imprint of Wildside Press LLC

MMIX

CHAPTER I.

IT was at the beginning of February 1938 that the bolt of war fell suddenly from the skies on an astounded, bewildered world—a world that had talked too glibly, or turned aside too obstinately from that in which, even while it cleared the stage, it had never really believed. It had been a nightmare too dreadful for the reality of the cheerful, trivial day, a thing too incredibly foolish for men to do, too horrible for Deity to permit. If it should threaten too close a cloud, sensible men had a line of defence which could never fail. They would refuse to fight; and the warmongers would find themselves foolishly regarding one another in a world too peaceful of disposition, too sane of mind, to allow itself to be blown to bits or choked with poisonous gas. It broke first by night over the ancient city of Prague, which a German air force had reduced to burning ruin when morning came.

That was on the night of Friday, February 4. The next day the chancelleries of Europe were confronted by the fact that Czechoslovakia had ceased to exist. Poland and Hungary had received those cuts from an ample joint by the promise of which their friendly neutrality had been bought, and Germany had absorbed the major extent of a short-lived State.

Had the Berlin Government felt assurance during the following hours that Europe would accept the event with the passivity of its reaction to the Austrian coup of a few months before, it is possible that the war which no mortal wisdom of other lands could permanently avert would have been delayed for another year; for the plans of the High Command were not yet fully matured, and they would have preferred that Europe should wait, as a bullock waits the butcher's convenient time. They would have preferred to avoid each of the displays of truculence by which Germany had disturbed a half-frightened, half-resentful Europe during the three previous years; but they had been overridden by the urgency of politicians who had felt it necessary to placate a population reduced to ill-fed servitude in anticipation of national ascendancy by providing morsels of the expected meal.

But it found that the world stirred ominously, moved both by apprehension of what might be its own fate on another day and hatred of an act abhorrent to all decent and kindly minds; it stirred in what might soon become a menace to those whom it was not yet wholly tutored to call its lords, and if it were inclining to present war—well, it should not be first to begin! Confident in her secret alliance with the atheistic tyranny of Russia—so different in its outer garb, so similar in its inward soul—Germany would be instant to separate or reduce the total of her potential foes.

With this object, as the afternoon waned she had sent an ultimatum to the British Government requiring an instant declaration of neutrality against the possibility of the annexation of Czechoslovakia being made the occasion for continental war, and the temporary surrender of Gibraltar and the control of the Suez Canal as guarantees that that neutrality would be observed.

It is not a necessary conclusion that, had that assurance of neutrality been received, with the surrender of the guarantees which had been required, the Russo-German alliance would then have fallen upon the nations of Central and Southern Europe, as they actually did on the next day.

Had London yielded now, it is possible that Paris would have received a similar ultimatum; possible that, had she yielded in turn, as she might then have felt compulsion to do, Germany might have been content, for the time, to consolidate her mid-European power; and probable that it would have been done without disclosing the secret alliance that she had formed, which she might have preferred not to invoke until her own strength had increased in that comparison also.

But with a caution born of the experience of the last war, she would have preferred that the British Empire should be paralysed into passive acquiescence rather than roused to active hostility, while the fetters of political and economic servitude would have been fastened upon a prostrate Europe at whatever moment she might feel opportune to make her intention plain. After that subjugation had been completed, it would have been needless to look beyond her own professions of political moralities and expediencies to learn what the fate of England would next have been.

It is even likely that she would have preferred at this time to have made alliance with one or other of the great maritime powers—either England or the United States—by offering them a share in the spoils of a plundered world, had she not anticipated rebuff, and known also that the isolationist policy of the United States would have ensured the rejection of any offered alliance, even apart from any issue of morality, or of the motives or merits of the proposals it might receive.

There is, at least, little doubt that the abrupt ultimatum was delivered in confident anticipation that the British Cabinet would lack courage to face the prospect of instant and single war. To the German mind, always curiously obtuse in appreciation of values differing from its own, the futile chatter of English pacifists in a country where conscription was not imposed, though all Europe had armed for the coming war, was conclusive evidence of a national decadence which, while its existence could not be denied by anyone who looked with impartial eyes, might yet be consistent with the survival of a sound and most stubborn core. The sword had slipped from a slackened hand, and its rust was easy to see. But who could say how deeply it had eaten into the blade, or how far it had dulled its edge?

Actually, though that monstrous ultimatum was received by some members of the British Cabinet with mingled feelings of incredulity, irresolution, and fear, which were of less fortitude than the occasion required, the possibility of accepting it, when its details had been announced, was not even discussed. It would have been a betrayal beyond their power, as it would have been beyond the possibilities of their own minds. Had they issued such orders, it is not reasonable to suppose that they would have been obeyed, either at Gibraltar or Suez, for the ultimate loyalty of those who command her garrisons abroad is due to England, and to them only so far as they remain loyal to her.

When the next morning came, the central city of London and much of its eastern end was a sea of flame, which the changing wind and heavy rains of the next day would be only partially able to check; while her gallant outnumbered air forces were driven back or reduced to intermittent sporadic efforts to defend the vital nerve centres and arteries of a land which had failed to make them equal to meet their foes.

France, delayed through the fateful midnight hours through desire to have Russian backing for what she did, learnt in the time that preceded the dreadful dawn that the Russian Air Force had indeed taken the skies, but were approaching her own frontiers to scourge her with hostile bombs. And in the following days, upon Southern Europe and Southern Asia, like a winter tempest out of the north, the swift tide of invasion came. In the protective arming of other lands there was nothing which could hold back the gathered might of these two nations, which, during the three previous years, had been solely organized and intended for war.

CHAPTER II.

IT was on the evening of February 11, 1938, seven days after the destruction of Prague, that Prince Alexander Nicholas von Teufel, Commander of the combined Russo-German air forces, sat in his private room in the Lustgarten Palace, dining with Field Marshal Ernst von Hoffmann, the four-days' Commander in Chief of the German Armies, who had gained that exalted position by the nomination of Prince von Teufel, after the Air Marshal had shot the previous holder of that office with his own hand, as part of a process of assassinations, not previously unfamiliar in Nazi records, by which he had made himself the centre of absolute and most ruthless power.

Now they met to discuss the military position of a world war which von Teufel felt no doubt that he could direct to his own ends, being no less than the domination of a prostrate world. During the last three days he had surrounded himself with those who had been his carefully chosen associates in the Air Ministry previously—men who were loyal to him, unscrupulous, and now intoxicated by his success, both against outer foes and those at home who would have disputed his power; and in that space of days he had become recognized as the *de facto* head of a Germany well accustomed in recent years to the unbridled violences of those who rule her.

It was only a few hours before that he had given orders for the assassination of certain Russian statesmen who might otherwise show the will and ability to oppose his ascendancy in that country, which could be based there on no better right than that of a Russian grandfather, and the fact that he had been chosen by the two governments which he had overthrown for the command of the combined air forces in the war by which they had conspired to enslave mankind.

"I will not vex my mind," he had said, "to decide how or by what hand they shall die. I have no time for such details now. Let me hear of it next as a thing done."

Now he rose and strolled over to a large-scale map of the world which hung across the length of the one side of the room that was not broken either by window or door. He laid a finger upon the British Isles, as he said: "If they do not yield, you must make an end.

You can have two days, but no more. We have too much on hand to be hindered longer by them." But he said this in an almost casual tone, and his eyes settled more seriously upon the Mediterranean and the line of the North African coast. "It is here," he said, "that they will make head to resist our power."

The decision to abandon Southern Europe on the fourth day of the war—which the President of the United States had made an emphatic condition of entering the arena of conflict in the Eastern Hemisphere—was not reached without emphatic protests from among the heterogeneous convention of statesmen, ambassadors, and military experts who had hurriedly assembled in Washington, by land and water and air, with such credentials as the occasion allowed, to represent the opinions of the assaulted world; and it has been the subject of much subsequent controversy.

It entailed the surrender of vast resources, which fell into von Teufel's hands without the wastage of war, and it abandoned large populations to a servitude which he would use to recruit his power.

But it is at least probable that it abandoned nothing which could have been held for more than a space of days, and it gave an aspect of voluntary strategy to what might otherwise have been a demoralizing, compelled retreat.

It also saved immense quantities of war material and naval and aerial fleets which must have been destroyed or surrendered in the course of a stubbornly prolonged resistance, but which were now transferred to the North African coast by a decision which operated before von Teufel's armies could arrive in sufficient force, either by land or air, to restrain them effectually.

Like a migration of locusts, the remaining aeroplanes, civil and military, of the Christian lands darkened the winter blue of the Mediterranean skies. With ten thousand deep-wallowing holds, the Mediterranean shipping left the harbours of Europe empty as it fled to its meagre North African refuges, or crowded like flocks of stampeded sheep through the narrow Gibraltar straits, or the congestion of a Canal in which all the traffic was now moving in the same direction.

It was a disposition which gave a water frontier, deep and wide, to the Christian powers, and though the dangers of air remained, it must suffice to hold off the land attack of the vast Russo-German armies, so long as its navies remained supreme, and the two gates of the inland sea could be held secure.

It was the position that the murdered Field Marshal Wertner had foretold, and it was one that von Teufel did not fail to recognize as formidable, though he did not doubt that he would be equal to overcome it.

He ordered that Gibraltar should be attacked by aerial fleets of overwhelming strength, armed with all the chemistry of hell, and that an army should be assembled in Southern Spain in readiness to be transported across the straits. He ordered that the naval harbour of Malta should be subjected to attacks of a like intensity. But it was to the Eastern Mediterranean that he looked as the point where he must strike the decisive blow which would leave him at the head of a prostrate world. Here was the gate of Africa. Here, equally, was the gate of Europe and Asia, if his enemies should become of a disposition and strength to endeavour to break it through.

The naval harbour of Alexandria, the narrow isthmus of Suez, the great island air base of Cyprus, which England owned, and which had been better prepared for this day of fate than either he or most of her own people knew—he looked at them, and saw that he had only to win them now to control the world. It would enable him to overrun Africa before sufficient armies could be assembled for its defence. He calculated that the subjection of Asia was no less than the certainty of an early day.

The New World might think itself to lie apart and secure, but how long would it maintain an unbroken front against the full strength of the Old? Its fate would be sure and soon. It would be struck from the north. Struck both east and west when the time should come, where the Arctic seas are not broad. But that time could wait. Now he had no more to do than to destroy those keys that the English held. Gibraltar, Malta, Cyprus, Alexandria, the Suez Canal—keys that must be easy to wrest from relaxing hands while the life of England itself ebbed out from its mortal wounds. And meanwhile he would hasten to advance the strength of his armies towards the fertile Syrian plains, that no moment would be lost before Africa should be overrun. "Frightfulness and speed" must be the order for its subjection now that America had come into the war.

The War Council at Washington saw the problem in the same light, and that the same area might soon become the final vortex of war. Senator Ramsden, asking the President in a moment of relaxation what this fool talk about Armageddon meant, and whether there were such a place on the map, and being shown the ridge from which Mount Carmel rises to front the sea, remarked that the Hebrew prophet must have been a wise old bird, and mightn't prove to be so far wrong after all.

CHAPTER III.

PRINCE VON TEUFEL returned to the table, the Field Marshal following. They cracked nuts, which they ate with the aspect of men whose leisure was too assured to be disturbed by any outer affairs. Their thoughts, it is true, were upon other things than the kernels they ate, but it is true also that, among the scores of thousands of those who held posts of command or responsibility in the war which had suddenly spread over half a world at a pace which must be counted in minutes rather than weeks, Prince von Teufel, who had already seized a wider control than was held by any other on either side, may have been the one who was least conscious of pressure upon his time.

This came, in part, from the typically meticulous German care with which this monstrous assault upon civilization had been planned in detail before the first bomber rose to the midnight skies—a preparation gigantic in its original impetus, which must, however, decrease as its orderly process must become confused with the passing days; and, in part, because not having been accidentally thrust into, or suddenly seized, an unanticipated power, but having schemed for it from the first day on which the organization of the German air forces had been placed in his hands, he had his own plans as matured as were those of the High Command which was now subordinate to his ruthless will.

Now he said: "There is one point on which we must be assured beyond reach of doubt. We are agreed that the haste with which America has entered the war, which our High Command did not expect, renders it vital for us to possess the North African coast at the first moment we may, lest it become a ground on which the strength of the New World will be arrayed to augment our foes.

"That is what, if they be soundly advised, they will be active to try, and we must be the more diligent to prevent. But we must also look to the chance that their eyes will be drawn aside to the British Isles, thinking that they may be the better base from which to launch their attack."

Field Marshal von Hoffmann looked a doubt that he was slower to speak, and Prince von Teufel continued with an overbearing brusqueness which explained the Field Marshal's hesitation, though his prudence may have been falsely based: "Do you think me a fool?

Even so, it is a thing to be said. I must have your thoughts, if you are to be useful to me."

The Field Marshal, who had seen his predecessor assassinated by von Teufel's hand less than a week before, showed no surprise or any sign of offence at the manner of this address. He answered equably, as though the loss of von Teufel's temper assisted the stability of his own: "I thought it unlikely that such a choice would be made, but there may be reasons I have not weighed."

"Did I say it was not? But a small doubt is not to be left unprobed. We must be most certain in all we do."

"You would wish the greater energy to be shown in subduing the British Isles, if they would otherwise be used as a base for the landing of American troops?"

"So I might. Or I might wish to lure them to that which would be their fall. It is the fact I must have."

Field-Marshal von Hoffmann considered the military problem proposed, which he saw to involve others of air and sea. He said: "It is surely Africa they should use. Their advisers will tell them that. You may count it sure. But we know what the politicians are likely to be. They are dogs that the tail will wag, for those lands have no men who rule with better right than the counting of heads. They may say that England must be sustained, that her kindred shall not lose heart in their distant lands."

"It is not that which I wish to hear. I said we must know."

The Field Marshal might have replied that it was a matter for the Intelligence Service, and that he would see that it had their attention. Strictly, it was not his matter either to make inquiry or to give orders thereon. But if Prince von Teufel chose to make him the instrument of what, in all but name, had become an absolute power, should it be his part to object? Besides, it happened that he knew a very apposite fact, and one which would entail a responsibility of decision which he would be pleased for von Teufel to take, rather than that it should be his.

"There is one man," he said, "who might be trusted to find out what you wish to know. That is, if he should be trusted at all."

"He is a spy whom there has been occasion to doubt?"

"Apparently not. He has just brought news of the situation of the secret aerodrome which we desired to locate. It is in Wales in the Brecon Hills."

"Still, if you have had a doubt, he should die. Spies are venal men, most often selling secrets to either side. You should not doubt them a second time."

"I will remember that. But this is not an ordinary spy, or a common doubt. You may remember the name of Zweiss—Adolph Zweiss. He was a flying ace in the last war. He did feats on the Italian front hard to believe, the aeroplanes being what they then were."

"I have heard his name. What of him?"

"He disappeared shortly after the end of the war. It was supposed he was dead. Two weeks ago a man was caught who would have been shot for an English spy, as, indeed, he did not deny that he was. But he said that he was Zweiss. He said that he had abandoned his identity nearly twenty years before, and joined the British Intelligence Service, which he had loyally served for that time, but solely that he might be ready to give us exceptional help in war—for which he had waited in assurance that it would come."

"But he was not fully believed?"

"His identity appeared to be proved, even to body-marks such as a mole which he could not fake."

"Then where is the doubt?"

"He was spying for England when he was caught, having penetrated one of our secret aerodromes in the Bavarian hills in a very bold—I might say a most impudent—manner. He was in the uniform of a German soldier, whom he had actually killed to obtain the disguise."

"That must have been hard to explain."

"He said that it had been necessary, so that he should not lose the confidence of his English employers, and all his eighteen years of preparation be thrown away just as war was about to come. He asked what was the life of one German soldier beside the service which he could render while he was in the British Intelligence Service, and unsuspect."

Prince von Teufel considered this. It was a ruthless argument such as would have been sufficient to himself in a like case. He did not think the worse of Adolph Zweiss for that, nor was he less disposed to believe his tale. He asked: "You have trusted him since, and he has not failed?"

"It was not I. It is a tale I have heard no more than a few hours ago. He was allowed to fly from Nürnberg in the uniform of a German private, taking with him an English girl of good family, who was anxious to escape rather than be interned here. She was nothing to us, and his taking her was to give confidence to those in England who must not suspect, or his use is done. They cannot have had a doubt, for they let him return, with this information which we had required him to get."

"You are satisfied that it is not false?"

·"Yes. It is corroborated by what I have learnt from another source."

"I will see this man for myself. Have him sent here in an hour's time. I shall be occupied until then."

Field Marshal von Hoffmann took a plain hint, and left at once to attend to this and other, as he may have thought, more important affairs.

The Prince said to himself: "If I should be assured, I must trust him much. But if there be a doubt, though it be of no more than a grain's weight, he shall surely die. For I must be certain in what I do."

He passed into an adjoining room, where he dictated to two secretaries for half an hour, thus duplicating the orders he issued, that there might be no error or alteration in what he said, and it would be at their peril that the copies should not be alike. He received some telephone reports, which were restricted by his command to the bare outlines of the movements that shook the world. He rested for a short time, according to the resolution he had made that the pace at which war swept over the earth like a forest fire should not confuse the stability of his own mind. Then he went back into the room to which he had ordered that Adolph Zweiss should be brought, and found that he was waiting there in the company of an officer of the Intelligence Service, who saluted and introduced himself as Major Luther.

CHAPTER IV.

PRINCE VON TEUFEL looked at the man who said he was Adolph Zweiss, and the man looked back at him as an equal might, but as he had not supposed that a spy would.

Adolph Zweiss saw a man whose face was familiar from many prints. He saw black, straight, rather coarse hair brushed back from a white bony forehead of no great dignity, over black eyes that were normally those of a dreamer rather than of a man of active affairs, but which would become piercingly intelligent and alert when his mind was outwardly roused, or alive with a dreadful menace when anger stirred. The nose was straight, short, thick. The thin-lipped mouth was hard and set in repose, and the jaw heavy in cruel lines. But these details were merged in a personality strangely magnetic, and in a coldly intense, dominating manner under the influence of which few could come without being moved to devoted service, or repelled to a sharp aversion, which would be commonly allied to a great fear.

If it were true, as was to be said in the following days, that he was possessed by the archenemy of mankind, then it must be allowed that the devil could give him great, if sinister, dreams, and the driving force of a most ruthless and implacable will.

The man upon whom von Teufel looked was of a very different, though hardly opposite, type. He had a lean, tired face that had been deeply lined by stress of living, either through mental or physical strains. He was rather tall, with a spare, muscular frame, and of such an aspect that neither his nationality nor his age would have been simple to guess. When he spoke, his German was idiomatic, and its accent that of the Prussia in which Adolph Zweiss had been born. He spoke English with equal ease.

The Prince asked with abruptness: "You are Adolph Zweiss?"

"It is a name which I once bore, but is best unsaid. Every time it is used it is an added danger to me."

"Are you so easily scared, being in the occupation that you profess?"

"So it is. All my work, and the preparation of half a life, may be spoiled by this chatter of who I am."

"You would not expect to be trusted here without assurance of who you are?"

"It should have been asked once, and no more."

"But your chiefs in England must suppose that you have some status or footing here."

"They do not know what it is. They leave that to me. We are not trained to talk or explain, but to be frugal of words."

The Prince made no comment on this. He asked, in the same abrupt way as before: "Are you armed?"

"No."

The Prince opened a drawer at his side, by which action an automatic was near his hand. He said: "You are discreet." He turned to Major Luther: "You may go. But wait near. It may be that I shall need you again."

When he had left the room, Prince von Teufel asked: "You have the confidence of your English employers? You are not doubted by them?"

"So I have reason to think. Otherwise they had not released me and sent me here."

"With what mission have you come back?"

"By your leave, it is a matter of which it would not be prudent to speak."

Prince von Teufel stared in an angry surprise. "You will be good enough," he said, "to reply in another way."

Adolph Zweiss, if he should be called by that name, appeared undisturbed by the anger that he had roused. "It is a question," he replied calmly, "of whether I am to return there."

"You will explain that."

"It is simple enough. If I am to go back, and in such a way that I can be of further avail to Germany and to you, I must be able to show that I have done that for which I was sent, which, if I say what it is, I suppose that I shall not do. But if I am to remain here, it is a matter which I may wisely betray."

"You may tell it to me. None can overhear, or will be informed, unless by my own will."

"Pardon me, but I think it were better not."

"That is for me to judge."

"When I had said what it is, it would be too late."

"Do you set your judgment against my own, and my stated will?"

"No. For if you had the same knowledge, I am sure that your judgment would be the same."

"Do you know that if you fail to give satisfaction to me you may be near to a quick death?"

"I believe that. But you will see that I am not taking the course which would be chosen by one of a false mind. I could have told you any one of a dozen lies as to what I have been ordered to do. In fact, I trust your judgment as I should be unlikely to dare if I spoke to a lesser man."

He watched the Prince as he said this with an anxiety which he must not show. Was he a man, as so many are, on whom flattery would work in a subtle way, even though it might have no instant effect? Whether his heart were with Germany or her foes, he knew his argument to be sound, but it was not such as one accustomed to be obeyed would be likely to accept with a good will.

Now it was hard to judge the impression that he had made, for von Teufel ignored his reply, turning the subject aside with the abruptness that he had used before. He asked: "By what name are you called now?"

"Richard Steele."

"Very well. We will call you that. Are you sure that the service which you can render to us is greater than that with which you will serve our foes?"

"How can I answer that, till I know what you require? If it be less, so I will say, and explain all. Except I can be of a great use, I have no desire to go to England again. It is a hazard greatly increased by the chatter here, which their spies may learn."

"Apart from that, you would feel secure?"

"Yes, I should."

"Who do you suppose will have the last success in this war?"

"Am I to say what I think, or that which all of our race are disposed to persuade themselves?"

"You must speak your thoughts, or you insult me by what you say."

"I think the war must be quickly won, or it will become harder to do. Our enemies will become stronger should we delay. But I do not know all the weapons that you may have."

"It is soundly thought. Is the resistance of Britain done? Is her strength spent?"

"She is on her knees, but she has as yet no will to submit."

"So I believe it to be. Can you penetrate to the counsels of those who are in control, and to the plans of their allies, of which they must be largely informed?"

"Yes. It is likely that I could do that."

"Will you find for me whether America will use that country or let it go?"

"I suppose I could."

"That is well. You have my commission for that, and you have my trust. *But it must be done*. I call failure and treason by equal names, nor will the world be so wide, in a space of weeks, that the meanest man can hide, or the swiftest outrun my wrath. What reward do you ask for this?"

"I ask none. I suppose that you will give with a just hand."

"You are right in that. How soon can you do this? These are swift and most fateful hours."

"I will lose no time. But I must first have three days here. I must go back having done that for which I was sent, or at least be able to show that I have made a worthy attempt."

"You can have two days, but no more."

"They will be enough, if I am unmolested and unobserved."

"You ask much."

"I wish to succeed in that which you have required me to do."

"I will give orders for that, after which Major Luther will arrange for your return to England by a sure route."

"Is it wise? I suppose I could find my way."

"You would run a risk which you need not have?"

"It is one I should be likely to overcome. And the more risk on the way, the less there would be when I arrive. If I am to do that which you require, it will not be by an easy path."

Prince von Teufel remained silent for a moment. Then he said: "You shall have it all as you prefer. But you will understand that, after that, I expect success, and that excuses will not be heard. Do this, and you will be paid from a full hand. But I will forgive neither failure nor long delay."

He took a tablet, on which he wrote a single word, which .he passed across the table for Steele to read. "Do not speak," he said. "Only read, and do not forget. That word, whispered to any officer about my doors who wears two white chevrons, will bring you quickly to me."

He tore the leaf from the tablet and cast it into the fire. He summoned Major Luther again. "You will provide all without stint that Herr Steele may require in the next hour. After that you will not see him again. Nor is he to be watched or molested while he is in Berlin on any pretext at all. You will let this be known to those whom it may concern, for disobedience and death are the same word."

CHAPTER V.

RICHARD STEELE, or No. 973 as he was known to the Secret Service of England, left the Lustgarten Palace in some confusion of mind, and walked two random miles west and south to Potsdamer Street, and sat for some time in the Haus Vaterland Café, before it was clearly resolved.

When he had been summoned to von Teufel's presence, he had known that he walked on the fine edge of the pit of death, and even after he left he had some doubt of whether he had won his life or was marked to die, for he saw that he had met one who could be devious and secret in what he did, and whom no scruples would hold.

But he had resolved before the ordeal began that, whatever his real identity, and wherever his true sympathy might be, he would speak, and even think, while in von Teufel's presence, as Adolph Zweiss would have been likely to do, irrespective of consequence, which he must make his later concern.

He supposed that, by that attitude of mind, he had removed whatever suspicions had been attached to his name, as it had been vital for him to do, but now he must adjust what he had said to what he would actually have preferred. He must weigh losses and gains.

If it were indeed true that he would be allowed to move for the next two days "unmolested and unobserved," he had gained more than he could in reason have hoped. It might be said that he had gained all.

But it was also true that the price was high. Adolph Zweiss, fearful of arousing the suspicions of the British Intelligence Service, which he planned to betray, might have thought that it would look better if he should appear to escape from Germany in a furtive way, but Richard Steele knew that if he should return to his own land by German airship or submarine, it would make no difference at all. It may be said that he had acted his part too well, even to the misleading of his own mind. But he must rest content, as his occupation taught him to do, with the extent of his present gain. Two days hence there would be time enough to consider that! Let him use the hours that he had.

He rose as the café showed signs of preparing to close, and took an omnibus down Stresemann Street, at the end of which he changed to another, which carried him well into the poorer quarter of the southeastern city.

He looked down the while on pavements which had been crowded throughout the day with those who were filled with sanguine excitement by the news which each moment brought, but now thinned at a late hour. Seeing them, he contrasted, in a cold bitterness of mind, a city which might be aware of the sudden war which it had thrust on a shaking world, but could still retain much of its gaiety, its amusements, its comforts of normal life, with that of London, crouching in darkness, now that the fires had died which had left most of its East End and half its centre no more than "a heap of ashes slaked with blood," but still gallant, desperate, licking its dreadful wounds.

Here, truly, there was awareness of war. Any woman or man not in uniform of some kind would have been a conspicuous figure, for Germany had been organized for this hour to the last man, the last woman, the last child that was of age to balance itself on its own feet.

For the first three days Berlin had known the ignominy of darkened streets, and Nürnberg had even heard the bursting of hostile bombs. But such days had been quickly done. The shattered remnants of the air forces of Southern Europe now fought rearguard actions among the clouds, lurked in hidden aerodromes mending their damaged wings and waiting for a dark hour that would aid escape, or were already gathering, like flocks of migrating birds that had been blown apart by a hostile gale, in Morocco, Libya, and the Sudan.

At Cyprus, at Ceuta—even at Malta—there might be nests of wasps whose venom was not yet spent, but they would surely preserve their stings for their near and most active foes. If the Christian nations had bombing-squadrons which were still of unbroken strength, they would have occupation more than enough in vexing the long battle-front which moved southward to the Mediterranean coasts. Certainly they would never reach to molest Berlin, through skies which were patrolled by swift-flying scouts, and possessed by fighter-squadrons against which the strongest bomber would have little hope of surviving in a close-fought fight, and insufficient speed to escape its foes. No, Berlin had no reason to dim her lights as she came to the second week of the war.

Being convinced, after alighting from the second omnibus, and having taken one or two sudden turns and cut through a narrow passage, that he was indeed unfollowed, Richard Steele went on to a quiet side street, from which he entered a covered alley in which the light was so dim that it was rather by feeling than sight that he came to the door he sought—and here, for the next half-hour, he knocked gently, and then more firmly, without reply.

It was a confronting silence, by which he was disappointed but not surprised. It was indeed a natural sequence to that which he already knew. The door, as he had been told, was the sole entrance to the two-roomed dwelling of Martin Blatz, a confidential clerk in the service of the German War Office, and secret agent of England since he had settled in Berlin under that borrowed name fourteen years before.

Two years previously he had installed, in the solitary apartment of another espionage agent at Nürnberg, a radio transmission set working on microwaves not otherwise used, by which secret code messages would be sent from time to time to London, based on information which he would obtain in the course of his own confidential employment and send to Nürnberg through an intermediate agent. But this medium of communication had been most sparingly used; the first object being to have it available if there should be the outbreak of war which had now come. Two days after the commencement of war a message which was being received in London had broken off in mid-sentence, and no further sound had come through.

To discover what had occurred—to ascertain whether the secret transmission had been detected—whether Martin Blatz or his subordinate agents, all or any, had been discovered for what they were—to re-establish communication if it should still be possible—such was the desperate enterprise which Richard Steele had undertaken; and to do this while maintaining also the character of Adolph Zweiss, so that his presence in Berlin must be known and his movements (he had supposed) almost certainly watched, in consequence of the very natural suspicion of his own nationality which was felt by the Berlin military police.

Now he could feel content that he was free from such surveillance; and even if contrary orders should have been issued subsequently by von Teufel, it would still be probable that his movements would be unobserved until he should return to his own hotel, which he was resolved that, until the completion of this investigation, he would not do.

Yet what alternative had he? The night was becoming bitterly cold, and in the street without a thin sleet had commenced to fall. He had no means by which he could break open the door, even if that would have been prudent to try. To walk the streets through the night might be to draw the attention to himself which he must avoid at whatever cost. Considering the magnitude of the issues involved, he saw that his own comfort or health could be of weight in such scales only as they would affect his efficiency for that which he had to do. He sat down on the wooden step of the door, congratulating himself that it was not stone, and took such rest and shelter as could be found in the corner of door and jamb.

He waked from the uneasy slumber that the position allowed before the late February dawn had lightened the eastern skies, and rose stiffly, having resolved what he must do next. He knew that no one could have opened the door during the night, and that the one opposite to it, to which his feet had been nearly stretched, had been equally undisturbed. But, as the morning approached, that opposite door must be likely to open at any time, and when that happened he would prefer to be gone.

He gave a few further knocks upon Herr Blatz's door, gaining no more response than he had expected to hear, and went out to streets which were now covered by a thin coating of snow. Fortunately he would leave no footmarks in the covered entry, and the street was empty and silent. In the dim light of that early hour he did not suppose that anyone would have seen him pass out, or attach any importance to the movements of one who walked coolly, as being assured of the credentials of what he did.

CHAPTER VI.

HE stopped at a coffee-stall for a much-needed meal, and continued to walk quietly about in the busier streets, making a wide circuit towards the place which he had in mind, so that he had no need either to loiter or to pass twice over the same ground until the hour arrived at which the smaller side street shops were beginning to open. Then he approached a delicatessen shop, and remained for a short time studying the contents of the window, as being in doubt of what he would buy, which in fact he was, for he was aware of the need of food, and his assumption of the identity of Adolph Zweiss did not include the German passion for the consumption of pig meat in twenty forms.

Having resolved this, he entered the shop, to be greeted cheerfully by a small, pot-bellied elderly man, who bustled forward to serve him.

"Max," he said, "I will take half of a roast fowl, and some bread with it, for I must buy if I come here, and must then find somewhere to eat a meal. Show me some other things first which I will not take, for I have questions to ask."

As he spoke, he observed a man whose face had changed from the first word, for Max was his middle name, which was not over the shop, nor was it commonly known. It could be used without difficulty of explanation by anyone who knew that it was his, but in fact, it was only employed as a sign that he was addressed by another of the secret fraternity to which he had thrilled tremblingly to belong in less dangerous days. But for the last week he had been in a condition of panic fear, expecting every moment that those would enter the shop who would take him away for the perfunctory trial which would mean his death at the following dawn. Was this a trap? He would take no risks.

"Sir," he said, ignoring all but the order he had received, "chickens are dear and few, but if you have space on your card, I shall be pleased to serve you with what I have."

Steele recognized a difficulty he had overlooked, but saw it to be one which would provide the present excuse which he required. It had become the custom in Germany at this time for every citizen to have a general food-card, on which particulars and prices of all he purchased must be entered by the shopkeeper from whom he bought, to a total which he could not exceed. It was a method of control which had proved to have many advantages, especially in reducing the prices of fancy foods, but it was not adapted to the requirements of a stranger who did not wish to return to his own hotel.

"I have no card," he said. "I am a visitor here. So for the next few minutes I must be begging for food which you will not give, or, at the last, perhaps some scraps, if you can. That is what you can say if you should be asked why I have called here, which you need not expect to be, for I am Adolph Zweiss, who was a flying ace in the last war."

"I do not care who you are," the man replied, "nor know why you tell me this, but if you have no card I cannot serve you, and you had better be gone. There is the Food Bureau to which all may apply."

"I know who you are, and I can see that you are less certain of me, so I will speak in plain words. Do you know why I knock for hours on Herr Blatz's door, and have no reply?"

"Why should I be expected to know that?"

"Have you heard from Nürnberg during the last week? *Do you know whether No. 428 is well?* It is that which I have come from London to ask, for it is of importance to us. I am No. 973, of whom you may have heard something before now."

Max looked at the speaker with puzzled, frightened suspicious eyes, as he heard this. He knew that a mistake would be his death, but he was a shrewd though a timid man, and he saw cause for belief. Yet his answer was still very cautiously framed.

"I understand little of what you say, but there is talk of Herr Blatz—if we both speak of the same man—that he was caught in some treason against the State, and was beheaded a week ago. He was no friend of mine, though he would come here for some things for which I have a name that I cook well."

"There is no doubt that we speak of the same man, and it is news which I am sorry to hear. But my point is that the Nürnberg transmission failed—it may have been two days after that—by which you will see that there is a probability that it came to the ears of the police by the same channel as that by which Herr Blatz was shown to be serving us. But it is not enough to guess. We must know."

The old man had turned away as this was said. He fumbled under a shelf. He rose with a parcel wrapped in newspaper in his hand. "Here is half a chicken," he said, "and a piece of bread. You can call it scraps, and I have made no charge, as my till will show. But I can do no more. I shall be glad for you to leave."

"So I will when you have told me how you communicated with 428, and give me his address, which I have not got."

After he had said this there was sufficient silence to allow time for Steele to conclude that the man would not talk of his own will, and to consider what form of pressure he could apply. But after a while the man said: "I suppose they do not suspect, or they would have questioned me. It was of other matters that Herr Blatz was accused—as a spy of France. Yet if it be as you say.... The address is Paulborner Street 529. I suppose that there may be other apartments there. But I will give you a key which has been left with me against such a moment as this."

He went into a room at the rear of the shop, with the parcel still in his hand. He returned in a few minutes, saying: "You will find a key there under the bones. I can do no more. I have been watched by the police for three months and perhaps more, but they have no charge they can bring. They will suspect much if they see that you have come here, which may be fatal to both. But I can tell you this—the last letter has not come back."

He handed the parcel across the counter, and as he did so another customer entered the shop. Steele said: "Well, a hungry man must take what he can get." He went out, thinking that there was no more there to be learnt or said.

It was bad news that Max was being watched by the police. It might mean that his own visit would be observed, even though they might not be looking for him. And as to proof being required, he did not think that the German police would be much troubled for lack of that. A mere suspicion would be enough to put the man behind solid bars at such a time, even if his life should be spared—unless, of course, he had been left as a decoy to draw better spoil into the net. But more probably he was not suspected at all. It might be no more than the baseless fear of a frightened man.

With these thoughts, he entered a beer-house to which he came. He ordered a glass of lager, which could still be had without stint, and spread the parcel of bread and chicken open upon his knees. In that position it was a simple matter to abstract and secrete the key, which was a small one of the Yale pattern.

He saw now that he must go to Nürnberg, which he would have preferred to avoid. And, for several reasons, he must go by rail, which was also against his will. For one who wishes to elude the notice of the police, to enter a railway station is not the ultimate folly, because he may board a ship, which is insanity in an extreme form. But it is bad enough. And it was especially so at this time, when all human transit was more or less under the surveillance of the military police.

If he must do that, there could be no purpose in absenting himself longer from his hotel, to which, indeed, it might be discreet to return. Let those who watched (if such there were) suppose that his secret work had been done while he had eluded them during the night. After all, he had undertaken to find his own way to England, and Nürnberg was a step in that direction by the more southerly line. He could raise no suspicion by going there, especially if he took a single ticket, as it would be prudent to do. Besides, whatever he might be going to find, it was unlikely that he would wish to return to Berlin. In fact, he would be glad to think that he was seeing it for the last time.

He went out and signalled a passing taxi. The police could question the man as to where he had taken it if they cared to do so. They would learn nothing from that.

It was only a few hours later that he entered the Nürnberg train. He could not say that he was unobserved, but that he was unobstructed was certainly true. Two men who entered his compartment were required by a police official, with polite firmness, to remove themselves elsewhere. The ticket inspector passed without entering the compartment, or appearing to observe his presence. He concluded that von Teufel's orders were being strictly obeyed. For the first time he regarded it as more than a remote possibility that he might see England again.

CHAPTER VII.

IT was dark and the snow was falling thickly when Richard Steele entered Paulborner Street, having spent a perhaps needless hour in making certain that he was not trailed; which would, indeed, have been almost impossible without his knowledge in the weather through which he came. But he had a double need for precaution. For if he were followed, he would be leading the police to the last place of which he would wish them to know, and perhaps bringing death to one on whom no suspicion might yet be laid.

Perhaps. That was the word. It was hard to guess. The method of communication which Martin Blatz had instituted had been that he would write a letter in code, having no designation or address, and pass it over to Max while he would be making a purchase of liver-sausage or brawn, and when there were no other customers in the shop. Max, in his back room, after his visitor had left, would put it into an envelope addressed to Wilhelm Lotz, Paulborner Street 529, Nürnberg, and drop it into some letter box in the city, now here, now there, as he would wander about after dark, and when he was certain that he was not observed. The letter would arrive safely, as, indeed, why should it not?

Wilhelm Lotz was not one upon whom any suspicion had over lain. A quiet, elderly man. An outworker, engaged in the carving of toys. A childless, unmarried man living a very solitary life. One with skilled, sensitive hands, who could have as much work as he would be likely to do, but if he should fail to canvass for it among the half-dozen firms by whom he was intermittently employed, which of them would take notice of that?

He had an English mother who had died by his father's brutality forty years before. But was that a matter to be recorded, even in the official-ridden country to which he belonged. He was a simple German citizen with a blameless record: one who had never been of any interest to the police.

The fact that Martin Blatz had been discovered in a separate treason against the State might seem likely to pass him by, and to leave the radio set which was in his charge unsuspected and undisturbed, and the fact that Max was still free gave this probability strong support.

Against it was the fact that the transmissions had broken off abruptly a short time after Blatz's arrest, and had been silent since. But here again a contrary argument could be used. Had it fallen into German hands, would not an attempt have been made to send false messages, or to draw London to indiscreet disclosures in its replies?

Steele climbed the ill-lighted stairs of the shabby apartment-house with a most doubtful mind as to what he would be likely to find.

The first floor gave him no occasion to pause. He heard children's voices within the rooms. He saw a supper-table through a half-open door around which several people sat, and they were loud in some trivial dispute. He went on quickly, content to think that he had not been noticed by those within.

The next landing was investigated with equally definite result. Dimly lighted, it showed names painted upon the doors, none of which was that which he sought.

On the next landing he must stop, for there was no farther to go. He had reached the top. There was a single door here, bearing no name.

He listened for some time, and then knocked. Having done this several times without response, and hearing no movement within, he ventured to try the key.

The lock yielded at once, but the door did not. Pressure showed that it was bolted both above and below.

It was an unwelcome rebuff, yet one which seemed to indicate that there must be someone within. He considered that Wilhelm Lotz, guarding the secret he did, might not welcome callers whom he had no cause to expect. Had the door been unsecured, but for the lock, a pistol-bullet might have been a more probable greeting than an outstretched hand. It might be as well as it was. He knocked again, more loudly, but with no better result than before. He did not wish to raise a commotion which might bring up those who were at the supper-table below, or others from the nearer floor.

But neither did he wish to wait there through the midnight hours. He had spent one night at a closed door, and it was more than enough. He had no light but that which could be gained from a torch that his pocket held. His heavy coat, from which he had shaken a shower of half-melted snow, dripped audibly as he moved.

He tore a blank leaf from a pocketbook and wrote a short note in code, which No. 428 could not fail to understand, and pushed it under the door. Then he went down to the stormy street and sought an ironmonger, from whom he bought a stout chisel so that, if it should be necessary on his return, he could force open the door.

He mounted the stairs again without encountering anyone, and having knocked for some further minutes, though not loudly, without response, sat down on the cold landing to wait till sleep should come to those in the rooms below before proceeding to force the bolts.

It proved to be slow and difficult work, for he was careful to make the least possible noise, and wished also to do the work in such a way that the door would not be materially damaged. Fortunately, the jamb to which the bolt-sockets were fixed, which was of greater age than the door, had softened sufficiently to release the screws under the steady pressure of a chisel that did not relax.

Finding that his first effort had such definite effect that the chisel could be more loosely inserted, he continued to apply the pressure, now high, now low, in preference to the more vigorous action of shoulder or foot, and had the satisfaction at last of swinging open the door on undamaged hinges. But not noiselessly. It opened with a long whine, such as surely must have alarmed anyone within, even had he been unaware of the long-drawn creaking before.

He darkened his torch and stood aside as he pressed open the door. He did not know what might be the significance of the silence and the shot bolts, and though he did not expect that an actual enemy would be there, his pistol was in his hand. But the silent darkness was all he met.

He felt round the jamb of the door while still standing aside, and his hand stopped on a switch. Instantly the room was alight.

He saw a workbench littered with small carvings and tools, a table, two chairs, and a heavy chest. There was a small dresser with shelves above it, on which some odd crockery was neatly arranged. On the right-hand wall there hung a coat, an apron, and two hats. It was plainly the living- and working-room of a single man, and one whose habits were simple, tidy, and clean.

The room had an appearance of having been deserted rather than disturbed. But, if that were so, how came the door to be bolted on the inside?

Looking down, Steele saw his own note on the floor, with another beside it. Picking this up, he observed the Berlin postmark, dated February 6—evidently the last letter from Max, which had lain undisturbed since the postman had pushed it under the door.

There was a closed door in the farther wall, and the absence of sleeping-accommodation made it obvious that it led to a bedroom beyond. Presumably whoever had bolted the door was there.

Calling out, with no expectation of response, "Herr Lotz, I am a friend from London. Are you there?" Steele proceeded to further investigation.

CHAPTER VIII.

THE man must have been dead for some days—dead perhaps within a few hours of when he had collapsed at the moment that the transmission had broken off. He appeared to have crawled to the bed, against the side of which he had propped himself, perhaps not having had strength to climb upon it. There he had died unrelieved. Perhaps unable to call for help. Perhaps loyal to the trust he had undertaken, and unwilling that any should set eyes on that which occupied a long attic that extended beyond the little bedroom where he had died. Perhaps thinking only of the danger to himself, if there should come those who would denounce him to the police.

It would have been a pathetic sight at another time, this lonely, untended death, but now, when the cry of a million woes that itself had made went up from a tortured earth to a Heaven that would not hear…anyway, he was dead now, and his woes were done.

Having been dead for that time, he was not pleasant to see, and would become worse.

Steele was a tired man, but he saw that he must not sleep. The night was still young, and for the time, at least, he might expect to be undisturbed. He must think first, and might find that there would be much to do before morning would come.

He closed the outer door, which would still lock, though it would not bolt. He searched for food, and found some good bacon and musty bread. He switched on an electric stove, and soon had a meal that was good enough. He had learnt that in such emergencies, if there be the chance of a quiet meal, it should not be missed. It is an insurance of strength of body and balance of mind for whatever may be ahead. And while you eat you can think, which is better than to act on the impulse of sudden moods.

The dead body could not remain there indefinitely without discovery being assured. Neither could people be called in for its removal without the probability that there would be disclosure of the radio apparatus in the further attic.

Yet that might be inevitable now. The simplest course might be to break it up, to destroy any documentary evidences by which codes might be discovered or other agents involved, and to walk out, leaving the door open, and the dead man to be found either soon or late, as the chance might be.

Otherwise—but suppose he could get through to England now? Suppose he could get instructions that would put the responsibility of decision where it could be made with more knowledge than he possessed?

He examined the transmission apparatus, which appeared to be in good order, as was the reception also. He saw that the power which they required had been tapped, without formality of a registering meter, from the city current. He wondered whether an aerial were necessary for such transmission, and, if so, how it had been erected without suspicion being aroused; but it was not a matter which he was likely to investigate to his own exposure.

There was no difficulty about the code, which was one of the arbitrary variety, easy to remember, and very difficult to resolve. It was only necessary to look up each word in a twentieth-century dictionary, and then—with some necessary qualifications, needless to detail—to substitute a previous word, selected according to the figures of the years from 1912. The word before—the ninth word before—the word before—the second word before—the word before—and so on, going forward through the years indefinitely, according to the length of the message sent. It was a cipher which could be coded and decoded with equal ease, and after finding the expected dictionary, standing among those of other languages on Herr Lotz's single bookshelf, it took no more than a short hour to prepare a concise summary of the position, including his interview with von Teufel and the mission he had undertaken from him. He dispatched this, and had repeated it twice in the silent interval that followed, before he received reply: "*Djereed nosology leather oesophagus Yorkish camphire retaille contriturate oes rade ancome transmarine unleisured relay substernal autotype expatriate ouch messs dysuria micturition yoni timbrology wawe wile installation Yorkish impudent dudgeon coupure wharf tittup infold inordinate acknow.*"

He might have observed from the incidence of this cipher, had he had leisure for such reflections, how large a proportion of the words in the English language are not in general use, and how much the shorter of them prevail in colloquial speech, for the message, on being decoded, read: "*Do not leave if you can retain control of radio and transmit unless reliable substitute available expect our messages each midnight your time we will instruct you in due course what to inform inquirer acknowledge.*"

He considered this blankly for a few minutes. There would be the dead body, already putrefying, to be disposed of in such a manner that not merely would he be unnoticed in what he did, but so that its ultimate identification would not lead to the eye of inquiring authority being directed upon these rooms where Herr Lotz had lived, which would be the natural sequel to such discovery. There was the question of how he could continue to occupy the rooms of the dead man without arousing the suspicion which must lead to inquiry, arrest, or instant flight. There was the certainty that if he were discovered to have remained here when more than two days had passed, von Teufel's vengeance would put a quick end to a life he loved, though he had been prepared, for that which he must regard as a greater stake, to risk it with every hour. There was the final prospect, if all these difficulties should be overcome, these dangers subdued, that he must face von Teufel again, not only with a lying answer (as it was likely to be), but with what must be an invented tale of how he had visited England, and returned through the German lines. It was a programme which the boldest, even the most foolhardy, of espionage agents might regard with irresolute eyes; and

Richard Steele, whose long immunity had been won by no headlong courage, but by the patient thoroughness of his preparations for the hazards he undertook, sat for some minutes in a dubious silence before he reached for the dictionary, wrote out the message, "*Shale statute busy prosopopeia succedaneous pood.*"—"*Shall stay but prospect success poor*"—then spoke it into the transmitter with the pauses which a verbal cipher requires. He received an answer a few minutes later, which he decoded to: "*Your decision greatly appreciated,*" and was moved by it to a moment of irritation. "Wasting time," he muttered, "on such piffle as that!" And then went on, in a better mood: "Well, I have succeeded before. Several times. I must fail once." Sooner or later, what did he expect? What had he ever expected? Soon or late, he must fail once. And in time of war—and of such a war as had now fallen across the world!—a spy has no chance of failing a second time.

He looked down on the putrefying body beside the bed. It must be removed. That was sure. But could he carry it out into dark streets that were strange to him, and hope to dispose of it there in an effectual manner? The storm, which still raged without, would favour him to a point, but how could he proceed in a way that would provide against identification? And against the inquiry which would be certain to come to a door that would be fatal, if not to him, to the purpose for which he stayed? If there were a way, it was one of which he could not instantly think.

"No," he said, regarding the remains of Wilhelm Lotz with a natural repugnance, from which human pity was not divorced, "we must be companions here for another day, if not more."

He went to the outer door, and fixed a broomstick under the latch, so that he should have some notice of the entrance of anyone who (unlikely enough) might have a key and the disposition to enter during the night.

He came back to the dead man, on whose shoulder he laid a hand, so that the awkwardly half-recumbent figure fell stiffly away from the bed against which it leaned. He had cast his wet great-coat aside when he lit the stove, and he lay down now in the clothes he wore, and had passed next moment to dreamless sleep.

CHAPTER IX.

He awoke late, as he had purposed to do—for sleep, like food, should not be missed when the chance allows—and found that the long sleep had clarified his thoughts, as it often would.

It required no directions from others now to enable him to see that his place was here. Given the wireless installation—and perhaps even without—he would be of greater potential use to England here than if he should return to do one man's part in the defence of its threatened shores. That von Teufel might learn at last of the most impudent use which Richard Steele had made of the freedom which had been granted to Adolph Zweiss, and that his vengeance would not be pleasant to meet, were considerations which must be put lightly aside. They were no more than the professional risks which he should always be ready to take, and against which his wits must protect his life, as they had been practised to do. And was it not for this hour, dimly foreseen, that he had been preparing through the patient diligence of earlier years? His long previous residence in Berlin, in an assumed identity too humble to draw attention upon himself—the care with which he had perfected himself, not only in the German language but even in some of its local dialects—his study, to minutest detail, of German ways, even to their habits of thought—his trained thoroughness which left no detail to the decision of friendly chance—must they not come to fruit at this crisis hour, or be the mere waste of a worthless life?

He must have an identity. That was the first imperative need. A name to give, if he were asked. Papers to show. A recognized food card, without which he could live only by continual theft in this land of slaves. And for all this the dead man was at hand to supply his need

Even in this highly organized State, where each man had his numbered, allotted place, the disappearance of Wilhelm Lotz from any war-time part he might be expected to fill might not be probed, or at least not to a point that would force his door. There must be much which would be confused or left to its own drift in these whirlwind hours.

Not to the neighbours, of course—not to those who had known him—but in street and shop, and anywhere that a name must be used, he would be Wilhelm Lotz, and if he were careful how, and at what times, he went up or down the stairs, he might pass unnoticed, or taken for a visitor of one who had presumably led a very unsociable life, with which his co-tenants were not likely to have had any intimate contacts.

Having decided this, Steele proceeded to adopt the identity of the dead man as closely as he was able. He could not hope to assume a voice that, most unfortunately, he had not heard. But he stripped off his clothes. He examined the contents of his pockets, which he adopted for his own use. He searched for the meagre correspondence, the few personal records, the rooms contained. He discovered surprisingly in the locked chest a collection of Asiatic postage stamps which appeared to be the accumulation of many years, and upon which a large sum must have been spent. He thought that its present value must be great—or rather that which it would have commanded a fortnight before, for who could say what values would stand in tomorrow's world? He wondered whether it were gratification of this secret collector's passion, rather than hatred of a brutal father, or love of a mother's land, which had led the man to take a spy's perilous pay. But that was a question to which there could never be answer now.

The man had not been unlike himself in height, and his clothes were decent and clean. By their creases and the way they hung, he judged that Wilhelm had walked with a slight stoop, which he practised. When he had worn the clothes for some hours, he had learned to move so that they fitted easily to his own limbs.

He found a receipt which showed that the rent was paid in advance for some months to come. The electricity, of which there had been legitimate as well as illicit use, had also been recently settled, and the meter was placed on the landing, so that it could be read if Wilhelm Lotz were "away," as no doubt he had explained that he often was. It was clear that he had taken all precautions against his rooms being entered, whether he were absent or not, and in that way Steele could not have come to a better heritage for that which he was attempting to do.

In the dusk he went out, wearing the dead man's clothes, and glad to separate himself for a time from that naked corrupting corpse on the floor of the inner room, with which he had still to deal. He met no one upon the stairs, and in the streets he was no more than a humble citizen, obviously German in gait and manner and speech.

The skies had cleared, and thaw had followed a veering wind. The main streets had already been freed from the melting slush, showing that local efficiency had not relaxed. Nürnberg had become a munitions town, and its population had not been greatly reduced by the call of war. As the shifts of workpeople left the factories, they crowded the pavements, talking in excited groups, or filled the cinemas, which were now devoted entirely to news-reels showing how rapidly the Russo-German allies moved on to possess the world.

Having gone far enough from the shops at which Wilhelm's food-card showed that his recent purchases had been made, Steele bought boldly and was readily served.

The cards were issued monthly. The one he had would last as long as he would be likely to need it, or so he thought, supposing that this would not be a long war; and, in any case, that he would be required to see von Teufel again within that time, after which—but it was a mistake in his profession to reflect on that which was far ahead, and might be quite different at a nearer view. The last purchases had been made on February 4. He wondered whether he would be questioned as to how he had lived since then, and had prepared a reply, but those who served him took it without remark. His card was in order, his money good. Beyond that it was no business of theirs. And besides that, he observed that the men around him were not suspicious of mood. They were not fearing bombs from the skies, or looking for treason in the faces of those they met. If there were any spies in Germany now, the Government would be quite equal to dealing with them! Their thoughts were on other things. On the events, which each hour announced, by which Germany climbed to seat herself on the world's back; as did Russia also, but there was less mention of that.

There was a growing realization—it was implied rather than said—that von Teufel controlled all, and though he had a proportion of Russian blood, he was German by nationality and descent, and they felt that it was for her that he took the world by the throat. It was an excited, brutal, good-humoured crowd, relaxing from hard work, which, in so great a cause, it was very willing to do. Steele bought newspapers also, from which he might learn much, though he knew that they would contain no greater leaven of truth than the Government felt it good for the people to have, and such lies as might be useful for them to believe. He did not look at these in the street, as was being commonly done, but reserved them for a later hour. His mind was upon the problem of the disposal of Wilhelm Lotz's remains, which must become more urgent with every hour, and he could observe no place in the neighbourhood of his rooms where he could dump such a burden without the certainty that it would be promptly discovered, which he was resolved to find some way to avoid. And to carry it without remark, even the length of the street, would not be easy to do, whether it were attempted in crowded hours or in the solitary night. It would be a burden to excite the curiosity of any night-policeman, even if its odour did not announce the nature of what it was. He might, it was true, throw it down in such an event, and escape by violence or speed. But if it were subsequently identified, as was likely, being dropped in the street where William Lotz had been lodging so long, the advantage would not be much.

There was one alternative to the streets, which he did not like. There was a dormer window in the roof of Wilhelm Lotz's attic, which he had found to be strongly bolted, and with the appearance of not having been recently opened. But he had noticed that the latch and bolts had been kept oiled, so that they could be quickly and quietly withdrawn. It was a reasonable inference that Wilhelm had regarded the roof as a possible direction of flight, should there be those knocking upon his door whom he feared to meet.

Looking through panes which had not been cleaned for many months on the outside, Steele had been able to see no more than that the roofs were tiled, rather steep, and crowded closely together.

As an emergency exit it was good to have, but as a road to take with a burden awkwardly shaped, and of little less than his own weight, it had a forbidding look. Yet, being in the desperate position he was, he had not put it wholly aside until he had considered that the tiles would be slippery from the frost, and had recognized that he wasted thought and that he could observe no sewer-access in the neighbourhood of Paulborner Street, such as might have taken a dead body with the reasonable chance that it would be swept unnoticed away, it seemed that it must be considered again.

Anyhow, there were two things that it might be useful to have—a good length of rope and a large sack. These he bought, while he was still a good distance from the place which he must call home for the coming days, and returned for a much-needed meal, and to decide what must be essayed at a later hour.

CHAPTER X.

As Richard Steele entered the door which had become his by a war-time right, coming from the clean night air, he perceived the foul stench of decay with an acute revulsion far exceeding that of which he had been conscious before. He saw that, apart from any question of his own capacity to endure that which already approached the intolerable, the risk that it would penetrate to the floor below and rouse inquiry he could not meet, gave an urgency to the disposal of Wilhelm's body which must not be longer deferred.

Yet, even so, he must wait until a later hour; and meanwhile must eat with such appetite as he could contrive. To assist his mind toward unconsciousness of his unwelcome companion in the adjoining room—who yet had a clearer right to that occupation than he himself could claim—he was glad to open the newspapers that he had brought, and study them while he ate.

He read that a patriotic riot in Milan had been repressed with a "firm"—it might be said with a very pitiless—hand; that General Hagen had flown to Rome to "advise" the Government there upon the dispositions of their forces of land and air which the war required; that the Turkish Army had taken to headlong flight without awaiting its foes; that a Russian Commissar had been appointed to take control of that country, in which, as in all occupied lands, conscription both for military service and civil occupations was to be immediately imposed.

Gibraltar, he read, had not yet fallen, but was expected to do so on the next day, being subjected to concentrated attacks from the air, which had already destroyed all the shipping its harbour held, except such as had run for the open sea, where the German submarines were waiting.

"Well," he thought, "so they say; and so, more or less, it may be. But they do not mention Italy's fleet, which, it is a most sure guess, will have joined its force to their Christian foes; and as to the Turkish Army turning tail before it has shown what its teeth can do, it has a reputation for better things. It might be truer to say that it has been withdrawn to a backward line, and that with such speed and skill that even its rearguard was not engaged. And as for Gibraltar's fate, there is a proverb that tomorrow will never come. Its harbour might not be a place in which to remain when the bombs fall, but for submarines—I have heard it said that the Mediterranean is for them, from end to end, a most unsuitable sea; and we have some too which will be likely to do their part."

So he fought with a stubborn mind, as did millions of others throughout an assaulted world, to maintain the fortitude on which much more than on cunning schemes or stored munitions of war, victory must at last depend; and turned from troubled though half-sceptical reading of the destruction of the English troops attempting to storm the camp which the Germans had established at Bridgnorth, and were hourly reinforcing out of the clouds, to perusal of proclamations of a different, and possibly more informative, kind.

The German Government, it appeared, still desiring to show its moderation, its hatred of avoidable war, and its care for the cultural development of the world, had offered terms of accord to the United States. They were simple and short and had a generous sound, proffering much which, it might be observed by those most nearly concerned, was not Germany's to bestow.

If the United States of America would leave the Old World alone, she could have the New, with Canada being thrown in, together with the Guianas, the Falklands, and any other fragments or islands of which the already, or soon-to-be, subordinate European States had had possession. There would be no cavil for such trifles as those. Let the three nations that led the world dwell in accord, as great neighbours should, taking their own continents under control, with the wide oceans to keep the peace.

If this should be agreed, it was plausibly said, resistance in the Old World would be quickly done, and there would be a soon end to a war which would otherwise go far to destroy the civilization of many lands, which—if her supremacy were allowed—Germany had no wish to do. But if America should be obstinate to intrude upon a quarrel and a hemisphere which were not hers, the moral responsibility for prolonging the war, and her own ruin, must be laid at her single door.

It was easy to guess that this offer was made with the design that today's ally would serve for tomorrow's meal, but might it not also show that the German High Command was already concerned to reduce or divide its foes?

Reading it, Steele felt a faint stirring of hope, which was not lessened by contempt for a diplomacy which was so singularly and characteristically unable to appreciate the ponderance of moral standards it did not own. Nor was his judgment changed when he read that the Russo-German allies had made a similar offer to Japan. Let her call off her forces of land and air, and Australia should be hers. Could there be stronger evidence, it was urged, that the allies were without greed either for territory or power, desiring only to bring the world to a settled peace, beneath which its leading nations could impose their cultures, as it would be beneficial for them to do?

But after reading these declarations of the world-policy of the Reich, he came upon another which was of a more sinister, because of a less obviously futile, kind.

"The following," he read, "is the text of a proclamation which will be distributed, over the signature of Prince von Teufel himself, in all countries of Southern and Western Europe, including the British Isles, wherein resistance may be prolonged beyond the end of the present week:

DECLARATION OF CLEMENCY AND OF DISCIPLINE

(1) The families and dependants of all men of whatever nationality who give loyal service to the German Reich, whether by conscription or in a spirit of voluntary obedience, are hereby assured of immunity from outrage, wrong, or molestation of any kind, and of due provision being made for their shelter and sustenance, they being hereby accepted as citizens of the Reich, and entitled to its support and protection, so long as their own words and actions remain loyal thereto.

(2) The families and dependants of all men who fail to submit themselves to the irresistible might of the German Reich, whether by continuing armed resistance thereto, or by contumaciousness of whatever kind, are hereby declared to be outlawed from all civil and legal rights, and at the disposition of the constituted authority in the districts where they may be found, both in their persons and properties, and available for the use and service of loyal citizens at their discretion without redress.

ALEXANDER NICHOLAS VON TEUFEL,
Prince of the Power of the Air

Steele considered the dreadful vagueness of this threat against the civilian populations, or at least against all such as might be relatives of men in arms against the violators of their native lands, and saw, even more clearly than he had known it before, that he watched a war to which there could be no end until one side or other had been finally and utterly overcome. He wondered whether deliberate wholesale massacre, or merely plunder and starvation, perhaps leading to some form of slavery, naked or disguised, was the policy which this proclamation forecast. Or might it be a threat deliberately worded in such a way that it would arouse fears beyond anything that was intended, to induce the submission of fearful men?

It was a sanguine interpretation to which the ruthless horrors which had opened the war gave little support, and it disappeared when he turned the page to find an editorial, officially inspired as he knew that it must be, which was explicit in explanation:

Looking [it said] beyond these brief days of war, as good statesmanship must, to the permanent pacification of Europe, it becomes of an evident importance that future generations shall not be allowed to breed the spirit of insubordination or of hostility to the Reich. To secure this paramount consideration, it is intended to remove the female members of the families of those who persist in armed resistance to the hegemony of Europe, in whom the spirit of bitterness might survive, and to distribute them in far-distant lands, where their crossbred offspring will have no race but that of the great new nation that is to come.

It is not intended that this policy shall be enforced in those countries, such as Holland, and the Scandinavian lands, which have given prompt and ready submission, unless it shall be found that a considerable number of their nationals have left their own countries to join our foes, in which event individual orders may be issued for the arrest of their wives and daughters, and for their ultimate disposition, after a sufficient interval has been allowed for their husbands to return and claim them. In the British Isles it appears probable that a substantial movement of population will be required, and it is the intention of our Government that the most part of these women, being of Aryan blood (excluding any which may prove to be of Semitic or Slavonic origin, who may be more suitably utilized for the adulteration of Negro tribes), shall be distributed as concubines among men of loyalty and worth in the German lands.

For the assurance of German wives, who might otherwise resent the introduction of these women, a stringent edict will provide for their proper subordination, and for the drastic punishment of any of them who may become causes of discord, or fail in due respect to their mistresses, or in diligence in their allotted tasks. As, in the legend of Christian superstition Adam was given control of an inferior creation and

had dominion over them, so will the German house-
wives be given dominion over these females to chas-
ten them to the service and humility which, by the
long verdict of history, must be the lot of a conquered
foe. But, apart from and above all personal considerations of whatever kind, German wives will not fail to
recognize with submissive loyalty that the introduction of these women is to the glory of the German
Reich, and that their fecundity will increase its
power.

It may be added that, in the spirit of lofty and
impartial equity characteristic of German culture the
sanctity of the homes of those who make docile submission in the occupied territories will be protected
with all the rigour of martial law. Every man who re-
ceives a submission card, and whose subsequent conduct is consistent with the obligations which will be
set out thereon, will find it all-sufficient for the retention of a legal wife, and for the protection of his legitimate daughters; and all women who may be ar-
rested under the provisions of this edict will be
granted, on their own applications, sufficient period
of suspense, during which they may be claimed by
husbands or fathers whose submissions have been
satisfactorily made and accepted.

Steele read this with a hardening anger which made the disposal
of that rotting body in the next room a mere matter of routine, in
which he was assured that he would not fail. Was it possible, he
thought, that the loud-boasted advance of civilization had led it forward no farther than to such barbarism as this? His reason answered
honestly that it was not merely a possible development, it was one
that should not even arouse surprise. It was no more—it was, indeed, much less—in its calculated barbarity than were other things
that had been done during the last two millenniums, even by those
who had made profession of Christian faith. And the Russo-German
allies had repudiated Christianity and all that it had attempted to
teach the world.

Indeed, their attitude went beyond that, casting contempt on all
that spiritual religion had meant for men, setting up an affirmative
atheism against which Jew, Christian, and Mohammedan might
unite, as having a common faith and a common cause. And even in
Christian lands—the callous brutalities of the Spanish conflict—the

bloody roads of England and France, where lorries speeded and children died by a crime of slaughter faced, tabulated, publicly announced and allowed!—Perhaps had the hands of the Christian nations been cleaner from most innocent blood this nightmare of oppression would not have fallen upon the world.

It was true that this threatened wholesale expatriation of women, and their enforced submission to the embraces of alien men, was a brutality of a kind without exact parallel even in the Spanish War, but could it be said that it sank to a lower plane? After all, death was the worst fate that any woman need have to fear. She could kill herself, if she would! And she had a choice here, which was more than came to thousands who had been massacred in Spain, and that not only by atheist hands. It was true also that the German edict offered something better than the barren promiscuities which, if they had not been widely practised in France and England, the current literatures of both countries had openly condoned.

All these things might be true, but there are matters on which feeling and logic are widely apart, and it was true also that such action as the German edict forecast would not have been even contemplated by the Christian allies, had their armies entered the territories of the aggressors.

Their fault had been that, after one bitter lesson, and the loss of a million lives, they had allowed an unrepentant Germany to rearm—their fault, or at least that of their statesmen, who had presumably read the Treaty of Brest-Litovsk, and knew what the attitude of Germany had been to a prostrate foe.

Steele thought: "If this war endure for no more than a month, it will become one in which mercy will be a forgotten word." He went on, with the particularity which would be the reaction of millions who would read that proclamation during the next week, to consider what might be the position of one from whom he had parted in England a few days before, one from whom he had parted after no more than the brief fortuitous association of a common escape, and with no more than the half-conscious regard of a mind burdened with urgent, momentous things. Would she be one to be caught in this net of shame? How would she react to the ignominy which it proposed?

There had been a moment when he had thought her coward: when her courage had faltered from a parachute descent which had seemed the path of obvious safety to him. But in other matters—in different ways.... He wondered what she might be doing in England now. But it was unlikely that he would ever see her again. All these years he had kept himself clear from a woman's claims, that when the time should come, as it now had, he should be single in what he did. But it was late now. He had sat long enough reading that with which he had no immediate concern, and thinking of what he read. The time for action had come.

It was long after midnight, and there had been no communication from London, which was not likely to be attempted without particular need. He rose and drew a pair of Wilhelm Lotz's socks over his shoes. He opened the dormer window and looked out on a night that was cloudy, but with a clear air, and some diffused light from the wide city below. He climbed out, and was absent for more than an hour, making cautious explorations, patiently controlled by a hard resolve that he would not fail.

After that he did some unpleasant and probably unnecessary work upon the remains of William Lotz, being resolved that discovery should not come through any lack of thoroughness on his part. He removed a denture. He cut off a finger on which a signet ring was fixed too firmly to be otherwise removed. The sack proved to be useless, being too small; but he was not now depending on that. He might not have used it had it been twice the size. The rope was a different matter. That was to be of vital use. It was three hours later when he came back through the dormer window a second time. He was exhausted by physical toil prolonged under conditions of constant strain, during which instant death must have been the penalty of relaxing muscles or weakening mind. But the thing was done.

The naked corrupting body of Wilhelm Lotz lay across the ridge of a roof which, to the best of his observation, was not visible from surrounding windows or street below. Its head and arms hung down on one side, and its legs on the other. And there it might remain to complete decay, or to become food for the prowling cats, until identification would become an impossible task. There would be some marks on the roofs, of course. It had been impossible to prevent that. But a brisk rain was falling. There might soon be little to fear from them.

CHAPTER XI.

FOR the next five days Steele remained quietly in his garret, and nothing happened at all. He might almost have deceived himself to the belief that he had cunningly devised a means of escape from the black danger which had fallen upon the world. It seemed that while he remained there he was lost from scrutiny of unfriendly eyes, and he had established a new identity for himself which might be difficult to disprove. He drew rations which he did not even labour to earn. He had no occasion to transmit to London, for he observed nothing of importance adequate to the risk of discovery which each message involved, and nothing came through for him. It seemed that, while his ration-card remained valid, he was in no peril, unless he should do some act to draw attention upon himself.

That he might have excuse, if he should be asked why he was idle at such a time, he cut his right hand, deeply in one place, and slightly in several others, with a sharp splinter of glass. It was still not beyond use at need, but it was hurt enough to make it reasonable that it should be bound up, and it made a show that should be sufficient to turn anything less than acute suspicion aside.

At this time he went out for no more than a short daily walk, both to avoid needless observation and to be at hand if a message for him should come through at other than the expected time. When he was in the streets he observed all that he could. He listened to passing words; he read the Government newspapers, apart from which all publications, whether of books or papers, had ceased among a nation that was now organized for the sole purpose of war.

He knew that the news he read, even as far as it might be true, was not worth transmitting, for it dealt with no more than matters on which the Christian allies would be likely to be equally well, if not much better, informed. It was not concerned with high strategy, or the movements of troops or fleets. The newspapers spoke only of what (they said) had happened yesterday on the wide front of the war.

True or false, it was a loud boast. It seemed that the Russo-German eagle had swooped, and its talons had grasped its prey. It had its beak in the neck of a prostrate world. It drank blood. Its broad wings beat down a yet-struggling foe. Under the hypnotic urge of this strident claim there was a visible change in the demeanour of the men, and still more in that of the women, who talked in the *biergartens*, or in the streets, or as they came out in excited groups from the cinemas, which showed little now but scenes from yesterday's battles of land or air, or of frantic disordered flights, or of vast quantities of war material, or strong artilleried walls abandoned to the armies of the advancing Reich.

For three years past they had been taught, controlled, disciplined, hardened, for the crime of which they were now a most willing part, and for the intoxication of its success. He heard them speak of England with exultation that she was low, and contempt of her damaged pride, of France with derisive jests that were heavy with a more bitter hate, of Italy as one that had kept its skin by making submissive alliance with the major power, as it would be likely to do. What it had gained for itself, whose armies must now bleed to make Germany strong, rather than for their own homes, was not easy to see, unless with myopic eyes.

But he heard on all sides that that which had been foretold, that for which they had endured privations, hard-drilled labour, and loss of all kindly freedoms of act and word, had most surely come. Germany had risen to rule the world, and the future would be bright with triumph, and easy with riches and many slaves. They did not talk of a world made safe for peace-loving men, as had been the dream of those who had held them back in the earlier war, or of a war by which war would end. They spoke of a world made safe for themselves, and which would lay tribute about their doors.

He heard some talk of the edict which was to transfer women of rebel kin to the ownership of those of more pliant necks, and particularly of the probability that a large number of English women would be brought over to Germany. Even among German women he found this edict to be well received, but with some doubt of whether the recalcitrant supplies could be equal to the demand. They did not appear to doubt that, with the aid of an active law, they would be able to keep them in a subordination sufficient for their own comfort, and the fact that they were to be distributed according to merits, military or other, of their husbands and sons, made them a more desirable acquisition. Jealousy, it appeared, would be directed less upon them than upon neighbours who might be more liberally supplied with these household slaves.

He heard no word of sympathy for these English virgins or wives who were to be delivered to their own tyranny and their husbands' lusts. The common opinion appeared to be that they would be coming to a better fate than their merits earned. There was talk, going somewhat beyond fact, of the meagre childbearing of English women. This, it appeared, was alone enough to justify their subjection to more virile masters than they had had. They were, by this sign alone, women of an inferior, decadent race. They would be brought now to a compulsion of better ways. Having avoided the production of English children, they would now become pregnant with those of a finer breed.

It was a judgment (to the measure of truth it held) by which innocent and guilty were cast to a common doom. But that, it is fair to observe, is an inevitable consequence of all national sins. An English girl whose instincts of motherhood were uncorrupted would be no more exempt than the married women who had bought comforts and cars at the price of their children's lives. For the fact was that however deeply the vice of birth-prevention had rotted the core of the English race, and to whatever measure (which was not much) the German women could claim a superior practice, they were not being seized on that issue at all, but to coerce the world to crouch to the German whip.

It was on the fifth night after that on which he had disposed of the body of Wilhelm Lotz that Steele entered a cinema to observe pictures which, however far they might be from giving a complete or attempting an impartial interpretation of the swift process of wide-fronted war, were yet capable of revealing much more to him than to the eyes of those who looked less keenly for that which they were not told to see, and who had been trained during three previous years to accept that which they were required to believe with passive, receptive minds. At this hour, when it seemed that all that had been promised to them was to be so richly fulfilled, were they likely to doubt the assurance of what they saw?

And, indeed, there was solid evidence enough that the German legions of land and air were on the heels of a flying foe. The triumphant entry of a strong mechanized unit of Bavarian infantry into Belgrade with a support of Hungarian tanks gave incidental glimpses of ruined streets, where the German air forces had scattered devastation and death, before surrender had closed the brief hours of hard-contested but hopeless war. Another, entitled: *The Maltese Air force having suffered heavy losses and fled, German bombers destroy Valetta*, was less conclusive in what it showed, having been taken from a great height, but it appeared that Valetta burned in more places than one, and the two harbours were bare of shipping. Another showed a German force, which had descended with its artillery from the skies, in possession of the railway junction at Lyons, it having been the strategic policy of the invaders to paralyse the railway systems of the countries they were invading in this manner, rather than to aim at the destruction of that which would be required for their own use when they had possessed themselves of lands from which their defenders fled.

It was only when the screen began to show scenes from the British Isles that land-fighting became a feature of the event. For the strategy of the Christian allies, which was withdrawing its mobile strength from Southern Europe to the North African coast, had avoided battle after the disasters of the past week had shown its immediate futility; and their pursuit came from the swift field of the air, from the heights of which they were strafed by great fleets at their focal points, and by hunting-squadrons of bombers that ranged more randomly through the skies. And these last would be caught at times, and driven downward to flaming death by some bold remnant of the fighting air forces of the allies that still made precarious effort to guard their retiring rear, trusting to speed, or the cloak of the friendly clouds, or to nothing more than the great expanse of the airfields in which they flew.

But the direction of this retreat was not intended, nor possible, for those who fought on British soil, and who must resist or yield or else die, as they largely did. There was no Africa at their rear. Having lost supremacy of the air, they must either submit to see their country a province of German power, which in a space of days would be organized as an arsenal of munitions in which they would be driven slaves, toiling for the destruction of their own friends; or they must resist from the ground with the maimed strength and unbroken spirit which still were theirs.

Steele looked at pictures which were not easy to endure with a quiet mind, and a demeanour suitable to those among whom he sat, whose excited murmurs rose to a clamour of approbation at what they saw.

London Still Burning. It was a picture of smouldering ruin, in the midst of which he had a clear sight, on the wall of a half-fallen street-corner house, of the sign *Elm Street E.7.* He took some satisfaction therefrom, as showing that London was still not in German hands, for had it been so there would have been widely different pictures from that. It was easy to believe that the conflagration which had devastated a third part of so vast a city had not been put out in a day, even though its course had been checked by rain and a changing wind. And he knew that it had been the East End and the docks that had suffered most from bombers rather than overhead, and there was sinister suggestion in that which he could not read.

One of the Frozen Regions. The screen showed a moving picture of desolation, in which there was no motion at all except that of the sliding landscape of death. It was a silence that could be felt. Here and there lay the stiff figures of men or of children or women as they had been caught by the freezing death. Or there would be a single horse, or a herd of cattle or sheep, stiffly postured with outstretched legs. There could be no resistance from any place which had been drenched by the freezing gas. But he told himself that there was a limit to the quantity that even the German laboratories could produce, and, besides that, it could not be satisfactory to them to destroy the land, as that method of warfare did. Who could say how long it would be before fertility would return to soil where not a blade of living grass, not a seed, not a worm, remained? Its purpose was to terrorize the nation against which it was so ruthlessly used, and if it should fail in that, it was likely that Germany would turn to other of the hellish means that her chemists knew.

Execution of Civilians Taken with Arms. Steele must look on at the parading of several scores of his countrymen, with some women among them, who were shot without mercy for what he could not suppose to be even a technical breach of the rules of war, in view of the armlet order which had been broadcast by the British Government during the first hours of the German invasion.

The Last of the R.A.F. It was a vision of fields seen from above, and moving across the screen. The fields were scattered with fallen planes, some in fragments, some blackened, burnt-out wrecks, some still smoking in evidence that the scene had been photographed immediately after the battle in which they fell. Once the camera dipped to give a close view of a giant three-engined battle-plane that lay crumpled, with its nose driven deep into a rocky soil. It dwarfed the surrounding trees, and made more vividly real the extent of the far-spread wreckage which had seemed small as it was photographed from the clouds. It was an unhappy picture for English eyes, but he knew that to call it the last of the R.A.F. was to go too far, and as that was so, who could set a limit to that which was no less than a certain lie? How did he know that all those wrecks, or even half, had been British planes? He had seen one. The others had been too distant to identify. He had seen enough of aerial warfare to be sure that a fleet of battle-planes will not be shot down without bringing some, at least, of their assailants to equal loss. The rocky scene had been Westmorland or perhaps—indeed, more probably—Wales. He remembered that he had been allowed to betray the secret aerodrome in the Brecon Hills that he might win von Teufel's confidence for a later gain. Was this a consequence of that which he had been permitted to do? No. It would be unwise to imagine that.

He got up, feeling that he could see no more for that time, but his eyes were drawn backward to the screen as he withdrew. *Sheffield Surrenders to General Bessel.* There was no faking there. He saw familiar buildings. A familiar street. He walked out pondering whether England were really so prostrate under the German heel in so short a time that organized resistance was at its end. Was that the reason that he had had no message for these five days? Was he waiting instructions that would not—that would never—come? If that were so, he must not wait vainly idle while better men were active to fight and die. He must consider how he could escape, or whether he could be of more use by remaining here. Should he dare von Teufel again with some audacious mendacity? He resolved to call up England. He could surely think of something which it would be useful to them to know. But what he really wanted was to ascertain that it was possible to get a reply. But he had no occasion for this, for, at the agreed hour; it was England that called to him.

He took down a long cipher message and gave no more than the reception signal in reply till he had decoded it to read:

See von Teufel at once. Inform him that there will be no attempt to hold the British Isles by landing American armies here. This information is true, and will have reached him from other sources. It is confidently hoped that it may enable you to obtain information of real importance, with which object you will make all possible excuses for remaining, transmitting what you learn as occasion requires. You will tell him that you returned by boarding German destroyer at Harwich, which was for some hours in German hands, but you were torpedoed within a mile of coast above Ostend. You swam ashore, and suppose yourself to be sole survivor. Destroyer 47B. Captain's name Kant, not Spener.

Steele considered this, and saw bad and good in a mixed bag. It were better to return to von Teufel with a true tale than with one which might prove, or which he might already know, to be false. With that evidence that his mission had been performed, there might not be too close a scrutiny into his account of how he had come and gone, for which he saw that he had been supplied with a likely tale. So far, so good; and if it had ended there, leaving him free to return either as a German spy or by his own wits, he would have felt that he might live for a week, and perhaps more.

But to stay in Germany, establishing contact with von Teufel again in his German guise, *and to transmit!* Did they realize that Nürnberg and Berlin were some distance apart? That it would be the end of his usefulness and himself if he were followed here, as he was so likely to be? That even to leave this place for more than a day, and then to return, might be to enter a waiting trap? Suppose that neighbours should observe that Wilhelm Lotz did not enter or leave, and break down a door on which they would first have knocked, thinking no worse than to give aid to a sick man!

But if he saw the risks with clear eyes, as it was his business to do, he did not fail to see also that the stake was worth the hazard of much more than a single life. It might be nothing or very much. It was his part to see that, should it fail, it should not be through lack of precaution or any forethought of his.

Thinking thus, he sent out a series of inquiries designed to fortify him with accurate replies to any questions he might be asked concerning the condition of the country from which he would be supposed to have come. He learned, beside many specific details needless to be recorded, that the spirit of the nation was still unbroken, and the most part of its territory unsubdued, although there might be little where either safety or peace remained. Apart from the broad tracts to the south of the Firth of Forth, in Worcestershire, and in Surrey, which had been utterly destroyed by the freezing gas, the parts which had suffered most, outside the London area, were the North Midlands, in which the Germans had established themselves at two centres, at Bridgnorth and on the Sheffield moors, where they had entrenched positions within which reinforcements arrived continually from the clouds. From these centres they were extending outward, like spreading ulcers, with the apparent objects of possessing themselves of the Midland industrial district, and dividing the London area from Northern England. The remnants of the R.A.F. which were still able to take the skies, and which had been joined by units from Scandinavia and the Netherlands, of no great strength, were too weak to prevent the convoying of the German armies, being more than fully employed in protection of vital posts and depots which still remained in British hands, and in rendering it dangerous for German bombers to venture destructive raids without the protection of a large force of their fighters.

But the Germans were finding that the resources even of their large transport air forces were a poor substitute for the facilities of land-transit available to them in Southern Europe, by which its territories were being so rapidly overrun, or for those of the sea which would have been theirs had they been able to subdue the British Navy to the extent to which they had driven out of the skies—though with losses they had not lightly endured—the outnumbered fleets of the air.

They were learning, too, as was the case on all fronts of the war, that the mobility of a highly mechanized army is dependent upon good weather and solid roads, apart from which its movements are more cumbersome, as they are more exposed, and more vulnerable to assault from the air, than is a force of more primitive equipment. But with the constant accession of men and material that they were receiving, they had become difficult, if not already impossible, to dislodge, and were gradually extending their positions southward, and advancing them towards the encirclement of the Birmingham manufacturing area.

Food, he learned, though its distribution was disorganized, was still abundant, and there was no fear of a general shortage, at least for some weeks to come. The idea, too lightly assumed in the considerations of pre-war literature, that England would surrender at once if her food supplies should be gravely threatened, had passed from the minds of men who faced the reality of what surrender would surely mean. But private ownership of the essentials of life had virtually ceased. The invaders found that they were not confronted merely by a small regular army, and a somewhat larger ill-equipped militia, but by a nation which this sudden monstrous shock of assault had united in stubborn purpose to beat it back. If food should become short—well, they must go short of food. What else would there be to do?

And with this stubborn defiant unity there was more self-reliance, more individuality, more initiative, than would have been found under like conditions among the more strictly driven and severely disciplined of continental nations.

Steele did not cease his questions until he had a clear picture of these conditions with much detail of incident, so that he would be able to talk convincingly of the visit to England which he must represent himself to have made. The process of communicating by a cipher which must be composed by him and decoded by those who received it before the reply could be prepared in the same way, and then, after transmission, decoded by him, was necessarily slow, and it was near to the late February dawn before he closed the conversation with a warning that, even if he should be successful in deceiving von Teufel a second time, it might be difficult to return to Nürnberg, which he would not therefore attempt until he should have something of high value to tell. He added that, as there would be an intervening possibility of the discovery of the transmission set, he would commence an authentic message with a code word, the absence of which would indicate that the call did not come from him.

He rose from this conversation to pace the room with the excitement that the prospect of action brought. He saw that if he could gain von Teufel's further confidence, as he had a good hope that he might, there were possibilities, vague but vast, of the aid which he could give to the Christian cause. He saw it as the moment for which he had prepared himself through the long monotony of the years of uncertain peace, when he had looked ahead to this war. But it was a moment for caution rather than haste. A meal was his first need, and he prepared and cooked it with no less than his usual care.

While he ate he read the messages he had received, pondering their implications and storing them in a retentive memory. Then he destroyed them, crushing each ash beyond possibility of recovering any word from a charred fragment. He considered how he should reach Berlin, and in what guise he should present himself before the dictator again. He had the clothes in which he had come, and those of Lotz which he now wore. He decided on the latter, which would enable him to leave without drawing observation from the lower tenants, if he should meet any of them upon the stairs, and which could be explained in one of a dozen ways, according to the tale of how he had come from Ostend, which he had still to invent. Probably it would all be wasted precaution! It was unlikely that von Teufel would have leisure for asking that, or that others, if he should be trusted by him, would have the right to inquire. But he was used to these elaborate mental preparations, of which ninety-nine would be utter waste, and the hundredth would save him from mortal peril he might not otherwise have escaped.

He would take nothing with him by which he could be identified as Wilhelm Lotz, or which could connect him with that garret, from which, apart from his own assertion, he would be entirely detached the moment that the street would be left behind. Even the key must be hidden rather than taken away. Lotz's food-card, his identity-card, all the contents of the pockets by which he had sustained that personality, must be left behind. He must put aside the mental habit he had cultivated of being Lotz, speaking as he would have spoken, thinking his thoughts. But he would take nothing inconsistent with that identity, lest he should find himself in a position in which it would be the lesser peril to claim it, or perhaps to assert that he had impersonated him after returning from England. Suppose he should say that he had killed him as a traitor to Germany, and with a secret purpose of using that short waved radio to the confusion of the British Secret Service, which so foolishly trusted him still? He could think of many plausible lies which could be adapted to the dangers he had to meet. But he could not think of too many for his own security. Such tales should be well prepared. They should not need to be improvised when the moment of crisis comes.

It should not be difficult to get unobserved to Berlin. The police were vigilant, no doubt. But their ranks were depleted now by the many calls of the war. And the general body of the people were not suspicious of spies. They were not in that mood. They did not feel as do those who crouch under the dread shadow of war. It had been different at first. It was scarcely a fortnight since there had been loud aerial battle above their heads, with falling of burning planes in the Nürnberg streets. But much had happened since then. Now the war had become to them a tale of victory moving ever farther away. On all sides their foes ran. They would not even have attached importance (had they been told) to the fact that the Christian nations planned to make a war-front of the North African coast. They might pause there if they would, till they should be reached by German bayonets transported across the straits, or by German bombs from the sky! But no longer than that. There was no fear—no thought—of Christian spies in the Nürnberg streets.

Steele walked out at a quiet pace, and with the slight stoop that he supposed Lotz to have used. He regarded none, having still much matter to tax his mind, and no man regarded him.

CHAPTER XII.

THERE is none so lonely as those who rule. Prince von Teufel had been a lonely man even when his office had been no more than to organize the secret air forces with which Germany had plotted to shake the world. He had had followers, adherents, men whose ambitions were centred upon himself, but few friends. Now he had none. If he would trust any man, he must rely on his passions, of false patriotism, or ambition, or fear, or greed. One of these would be potent with most. But they left him a friendless man. He may not have been greatly conscious of that, or at least not as a matter for much regret. Ambition burned in him with too hot a flame. At this time he was conscious of little but what he won.

But it is possible that the devil may have a dog which will be faithful to him, even to facing the nether flames, because loyalty is its own nature, and without caring whether his master be evil or good. Prince von Teufel had such a dog. He was an orderly, Lessing by name, who had been with him from humbler days. He was rather dull, illiterate, having no qualities likely to draw the envy of more brilliant or ambitious men. He was never likely to gain, or even to seek, a position of military or civil power. Had he sought such a goal, it is unlikely that von Teufel would have misused him in such a way. But he knew him to be obedient, silent, diligent to fulfil whatever instructions he might receive, and sufficiently intelligent to be trusted in simple things.

This man came to him when he was engaged with the three architects of most repute in Berlin, as no other would have been permitted to do. He stood at his side, somewhat behind his seat. "*Excellency*," he whispered, in a voice too low for the men at the other side of the wide table to hear, "*there is one here with the word*."

Prince von Teufel gave no sign that he heard, and went on with the instructions he was giving. In the last week his manner had become abrupter, more imperative than before, but his temper, unless he were opposed, remained calm, there being little to cross his mood.

Now he showed a great project to astonished men. He would have plans prepared for a vast palace, such as no man might have imagined before. It should be a square mile in extent, and in the very midst of Berlin, for which all existing buildings, shop or warehouse, palace or hall, were to be ruthlessly swept away. He pointed to an outspread map of the city, suggesting the position he would prefer. But he would leave all detail, even the site, to them. Only they must understand that it must be the best position, and the greatest palace they could conceive, and no consideration of what must be destroyed was to be regarded at all.

In a few words he had done. "Gentlemen," he said, "that is all. I shall require the plans in a week's time. You will not regard cost, thinking only of magnificence and enduring strength, for you will have the world upon which to draw. You may go now. Let your plans be bold, for in that direction you cannot err."

They saw that he did not invite questions. They had not been called there to give advice, but for an order to be obeyed. They went out, looking dazed.

As they went, von Teufel said, "Who is it? Have him in," and Steele entered by another door. As he came in, Lessing withdrew to the next room.

Steele gave the salute due to the army rank which Prince von Teufel held, of which the Prince took no notice at all. He said abruptly: "You are back? What have you learned?"

Steele answered with brevity, in prepared words, and von Teufel put the whole matter aside with: "It is what has come from New York. It is nothing now. But it is true. You have done well. Do they trust you still?"

"So it was to the last. But they would have had me remain, and, having your command to return, I slipped away. I do not know what they will think of that, if they learn. For the time, I suppose I may be best here."

"Are they likely to know?"

"I have some contrary hope. Or if they do, they will think me dead."

"How is that?"

"I came aboard the destroyer B47, which was torpedoed; from which I had some fortune to swim ashore."

For some time after that von Teufel questioned him about English conditions, and what capacity or will for resistance might still remain, which he answered as it seemed wisest to do, holding down with a strong restrain the natural feelings he had, and being unsure, almost to the last, of what impression he made.

His mind was, indeed, roused to a lively doubt when the questions turned to his experiences upon B47, and he had reason to be glad of the caution that had led him to gather what published details he could of that ill-fated destroyer before presenting himself for this interview. He had observed that the name of the Commander was given as Spener in the Navy List issued only two months before, but he remembered the hint that he had received, and when von Teufel said, "Spener was a good officer; one I am sorry to lose" (was it a trap? He would never know), he answered boldly: "It was Captain Kant who was in command, or so I understood his name to be."

Von Teufel corrected himself readily. "Yes, so I recall. Spener was transferred the previous week to a new boat. It was the better for him."

After that, von Teufel paused a moment, as though to reach a decision he did not speak. All the time he had not asked his visitor to sit, nor had he seated himself. He had stood at times looking across the table on which the map of Berlin was still spread. Or, more frequently, walking a few abrupt steps, now left, now right, as he shot out a further question.

Now he looked down on the map. He asked: "What do I do with that here? Can you guess? At a time when you will think my mind should be farther away, on the long frontiers of war? I will tell you that.

"I have had architects here. I have told them that I will have such a palace built as the world has not seen, nor yet dreamed. Such a one as will be meet for a city that centres all.

"Do you think me too soon in this? Or that I give my mind to the wrong thing? Then you see but a short way. For this design will be the world's talk in a week from now. It will take the heart from our foes. They will know that we are inflexible in resolve, that they have no hope of an abortion of peace such as they gave the world for its curse twenty years before. They will know that they must bend or else die, and that those who are first to yield may have less tribulation in what they do."

He turned his eyes, black, implacable, shining with a light that was exalted to the point where insanity walks arm-in-arm with inspiration, whether of Heaven or Hell, full upon Steele, as though he would read and possess his soul. He said: "I must have men I can trust. Men who answer only to me. I have tried you, and you have not failed. You have courage, and are one who can look at all with unblinking eyes.

"You are of the air, where your name was made, and it is by the air that I shall prevail. It is the arm that I love. I will tell you what will be yours. You will have no country to rule, for you must not be cumbered with that. They have no need of a part, who have all.

"You must have no wife, for you will be too great to be swayed by a woman's wiles.

"But you will be one of six who possess the world, and you will account only to me."

He touched a spring under the edge of the table, and a small drawer slid smoothly open. He took out a card. On it there were three small enamelled brooches, of ancient and curious work, such as would not easily be matched in a modern workshop. There were two blank spaces, against which names were written. He took off a brooch, and wrote the name Adolph Zweiss against the blank the removal made. Steele took from his hand a brooch enamelled with blue-black cloud that the lightning tore.

Used as he was to self-control, and to simulate or conceal emotion and thought as his safety required, Steele found it hard to decide what would be the natural reaction here, hard to meet the gaze of those probing merciless eyes, in which there was no kindliness even while he gave on a scale that sounded rather of demonic than mortal power. But he was relieved of that necessity as von Teufel went on: "Do not thank me in words. I am surrounded by lying tongues. You will thank me by what you do. I must have those who will tell me truth, and not that which they think it will be pleasant for me to hear.

"While that brooch is yours—and I do not take back what I give—you are my eyes and my ears, and there is none so high but he must do your command, for which you will answer to me alone."

His voice sank to a lower note as he took up a blank sheet of paper. "Write your name upon this."

It may have been the first time for many years that Steele came near to what might have been a fatal error. He had commenced the initial letter of his own name before he realized what he would be expected to write. He crossed out the half-written R, and wrote *Adolph Zweiss*, saying easily as he did so: "It is long since I wrote that name. I have trained myself to write in an instant manner that by which I have become known."

Von Teufel took that in the right way. He said: "So I was told. That you are thorough in all you do. This signature will enable you to draw all the money you will. It will be so ordered at the Reich Bank within the next hour, and you will find that there is no limit at all. I hold a war council at eight tonight, when you will not fail to be here."

He summoned a chamberlain, to whom he said: "You will provide accommodation for Air Marshal Zweiss, either in this palace or where he will, doing all that he may require." He said to Lessing, who had come back to the room: "Summon Secker. I will have his report."

Steele saw that he had passed from von Teufel's mind.

He followed the chamberlain. He must remember that he was an air marshal now. He supposed that he would be expected to dress the part, and his first thought was that an air marshal's uniform would be ill adapted for going anywhere in an inconspicuous manner. But he would be suitably dressed for the Council, which he must attend in eight hours from now.

He said to the obsequious chamberlain at his side: "For this night you can find me rooms here. Tomorrow I may arrange in another way, if I remain in Berlin. You will provide a fitting wardrobe, and all else that I am likely to need, in three hours from now. But first I will have a meal, and after that I will be alone for two hours."

The chamberlain led him to a suite of rooms which appeared to be already occupied by an officer of high rank, by evidences scattered about. He said: "This is the only worthy suite which I have. You will forgive that it will take ten minutes to clear."

It was cleared in less time than that, the chamberlain calling three menservants, to whom he said: "Clear out General Ficher's effects, with what care you can, but without delay. When he returns tomorrow you will refer him to me before he can come here."

An hour later, having had a most excellent lunch, Steele was left alone for the quietude he required to consider the amazing position which had become his.

He had imagined many results, good and bad, which this second interview with von Teufel might have. Many things, but not this.

CHAPTER XIII.

IT was not very easy to believe in a sober hour. He was an Englishman—an English spy (he preferred the direct brevity of the word to the "espionage agent" which had become its common substitute). He was not one who, being a butcher, would have called himself a purveyor of meat. Yes, he was an English spy who had spied upon Germany for twenty years, during which he had been most conscious of wasted efforts, and of gaining information at his life's risk which was disregarded or disbelieved. And now he was a German air marshal, and one who was to be in the special confidence of the arch-foe of his race and land. It seemed such an incredible thing.

Yet he saw that it was something different from the caprice of a random chance. It was the amazing, but yet possible, fruit of the dual identity which he had built up with such elaborate care in those years when there had been little notice of what he did. Fifteen years before, when he had had a mole grafted on his own flesh, where he knew that the army record of Adolph Zweiss would have it to be, he had sown the seed which was flowering now.

And from another angle, the development was less monstrous than, without consideration, it might appear. In the sudden eminence which von Teufel had gained through taking advantage of the world's crisis in violent, murderous ways, was it not natural for him to look round for those on whose personal loyalty he could rely? And how could he purchase this more surely than by raising others nearly to his own height who had not been in such positions before, and whose own security would be gone should he fall or his favour fail? Those who had held high office before he seized a place that was higher yet might be moved by jealousy or envy, might expect that their own positions would remain, and even be more secure, if he should be overthrown. But those whom he lifted up would be his, if not by gratitude, but by self-interest, as he had been shrewd to perceive. And then—it was not Richard Steele who had been raised to this sudden height; it was the man he professed to be. It was Adolph Zweiss. It was the flying-ace of the last war, who had lived all the intervening years for the hour when Germany would rise to regain her loss, with bitter usury for her foes to pay. No, the facts being as they were, the event was less fantastic than it appeared.

He went on from this to recognize the precariousness of the position which had been thrust upon him. He was secure while no suspicion disturbed von Teufel's mind, but how long was that likely to be? He judged him to be one who, if his own security were at stake, would have no scruple in what he did. If he should be in no more than a level doubt, he would not hesitate or pause to destroy, whether by legal process or the assassin's knife, or by such an order as would send him to certain death.

And he saw new dangers, new difficulties for himself in the conspicuousness of the position to which he had so abruptly come. He might learn secrets vital for England to know, but how should he become Wilhelm Lotz again? How should they be communicated? How should he disappear and be unnoticed in his absence or his return? It was not easy to think.

He saw that all his plans, all his forethought, had been wasted effort. Only that one solitary fact, the transfer of Captain Spener, which had been given to him, had been of use. Yet that frequent experience would not justify the lack of a like care for tomorrow's chance. With altered circumstance he must scheme afresh. First he must attend the War Council, at which he would sit with a modest mien. He would avoid making enemies, if he could. He would speak little and listen well. So his thoughts went till they were disturbed by a tailor's knock on his door.

Clothing himself four hours later in the uniform which had been so expeditiously made, he had a doubt of whether the brooch which was to be the symbol of his authority should be openly or secretly worn. But he considered that, if he were to have the great authority which von Teufel had promised, its source could hardly be a matter to hide away; and beyond that, that he would have spoken a warning word had he wished it to be concealed. The newly designed uniform of the higher ranks of the German Air Force had a close-fitting tunic of pale-blue cloth with facings of scarlet, and a small, two-headed eagle in black on the left breast holding lightning between its claws. He pinned the brooch with its streak of zigzag fire dividing the cloud beneath the bolt of the eagle's claws, which seemed an appropriate position for it to have.

The Council Chamber was a long, lofty room, in the centre of which was a table of sufficient size to have accommodated a more numerous assembly than those whom von Teufel had called together, whether for the benefit of their advice, or to receive instructions from him; and of those who had been his colleagues at the outbreak of war, only Field Marshal von Hoffmann remained.

When Steele entered, von Teufel was already seated with a pile of papers before him and a secretary at his side. The secretary was the only man there, with one exception, in civilian dress. He had the look of a keen-faced lawyer rather than that of a military caste, but Steele noticed that he wore, on the left lapel of his coat, a brooch similar to his own.

He would have moved down the table to take a seat which, being farthest from von Teufel, might be considered that which modesty would select, had not the Prince signalled to him with an abrupt motion of his hand to occupy one which stood vacant, only two removed from self.

As he did so he saw that his own name was already there, on an ivory disc inserted in the chair-back, and heard von Teufel's voice: "Gentlemen, this is Air Marshal Zweiss. He won a name, as you will recall, in the last war. It will be greater in this. You will know that he is not the least here."

There was a murmur of recognition which had the sound of cordiality. It was difficult to suppose that men such as von Hoffmann, who were accustomed to the highest offices in the State, would welcome such sudden elevation of others to their own ranks. Yet it is possible that envy was not alert. The sudden panorama of conquest was too vast, its opportunities too many, for the most greedful ambitions to fear that they need have less than a full meal. They may even have welcomed a colleague who appeared likely to strengthen them in control of the gigantic operations which must be successful if they were to have more than a soon-ended mirage of the power which von Teufel promised in such confident words.

This introduction having been given, von Teufel opened the proceedings by requiring his secretary to read a co-ordinated report of the course of the war during the twenty-four hours which had ended at noon that day. It was somewhat long, having much matter with which to deal, but Steele recognized that it was both vividly and concisely expressed, and that it must have been built up from many sources which had been synchronized with no little skill.

"Gentlemen," von Teufel asked, when the reading ceased, "is there more of which we should be informed? Or is there a matter here to condemn?"

The question was not productive of instant replies. The account had been one of constant advance, the German Command entering, city by city, lands from which their own outnumbered or beaten armies had either yielded or were flying across the seas. And, besides, the tone in which the question was put was that of one who had served the meal and required praise.

Yet when he had this and no more, he went on in a sharper tone: "Well, you may not, but I do. We hear the death-rattle in England's throat, but the Middle Sea has the look of an English lake. What have our submarines done in the last week? You may say much. But I should say not enough, though it were ten times that which it is. Klein, how many boats have you there?"

A short man, grossly fat, but with a face that open weather had bronzed and lined in days when he had walked with a leaner paunch, answered in a ready, literal manner, as one who gave what he was asked with indifference as to how it might be received: "There were twenty-two of our own, of which five are lost, if not more, and there are nine Russian, which I do not control. They have, of course, more in the Black Sea, where they remain."

"Which you do not control?" von Teufel echoed his words. "I will alter that. I will have no dual command in one place, be it land or sea."

Klein went on: "Besides these, there are about a score of Italian, which have surrendered, or which we have been able to seize, and two Greek. But they have crews that I do not trust. I would not commission these till I have supplied a leaven of surer men."

"Then it is two score at the most! It is not enough. They should be reinforced with as many more, and with orders that they must wage more diligent war."

Admiral Klein did not look pleased. "By your leave," he said, "I would give orders of an opposite kind. Is it well that they should be caught in a closed trap?"

Von Teufel frowned. He said curtly: "You will please us with plainer words."

"I should have said they were plain enough. The Straits are so guarded now, they are so netted and mined, that is it a peril for any boat to slip out or in. But the English are not content. They are working so that in ten days from now, or it may be less, it will be an impossible thing."

"Then you must send your boats in while you still can."

"But I thought to bring out those that are there now."

"Will you say why?"

Those who looked on saw that Prince von Teufel restrained himself with a hard rein. His was an anger that might break out at any moment to the ruin of the man who appeared stubborn to thwart his will. But the Admiral answered as though not perceiving the wrath he roused: "It is because, I suppose, you have given the post I hold to a competent man. The submarines would be more use in the wider seas—and they may be useful a longer time."

There was a moment of most ominous silence. Von Teufel appeared to be restraining passionate speech, or perhaps pausing before that which would be more deadly for its delay. But when he spoke, it was to say no more than: "How long do you suppose that the Straits will be in English hands? Do you know that Gibraltar is near to fall?"

"As to that, it is no province of mine. I must believe what I am told, and am glad to hear. But I would still remove our boats from that sea. It is too shallow and clear, and too well patrolled."

Von Teufel turned his eyes from the Admiral who challenged his orders so stubbornly. He addressed the Council. "Gentlemen," he said, "there are times when it may be well to conserve strength. There are times for prudence and times to dare, and I must have those around me who can judge rightly between these two.

"We are at an hour when the seconds count. It is of small moment that we may lose a score or two score of boats, if they are at first sufficient to vex our foes. They must be cast, at whatever risk, in the swaying scale. It is what they are for. If we hold them back now for fear of depth charge or mines or of nets in a shallow sea, they are no better than sunk, for how will they be useful to us when the war is done?

"We must press our foes where they make head, be the sea shallow or deep, and with the instant strength that we have, not on land alone, but under water as in the air. Shall we give them leisure for second breath? It is by that fault that most wars are lost. And who can pick the straw that bears down the scale?"

He may have meant to break a man whose will was not of the resolution the time required, or he might have been content had he been abject to acknowledge that he was wrong, but Admiral Klein met his gaze with a stubborn jaw and unblinking eyes. "Then," he said, "if you think that, I will give place to a more pliable man, and if you ask me back in a wiser hour, I shall be here to help you the most I may. But I had thought you to be one who could judge with a cool mind, and whose ears would be open to honest words."

"I will hear honest words, but they should be of a bolder tone."

"Do you call me coward? I am not on board. If I order as you would have me do, it is not I who should drown, nor could you blame me if it should go ill, when all have heard how you bear me down. But I say that we lose our boats in the shallow seas, while if we get them on the Atlantic routes they will not be so easy to sink, and they will sink more, which is, I must suppose, how you would have it to be. I would make America pay a most heavy toll if she will send her arms where they have no business to be. But you will give her a clearer way."

Von Teufel heard this and became silent again. When he spoke, it was to show himself on what to Steele, and doubtless to others there, was an astonishing side. He said: "We must thank you for good advice, which was boldly urged. It shall be as you say. For if the boats can be so used in Atlantic seas that they do more hindrance to the assembly our foes design than they could do as they are now placed, it is a disposition that should be made, and of this, it seems, you are very sure."

From this decision a discussion arose as to how promptly, and with what degree of safety, the boats could pass out through the Gibraltar Straits, and it was resolved to intensify the attack which was already being urged against that fortress, which, if it had not sooner fallen, was to culminate in a concentrated assault both by land and air on the fifth day, by which time the German submarines, and such of the Italian as were fit for sea, would have been assembled, and would endeavour to slip out at a time when those who would be glad to obstruct their course would be having other matters on which to think.

Up to this point Steele had found no occasion for speech. He was more than content to sit silent, and to listen and learn. He judged that Gibraltar was stubbornly resisting an overwhelming attack. Day and night bombs were raining continually upon it from the skies, endeavouring by numbers to overcome the difficulty of making effective hits on its knife-like edge. Batteries from the mainland were firing upon it as incessantly, and were being continually augmented with additional and yet heavier artillery. Its surfaces were being continually torn by high explosives and drenched with poisonous gases. Its civil population had been withdrawn into the rock. Its narrow airfield had been abandoned. Its harbours had been emptied of shipping, except for a few destroyers, which hid in a narrow anchorage blasted out of the rock so that they could not be bombed from above, or dared audaciously the air forces which must fly too high for accurate aiming, both because of the height of the rock itself and to avoid too great a loss from the anti-aircraft guns which were still active to bring them down.

For it was clear that its guns were not silenced yet. Its garrison had burrows no gas could reach. And there were batteries that gave it help from the opposite shore, and that were being strengthened by the allies. At times, too, there would appear fighter-squadrons out of the clouds, to the confusion of the bombers, and these would retreat too swiftly for the German fighters (which could not be continuously in the air) to bring them to an action which they would have been too few to sustain.

Steele judged that however fiercely it might be attacked, it would not be likely to fall before the fifth day would come, and that the plan which was now resolved would tend rather to lessen than augment the fury of its assault until that day should arrive. He saw it to be of vital moment that he should communicate the plan of this attack in time for the allies not only to be prepared to meet it, but that they might make dispositions to intercept the submarines, and perhaps cripple, at one decisive stroke, the power of Germany to menace their communications upon the sea.

But it was a thought which, in that assembly, he must not show, that it might be dangerous even to harbour within his mind. Let him even think now in a German way, till he should be able to think apart! And as he resolved this, he became aware that the talk had shifted in such a direction that it would be very easy to do. Easy, at least, to forget that which had been already heard. Less so to listen with the approving look, the ready supporting word, that his part required.

For they were speaking of England now. Of the foolish, obstinate resistance that she still made, though her air forces were beaten down or must slip furtively through the clouds, though a third of London was a ruin still smoking beneath the rain, and though German armies had come down from the skies and were establishing themselves and spreading over the land. Could she not understand that her day was done? Or, if she were unable to understand, how could she be most quickly and cheaply taught?

This time there was no doubtful or dissenting voice. No one denied that it could be done. The question was not whether, but how. Von Teufel said only that it should be without further devastation of factories or fields, of which there had been destruction enough. Let them strike at women and men, who could be more easily spared.

There was agreement here also, but allusion was made to the tens of thousands who had been destroyed by the freezing gas. Something, it seemed, must be done in a more spectacular way.

Herr Geibel, the only man there, besides the secretary, in civilian dress, spoke for the first time. He was a bald, elderly man with a very high, straight forehead and a heavy, sensual mouth, who had won infamy as the most ruthless of vivisectionists in earlier years, and was now the head of the German war-chemistry department. He had had a grievance during the past three years in that, though he had been given wealth with a free hand, he had not been raised to official rank. He considered that one who fought with gas and bacteria should be honoured at least equally with those who marshal clumsier, less deadly armies of men. In his heart he thought that a uniform was his right, and that an admiral or a field marshal was less than he. Now he waited impatiently for von Teufel to right his wrong, as he had some cause to hope that he intended to do. He said: "You should use the gas that eats out the eyes. I told you that six days ago."

Urging this upon those who seemed somewhat slow to respond, he became lyrical in description of what it did.

It was not merely the loss of sight, which would be inevitable from when the first particles, feather-light, drifted into the eyes. It was the sustained agony that it would cause as it hollowed out the sockets in which its special advantage lay. This was so great that pain-deadening drugs, even morphia, might have no more than partial or very temporary effects against it. He could show them dogs that had had enough morphia injected to render a man unconscious writhing and tearing the boards of their pens with frantic claws. It was most interesting to watch. If some thousands of people were put into that condition—a few hundred here, a few hundred there—it might have a most salutary effect.

Von Hoffmann asked: "It would require the distribution of a large quantity—a very large quantity—of the gas to be certain of such results?"

"It is not exactly a gas," Herr Geibel replied. "It is an extremely fine floating powder."

"Which, Herr Geibel, leaves my question unanswered."

"I should not recommend it without having sufficient quantities at command."

"But sufficient for what? That is what we should know, and how far it can be controlled. I have heard you say that it is extremely difficult, as well as expensive, to make."

"It is difficult to reduce the powder to the degree of fineness from which the best results are obtained. Had I been more liberally served during the last three years, there would have been no need for such questions now. The cost of a single battleship, which may outlast the war without firing a shot, would have provided enough to blind a city, and more than that."

"What I suggest is that your anxiety to demonstrate the doubtless most excellent quality of this powder does not enable you to consider its advantages in comparison with those of other methods of warfare with an absolutely judicial mind."

The words were moderate in themselves, and the tone of contempt in which they were spoken might have been unobserved by one who was not aware of the gulf of hostility which was widening between soldier and chemist in the prosecution of the war. It was not so much horror at the ghastly cruelties which the scientists so blandly contrived for the torturing of their fellow men, in regard to which a generation-long toleration of vivisection, under the base plea that it would relieve mankind of the pain which they inflicted on other creatures, was bearing no other than a natural fruit. It the same jealousy which had obstructed the exploitation of the longbow against the aristocracy of the battlefields of an earlier day, which had once caused two Italian armies to unite in massacring the harquebusiers that a too-enterprising leader had intruded into their war.

Von Teufel cared nothing for jealousies such as those. He would use every frightful weapon he could to possess the world. But it was a feeling of which he was well aware, and it had caused him, imperious as he was, to hesitate to dress Herr Geibel in the uniform and bestow upon him the high-sounding title that he desired. Now he interposed before the scientist could reply: "Then, von Hoffmann, what alternative do you recommend?"

The Field Marshal was confident in his reply. "I say the blinding powder may be an excellent arm, but I should hold it for a more local and particular need. Let it be known that we have such power in reserve, and it may do more to deject our foes than if it be used—which it seems is all that we can—in a small way. Will England yield for a thousand blinded or dead? After what we have seen in the last week, I should say not.

"I would advise that the edict already issued be put instantly and severely into force. When we occupy a town or a countryside—which we must aim to contain in a large way, so that there will be many who cannot flee—we will seize all women who are worth the petrol their transit burns, unless they be claimed by submissive men who will toil for us, and they will be brought to where they can be put to better use than if their eye sockets had first been eaten away."

There was a murmur of approval at this, but von Teufel hesitated, knowing that it was prejudice rather than reason that voiced the choice; and, being himself unsure, he turned abruptly to Steele, as his manner was. "Zweiss," he said, "you have the wisdom that listens and does not talk. You know the English as none other here can profess to do. Which should you advise it to be?"

Steele would not have thought that he could be startled so that his heart would miss a beat, as it did. He felt as though the dreadful dilemma the question brought must be bare to von Teufel's hard, questioning eyes. He had even an instant's fear that it was a trap to disclose him for what he was. And with that thought he saw that, if he were to do England the service which was already within his power, he must be bold and instant in his reply. And his word must either condemn hundreds of his fellow countrymen, and their women and children, to a most horrible fate, or expose he knew not how many women to a degradation beside which that of the Sabines was honourable, and such as should have given no cause for lament.

He was not aware of conscious choice as he answered: "I should say that Field Marshal von Hoffmann is right. The blinding powder, however horrible it may be, should be held back as a threat, or kept for a more apposite use. But the edict will strike in a larger way, and it is, besides, more fertile in its results."

He was master of himself now, of manner and voice, as he went on: "I suppose we who sit here may have a sufficient pick as the consignments arrive, and there should be enough variety to content us all."

He heard von Teufel's voice: "It is wisely said"—and knew that he had come through this first War Council without suspicion being directed upon him. And how much he had learned! And probably—indeed, certainly—the decision would have been the same had he not been there. Which did not alter the fact that, being there, he might have altered it had he spoken an opposite way. Or could he? Would not the edict have been enforced in any event, though perhaps it might not have been so instantly and severely urged. He became aware that the Council was breaking up.

He walked out at von Hoffmann's side. He was bold to ask: "Is Gibraltar really so near to fall?" The Field Marshal's shoulders rose slightly. "You have heard what the Prince said. You know the English better than I!"

"I know the air better than I know them. I know the winds over Gibraltar's height, and the air pockets that pilots dread. I do not envy those whose mission is to drop their bombs on the right spot, and to return for another load."

Von Hoffmann was friendly in his response. "I can see that we agree about more things than one. Yet it is that which it is most vital to win."

Steele turned the conversation aside. "When Herr Geibel spoke so lovingly of his blinding powder, I had a thought of the scientist of an earlier day who made the hollow bull which would turn the cries of the man who might be roasted inside it to a most natural bellow."

Von Hoffmann looked blank. "It is a tale," he said, "which I have not met."

"The scientist offered it to a certain tyrant, who, he had some reason to think, would find merriment in its use. The monarch said, with reason, that its quality could be proved by experiment only, and, as it was the scientist's idea, it was only fair to give him the opportunity of demonstrating what it could do. So he was put in it to roast, and as the heat increased it bellowed in a most natural manner."

Von Hoffmann smiled at what had been a rather hazardous jest, showing that the antipathy between soldier and chemist was no less than Steele had judged it to be. "And if the Prince should say that he would like to see a demonstration of the effect of the blinding powder, for which no more suitable subject than its inventor could be selected? It would be amusing to see his face!"

Von Hoffmann spoke lightly enough, but after that they became silent, for it was in both their minds that it was a thing which von Teufel might be quite equal to do, and this was not a thought to be spoken aloud. Steele had a further thought to himself. What would von Teufel's vengeance be like, if he should discover that he had made a confidant of an English spy? But it was useless to question that.

CHAPTER XIV.

THE rain fell from a leaden sky which no wind disturbed. But neither Perdita nor her companion had any quarrel with that. It gave them security from all but the most unlikely descent of a random bomb.

But there would have been little danger for them, even had the day been clear, for their work was in the wide Worcestershire area which had been destroyed by the freezing death.

They had been strangers before the day when the German air force had drenched the land with the freezing gas, and though they had escaped together, and had found companionship since in a common task, they were no more than friends who had been thrown together by the casual hazard of war.

Perdita Wyatt would have said that she was heart-whole, both of the living and of one who had died in Prague in the last month, whom she had been inclined to consider for the closest of human bonds. But if, in this present stress of physical toil, she had disposition to dream as a girl will, her thoughts would be likely to go to another who had the names both of an English and German spy, and who had aided her to escape from the fear of a German gaol. There had been a time when he had thought her a coward, if he had not called her that in an open way. Her mind dwelt much upon that. He had said that he would sacrifice her life without scruple if it would enable him to get back to England one earlier hour. She thought no worse of him for that, knowing now the reason that urged him on. In fact, she had no criticism of him at all, even when she thought of how she had followed him down the hill like a forgotten dog. Her discontent was with herself, that she had not been more equal to what he would have had her do at a great need. But these were no more than the idlest dreams, for was it likely he thought of her? Or that she would meet him again in this convulsion that shook the world?

Eustace Ashfield was not heart-free, either in fact or his own conceit. His faith was pledged to one who had no cause to blame herself that she had failed at her nation's need, having flown her scouting plane through the freezing storm to give warning of the course of the German fleet, till her petrol had failed and she had crashed in the night with her mission done. Now she lay in the Bournville Hospital with injuries of which she had been able to write in a cheerful pencilled scrawl, which had reached him by the precarious post still available for those—and who was not?—who were registered in the civilian army of men and women, which, loosely organized, and with no more uniform than an armlet cross, had united to resist the invasion that descended out of the skies. He had written back, and the letter might or might not have reached her, but he had done no more, though they were less than ten miles apart; for this was war in its starkest form, war without pageantry and with little of the discipline of the barrack-square, but waged to the bitter limit of human strength.

They had no glorious nor even dangerous task. It was no more than to enter, one by one, the long rows of houses which had been stilled by the freezing death, and to load up all the still-edible food that they might find into a lorry which must be driven to a North-field siding.

There were hundreds of others engaged in the same way, and it was to their honour that their loads should not be inferior to, nor less often delivered than, those of their competitors in this work of salving that which, though it had been frozen, was not destroyed.

They worked without the respite of settled hours, sleeping when exhaustion came in the house where they happened to be, and waking again to resume the labour that sleep had stayed. Even when Perdita would drive a full-laden lorry, there was no pause, for she would leave it at the end of a queue of those which stood for their contents to be transferred to the waiting trucks, and take an empty one from the other end of the line, and would drive back at a pace that had no regard for risks or restrictive laws, along roads that were silent and empty now, unless she should pass another lorry engaged on the same work.

She would drive between blackened fields which had become too utterly dead to wake again with the coming spring. It was as though the overbroad, concreted roads that had been cut from the living fields, and sterilized so ruthlessly for the sport of speed, had spread the infection of their own barrenness right and left till they had achieved an equality of enduring death; and they were, indeed, desolations nearly akin, being children alike of the slow-combustion engine with which a laughing demon had cursed mankind.

She drove hard, knowing that Eustace would be working the while to bear out further loads to the pavement, and the exhausting, unceasing labour of search and burden would be resumed. There was no thought now of forty hours being a week sufficient for all the work that the world required (it had never been enough, it had seemed, for the support of its children's lives, though what they need have lacked in shelter, clothing, or food, had they been nationally desired, had not been easy to see); for those days for this generation, if not for this civilization, were irretrievably gone. But to say that life had become less worth living might be a profound misreading of the calamity which men had contrived for others and for themselves. Rather, being threatened, its value rose. And its harder, meaner aspects of social competition were in suspense, so that, if the powers of hatred and cruelty walked abroad, there was also more sympathy, more comradeship—evil stimulating good, as it ever will.

And after the first horrors, the first piteous things that the silent houses contained had been looked at with steady eyes, it was surprising how little emotional disturbance their repetition would bring. Most of the houses had been emptied of human life. If their occupants had not escaped the wide range of the falling bombs, they had, at least, fled some distance from this part, which was in the very centre of where they fell. Usually there would be no more evidence of what had been than a dead dog, a stiffly distorted cat, or a mouse that had run a few bewildered feet from its hole before being overcome by the frozen air. And when they came on those who had been bedridden, or who had thought themselves to be safer in their own walls than in the open, congested roads, they had no more to do than to put a sign on the gate, so that the death-carts could make a halt, as they must also do for the frozen cat, lest there be corruption and plague for those who—but when?—would enter those forsaken houses again.

But as yet, in these few days since the bombs fell, corruption itself had been held at bay in a sterile land. Even the hard-frozen eggs in the larders had thawed to freshness again. The effect of the cold was most evident in such of the tinned provisions as had been liquid in their contents and had burst, often with a violence which had made confusion of surrounding objects.

They worked in the immediate silence of a land where no birds sang, nor was there a leaf for the wind to stir, a silence in which the fall of the light rain could be plainly heard in the intervals of the distant booming of heavy guns. For the German army which had its base at Bridgnorth, and was being continually recruited out of the skies, moved outward now like a spreading pool. It came down the right bank of the Severn, and was being shelled from the Malvern Hills. Yesterday's news had been that it had crossed the river, and that Worcester had been abandoned after a rearguard action continued long enough for the flight of those civilians who did not prefer to remain and make the submission that the invaders required, and for the destruction of such factories as would have been useful to them. But the flight of refugees did not come this way. It moved south and west: to Somerset and beyond, and to the security, such as it was, of the Welsh hills.

The low sound of the falling rain was deadened by that of a motorcycle ridden by a man in the uniform of the military police, and with a girl on his pillion-seat. He dismounted with a glance at the number the lorry bore, and met Eustace struggling under the weight of a sack of flour, being one of the major prizes found in the house of an old lady who had provisioned herself in a wholesale manner, and now lay in an attic bed where she had thought that piled blankets and height from the frozen ground would give her safety from that which the radio had urged her to flee while the hour allowed.

"Eustace Ashfield?" he asked briefly. "You are assigned to the forty-eighth V.L., to report at Savile Street, Wolverhampton, 7:00 P.M. today. This young woman will take your place here."

The girl of whom he spoke in a tone that lacked respect, if it did not indicate actual contempt, had dismounted beside him. She was rather plump and short, with black hair and a very white skin. Her face was coarsely attractive while void of self-expression, but would draw into ugly lines when she spoke or laughed. She stood now looking round in a half-sullen, half-speculative manner, as though uncertain to what she had come or what her reaction should be. Her glance went in sharp inquisition to Perdita, who came out at this moment clothed, cleanly enough, in a white linen overall which she had found in one of the deserted houses on the previous day, and bent under the weight of a flitch of bacon which she had triumphantly managed to get unaided upon her back.

Eustace had deposited his sack in the lorry by this time, and came back hastily to relieve her of the lighter burden. Being a few paces apart from those who had come, as they found a place for the flitch to rest, he said: "I'm called away for one of the new labour battalions. You know I put my name down for it when they sent us here."

"And that's the substitute I'm to have now? I don't think I shall gain much by the exchange!"

"Oh, you never know till you try," he answered cheerfully, glad of something which promised more opportunity than this job, which he yet knew that he had been doing as well as his unaccustomed muscles allowed.

The newcomer spoke to Perdita as they met. "This," he said, "is Miss Sarah Parfitt. She will take her orders from you, and it will be your duty to report if she should make trouble of any kind. I am to warn you that the enemy may overrun this part of the county within forty-eight hours, or they may leave it alone. Therefore, you should proceed with the utmost energy to collect what there is still time to remove. Should they come, it will be from the southwest, and you must retire towards Birmingham, preferring the more southerly roads. You must endeavour to save the lorry, and should therefore retreat in good time. You have, of course, no duty to fight, but you are warned that you should not fall alive into the enemy's hands. I am to give you this, which is the last that I have."

He took a rather heavy revolver and a belt of cartridges out of a carrier, and she looked at them without enthusiasm.

"It's not automatic?" she asked, remembering a weapon in an airplane cabin which, as it fell from a dying hand, had continued its deadly discharge while it had leapt on the floor like a living thing.

"No, it's too old a pattern for that." He explained its action while she belted it on without feeling much comfort in the cold barrel her fingers touched. It was a short time since she had handled a German service rifle with such clumsiness as to cause Richard Steele to change a plan which had been forming within his mind. But these were days when the use of lethal weapons was quickly learned.

"Do you mean they would want me to kill myself, if I couldn't get away?"

"Oh, I expect you'll manage better than that! But the fact is that the Germans are carrying off all the girls they can catch, and they don't mean them any good when they do that."

"I was in Germany," she said, "when the war began. They won't find it easy to get me back." With that thought, she had more satisfaction in the weapon with which she had been provided than she had felt at its first offer.

Eustace asked: "Should I have time to get to the Bournville Hospital, and still get to Wolverhampton in time?"

"The First Southern?" the newcomer asked in reply, using the name which was familiar to those who were old enough to remember the organization of the last war, when the university buildings had first been the hospital which they had become for a second time. "I suppose you could. Anyway, if I give you a lift back, and I don't see why I shouldn't do that. You're the last that I have to call up round here." He added: "But I don't suppose you'll get in. They're too busy now for anything they're not ordered to do."

"I'll risk that."

"Very well, come along." Eustace held out his hand to his companion, casual and yet intimate, of the past week. "Goodbye," he said. "I hope you'll get on all right."

"Oh yes," she answered dully. "I suppose I shall. But does anyone matter now?" And then, in a better tone: "Goodbye and good luck."

She felt lonelier for being left with this girl whom she had disliked at the first glance, and concerning whom she had had plain warning enough that there would be trouble to come; and the time was gone when those who parted could expect to meet, or even hear of each other, again.

"You'd better have one of these," the cyclist was saying, "though I don't suppose it'll make much difference to you." He handed her one of a bundle of leaflets of a proclamation he was distributing, and she looked down to read an order, signed by the Minister of Defence, intended to restrain reprisals which were being provoked by the brutality with which the invaders were conducting the war, and as she did so the motorcycle waked to noisy life and passed rapidly out of sight.

CHAPTER XV.

THE motorcycle pursued its rapid, explosive course for about two miles along the Birmingham Road, and came to a place where further progress had been barred by an elm, which, having been damaged in the bombing-raid of the first night of the war, had maintained a precarious perpendicular as long as it had been supported by the wind on its weaker side; but as the wind changed and fell, and was succeeded by gentle rain, it had leaned over, very gradually at first, and then crashed across the road so that, broad as it was, there was no space to pass beyond the width of a raised footway on the southern side; and this gap had become lamentably blocked by the first of a train of lorries loaded with trench-mortars, which the officer in charge, being desperately anxious that they should be over the Upton-on-Severn bridge before it should be blown up, or fall into enemy hands, had insisted should be pushed through.

Being assured that the road would now be cleared in a few further minutes sufficiently for them to pass, and there being already all the labour engaged upon the work that the position allowed, the cyclist spread his mackintosh on a wet kerb and proceeded to share both the sandwiches which his wallet held and the gossip which had become the principal medium by which news was circulated—or at least such as, not being suitable for enemy ears, could not be broadcast, or allowed to appear in the newspapers, which were still irregularly published.

Sergeant Fielder, as he gave his name, was a lean, grizzled, elderly man, probably far past military age, though still physically fit. In response to a brief account from his companion of how he had been removed from control of the works he owned at the outbreak of war, he said that he had been registrar, until four days before, of the East Birmingham district, when he had been notified that he must report for more useful service.

"I suppose," Eustace said, "they've got a woman doing it now?"

"No, it's just dropped. I should say the women can be no better spared now than the men. But, anyway, the registration of births and deaths—and marriages, if there are any now—isn't being kept up. To register deaths during the last week would be rather more than anyone could have hoped to do. I don't suppose there's been a war that has gone on at this pace before. And when it's over, we shall either be German slaves, when they can organize things their own way, or we shall have to make a fresh start. I believe that's the idea. Cancel out everything and divide what's left after the mess has been cleared up, among those who are left alive."

"You mean divide everything equally?"

"I didn't say that. I don't know."

"It doesn't sound as though it would be very easy to do."

"Perhaps not. But you might find it harder to think of a better plan."

Well, perhaps he would. He knew, though he had been too young at the time to observe it intelligently, that after the last war, by which the social order had not been profoundly disturbed, there had been shameful anomalies between those who fought and came back to a straitened, if not actually penurious, life, and others who had enriched themselves from the nation's need.

It had been as though two men had been in a cabin beset by wolves, one of whom had two guns and the other none. And the one who had the spare weapon had refused it to his companion except at a price that he could not pay, so that he and his children had become debtors for many generations to be. Between nation and nation the usurious burdens had been voluntarily cancelled or their payments denied, but between the rich and poor of a single land this admission of the radical fallacy of the principle on which modern industrial civilization was uneasily based had not been allowed to operate—could, indeed, not have been operated between individuals of the same race—except by clumsy obliquities of taxation and death duties, themselves almost as crudely unjust in their operations as the evils they were intended to tame.

And what had been evil in the economic fruits of the last war might be intolerable—indeed impracticable—as a sequel to this, even though the German menace might be subdued while the fabric of civilization stood. Now that all men were expected to throw their resources, large or small, into a struggle for national existence so instant, so severe, that there was no time to value or count the contributions they made, now that it had become evident that to delay for bargain between man and man, to debate the value of paper money, of which the producing and recording centres had disappeared, or to attempt adjustment of debts between those whose written wealth had been in banks (the clearing-offices of which had been reduced to smoking shells by the German bombs), would be as futile for the individual as it would be treasonous to the national cause—it had become impossible to contemplate an ultimate scramble for repossession of salvaged property as a satisfactory termination of victorious war. In how many thousands of cases, to consider one difficulty alone, would the title to a property be destroyed, or it be left in doubt of its living heirs?

No, if victory should come—which was much to doubt, while the growing ulcers of German occupation spread in the land despite the resistance of fevered blood—then, whether or no there should be a new heaven for which to hope, there must be establishment of a new earth from the wrecks of the ruined world.

Dismissing such futuristic dreams from his mind with the reasonable reflection that even if they should ever dawn there was small hope that he would live to see them (his own factory, now in Government hands, might be one item of property to which no one would make a valid claim!), Eustace left Sergeant Fielder's last remark unchallenged, and asked: "Why do they want me at Wolverhampton? The Germans aren't near there yet, are they?"

"I believe they're a good way on the road. They're coming south from Sheffield, with General Briggs shelling and machine-gunning them from prepared positions, and then falling back before they can make it too warm for him. They say the Germans are losing ten to our one by these tactics, but, as they're landing more troops every hour from their transport planes, I don't suppose they care overmuch about that."

"And at Wolverhampton we'll make a stand?"

"I know no more than you, and if I did—more than a guess—suppose it would be a thing that I ought not to say. But it's no secret that there's a lot of work going on there, and that the Germans will get some sort of surprise when they arrive."

"Well, I shall be glad of a chance of doing something better than filling hampers with odd tins of salmon and potted shrimps. But I should like to know how serious you were when you told Miss Wyatt that the Germans might be round here in a couple of days. It sounds, with what you say about Wolverhampton, as though they'll about close Birmingham in."

"I don't think anyone knows the answer to that. We know, as I've said before, that the German army which is based on Sheffield is advancing towards Birmingham, but the one that assembles at Bridgnorth has advanced, so far, down the Severn Valley, keeping, till they took Worcester, to the right bank; and whether it's aiming at throwing General Porter's army back into Wales and advancing on Gloucester and Bristol, or whether it will swing round upon Birmingham from the southwest, is a question to which we expect to have the answer in the next few hours.

"But if they come this way, the orders I and a lot of others have been distributing seem to show that we shan't attempt to hold the North Worcestershire country. Perhaps that's partly because it's already destroyed by them, and certainly won't have any crops on it this year. But I don't see that that means that Birmingham will be surrounded, let alone taken. I believe a lot of work's being done to protect the Coventry-London Road. They say everyone over ten is hard at work digging gun-pits and trenches there. If you'd seen some of the loads of shovels and picks going south...! I heard that the factories making tools of these kinds have preference for materials over all except those that are busy on airplane parts."

"Well, I hope, if the Germans do come this way, that Miss Wyatt gets clear in time. They wouldn't do her any real harm, would they, because she's collecting food?"

"They mightn't because of that. I don't know. But the tale is that they're catching every woman they can, and unless she can prove that her male relatives have submitted, or they give themselves up, so that their submission may rescue her, she's sent over to Germany to become a kind of white slave."

"They won't find it easy to get English women to submit to that."

"Perhaps not. But it's better to keep them here than to find out how they'll behave if they get caught. We haven't been altogether successful in that, if reports are to be believed. They say that some of the troop-transports that come down on the Sheffield moors are going back as fully loaded as they come. And it's to prevent more of that happening that I'm told to warn women near the front that they are not expected to allow themselves to get caught alive. There's a tale of them shooting some who wouldn't enter one of the planes, as an example to the rest."

"You wouldn't have thought that there could be so much savagery in the world in these days."

"These days? I don't know why we always talk as though they've been any less savage than those that have gone before, unless, perhaps, people always have done, at all periods, which sounds likely enough. Men have always been cruel, if there's any truth in history, for the things they have believed or wanted. And because those things have kept changing, it may have been easy to persuade themselves that they were more humane than the generation before. But look at Spain last year! And look at what our roads were like till the war came. We were killing children in such quantities that the Press found that it had ceased to be news when they were pulped on the road. And you were considered a pest by your neighbours if you even mentioned what was happening, as though it were not quite proper and necessary. No, if there's been a change in human nature, it's something I've not been able to see."

"I suppose, being registrar, you saw these things rather more plainly than most of us did."

"Yes, I dare say. As a matter of fact, I got so worked up that I wrote a poem about it that I thought might have done some good, but the papers didn't agree. Anyway, I sent it to about twenty, and it came back every time. I remember it began:

> The old gods are fallen. Now before
> A motor's bloody wheel we bow.

"It's sure enough now that it won't get printed!"

"I don't know how to explain it," Eustace replied, "but I don't agree, all the same. I think we are—or were—more humane than men used to be, in a score of ways. I say were, because it's hard to see what's coming now. And what about that proclamation you're handing round?"

"I didn't say that our Government has ever been as brutal as that of Germany. And to be fair, I suppose that lack of imagination was more than half the trouble. If the dead bodies had been left on the roads for a day or two, just as they were killed, it might have done good, and perhaps almost as much if there had been a regulation that every car must have the record of the people it had killed or injured painted large on its back panel. I suppose vivisection wouldn't have lasted a week if there had been a law that the laboratories should be glass-walled and set up in Trafalgar Square."

"You've certainly got some ideas!" Eustace answered, in response to this insight into the mind of a man who had spent the best years of his life in entering the records of human fate. "If you get any equally good ones for making the Germans jump, I hope you'll have a chance of seeing how they work out. By the way, what was wrong with that girl you dumped on Miss Wyatt to take my place?"

"Wrong with her? I don't really know. But about everything, I should say. She was ordered out of a factory where she'd been making trouble among the boys, and by the way she talked while she was up behind me, I should say that she was getting ready to make some more. But you heard me tell your friend to stand no nonsense from her."

"But would anything happen if she complained? I heard that the courts are closed, and that even the prisoners have been released, and that the gaols are being used as storehouses now."

"Yes, that's true. But it doesn't mean that it's easier to monkey round and get away with it. There's not much discipline in a way, and not much punishment going on, because the spirit's too good; but I heard of a man who deliberately scamped his work at a brass-foundry having his head held under water so long by his fellow-workers that they thought they'd drowned him, and it took an hour bringing him back."

Eustace would have liked to ask many more questions from a man whose different occupations during the last ten days had enabled him to hear more than himself of the surrounding drama of death, but at this moment there was a stir among the crowd of vehicles and cycles which had been delayed by the fallen trunk. It had been twenty minutes, rather than ten, but at last the obstruction was cleared aside sufficiently for the lines of traffic to move again.

CHAPTER XVI.

SARAH Parfitt was aware of merit which her companion did not perceive. She disliked Perdita with the instinctive perception that she herself was disapproved, which the best of women may be disposed to resent. Yet, no less, she had endeavoured to establish friendly relations. She had talked affably, as though oblivious of her auditor's lack of response. Surely there was virtue in that! Yet she would have been less actively disapproved had she been more sparing of words.

Perdita learnt her opinions on many things, and heard an account of her recent experiences which the narrator innocently supposed to have been edited into a self-flattering form.

Sarah had an obtuse strength of character which resisted the impact of circumstance more absolutely than a nature sensitive to its environment would have been able to do. She observed the coming of year with the alert and single regard to her own profit with which she had reacted to previous opportunities of fateful chance in a life which had been self-dependent from its earliest years.

Being put on a night shift, which she disliked, and to a monotonous occupation which she would not have undertaken readily even for a high wage, and which she was now expected to continue for a length of hours which her union perversely approved, and with no more settled remuneration than the assurance that her place of lodging was secure and her meals supplied, while the incidental necessities of life must be begged, borrowed, or exchanged, or were promiscuously distributed among those who were too arduously and too single-mindedly employed to be greedy for more than their present needs, she had been inwardly recalcitrant from the first, while warily observing the absence of any demonstration of similar resentment in those around her.

To the sharp complaint of a forewoman that her work was indifferently performed, she had replied that the glare of the electric light under which she worked affected her eyes. They were not equal to prolonged strain under unaccustomed conditions. It was a plea the weight of which was not easy to judge, though it was plain to see that she was not concerned for her own failure, but only that her excuse should avail. She was transferred to a day shift and put on to different work, with no better result. The next day brought two separate complaints against her: one of having stimulated a jealous quarrel between two youths who had become her working companions, to the detriment of their common output, and the other, not less serious, that she had complained to some girls engaged upon similar work to her own that they were exhibiting a needless diligence and setting a standard which she objected to emulate, especially with no reward of wages to follow.

The result was that she had been unceremoniously mounted upon the pillion-seat of Sergeant Fielder's motorcycle, with instructions to that officer to leave her in charge of someone—preferably a woman—who would be likely to deal with her in the right way.

Perdita, a year the younger, and having had little occasion or inclination to develop aggressive personality in the gracious security of her earlier life, might have been disconcerted to learn that Sergeant Fielder had looked at her with a sense of having arrived at the right address for unloading his charge. In any event, it was the last opportunity which had remained, after one or two less promising ones had been ignored or declined.

And for the first hour or two it went, apparently, well enough. Sarah conversed with a fluent effort at amiability which took only gradual heed of her companion's lack of response. She worked well enough while she was fresh to the task and its novelty pleased. The clearance of the store-cupboards and larder of the house on which Eustace had commenced—it was astonishing how much they held—and its packing into the lorry, in which Sarah showed a natural aptitude which rivalled Perdita's more practised methods, were accomplished without open dissension.

It was when they entered the next house, an old Georgian edifice of larger size than the newer surrounding residences, and standing farther back from the road, that trouble began.

Sarah looked around and was attracted by what she saw. She wandered up to the bedrooms. She explored clothes. To Perdita's urgent call from below that she would find nothing there, she replied that she was finding quite a lot.

Perdita, seeking her impatiently, found that she was exchanging her own garments for others of better material, though a worse fit.

"I shouldn't take those things, if I were you," she said. "It's the food that we've orders to get."

"I thought they say that everything's everybody's now, and you must pick up what you want as you go along. It's not such a dusty way."

"I don't understand it quite like that. I've no doubt it's rather confusing. It is confusion, of course, so that's natural enough. But if these people are alive and should walk in now, you wouldn't like them to see you pulling their things out as you are."

"That's what you say," the girl answered coolly. "If they do, you'll all get a surprise."

Perdita reflected that there really was some justification for this attitude, repugnant to her own habits though it might be, in the chaos which had fallen upon the world. And if the Germans might be here on the next day...! The thought turned her eyes to the window of the bedroom in which they were. The house stood high. They could see far. Outside the dusk gathered. The rain had ceased. The sky was a watery blue. The noise of gunfire, to which she had become so used that it was most often unheard, was surely louder, nearer, than before. Flashes winked in the west. If the Germans would soon be here, it might make it a matter of small account that the girl should pilfer the property of those who were absent and likely dead, but it also emphasized the urgency of what they delayed to do. Every pound of food which they failed to salve would not rot, but would serve to nourish the foe. And the needs of their own men! Who knew how great the shortage of food might be, how soon it might become acute, with the Germans closing upon them, as it seemed that they were about to do?

"Can't you see," she said, "that we haven't time to think of such things as these? That the Germans may be here almost at once, and we've got to get away all we can?"

"Garn! There'll be time enough yet. If you thought they were that close you'd have done a bunk before now. I'm not going to pull my guts out for whoever set us on this. I'll bet they wouldn't do it for me. But you needn't look so shirty for that! I'll lend a hand before long. But I should reckon by how you look that you've done enough for one day, and a bit more too."

"I haven't done enough while I can do more."

"Think not? Well, praise the Pope it's not catching. You won't see any spots on me. If the Germans did come, I don't suppose they'd treat us that bad. I wouldn't say but it might be rather a lark."

"If it had been like that, they wouldn't have told us not to get taken alive."

"You didn't fall for that, did you? Potty, I call it. If it's all true about how they're running the girls in, I don't see that we need lose any sleep. You might get with one who'd treat you real well."

"If you don't come," Perdita answered, in a voice that had become hard with angry contempt, "you won't need to wait for that. You'll find there'll be trouble now."

The girl gave her a startled, vicious, rebellious glance, and then her eyes fell sullenly before those they met. "Oh, all right, I'll come. But you fair give me the pip with your silly fuss."

After that, the loading of the lorry to the point to which its heterogeneous contents could be securely stacked was continued in a growing outer darkness, with little more than the minimum of unavoidable words from Perdita, though her companion, who did not seem to be easily roused to a lasting resentment, continued to be of a more talkative mood.

"We'll have to chuck it when it gets dark?" she had asked hopefully as the shadows closed, with a vaguely founded but not unnatural idea that the catastrophe which had destroyed all sentient things would have put systems of illumination out of action. But she had got for answer: "No, the electricity's on everywhere. Try that switch. The gas has gone, but not that. I don't know why, but that's how it is."

Half an hour later, Perdita said: "I'm going to take the lorry to Northfield now. That's not a long job. I just leave the one I take, and bring away another that's already empty. You can get everything that's worthwhile into the front hall here, ready for loading up. You might do three or four houses while I'm away, according to what there is. Most often there's next to nothing, and then you come to a six-months' supply. I'll leave you the keys. They'll open about everything except the Yale patterns. We've been forcing the windows if necessary. But it isn't often. If you find a house you can't enter, just leave it and we'll go back."

She drove off at a speed which had become usual to her on those familiar, dead, half-deserted roads, and came near collision with another lorry as rapidly, but perhaps less expertly, driven. It seemed that these vehicles had become more numerous, as though an extra effort were being made to clear the houses before the Germans arrived. She passed two that were standing in a road she knew to have been already cleared, but when she slowed down to call that information as she passed, she was answered with: "Yes, we know that. But it's metal, not food, that we're after now." She saw one that seemed to have whatever could first be seized loaded upon it, as though in the wild hope that all the wealth of a hundred square miles of desolation could be removed before the advancing enemy would be there.

There was a moon now near the full which made it easier to carry on through the darker hours. Easier too it must be for those whose advance did not cease with the fall of night on the Droitwich road, and who, as yet, were encountering little direct opposition the way they came.

But the English army that had been falling back before them towards Upton, and upon the Malverns, was now turning to press hard on their right flank as it swung round to the northeast. The sound of gunfire was ceaseless from that direction, though its volume varied. But it was surely nearer than it had been in the afternoon.

She had to wait for a few minutes, for the queue of empty lorries had shortened until they were being taken away as rapidly as they could be cleared. The officer in charge asked: "If I let you have this, are you good for another load? We shall have a few score more available during the night. They're on the way here now. But we want everyone to be fully worked."

"Oh yes," she said readily, though she had thought that the time for rest was about due. "If it's like that, I expect you'll soon see me again."

She drove back at a faster pace than before, and must search for the girl, who was not instantly to be found. When she came upon her, it was by the guidance of a light in the upper rooms of the house in which she had been left. She sat on the floor beneath a bureau, the drawers of which had been burst open. A glittering pile of pilfered jewellery lay at her side. But her eyes were on some prints which she had found in one of the locked drawers and, with an intentness which was oblivious of Perdita's approach till she stood looking down upon her.

The girl looked up startled, frightened for one visible moment, and then put on an indifferent air. "Gracious!" she exclaimed. "I didn't think you'd be back yet. Not for an hour. But, oh, my suffering aunt, you should see these!"

She held out the sheaf of prints, as a propitiatory offering against the anger of which she was inadequately aware; but Perdita did not even observe the nature of what she held. Back-handed, she struck her across the eyes.

The girl screamed as she went backwards, and then scrambled to her feet with a torrent of foul abuse. She made a motion towards Perdita, who stepped back, seeing that the girl's fear of herself was lost in the anger that pain had brought. She saw that she was near to an undignified and perhaps dangerous scrimmage with one who would be guided by no rules of decency in the way she fought, and as she stepped back she pulled out the pistol she had been given for a different need.

"No, you don't," she said. "I've got this. You'll pull your guts out, as you call it now, or I'll put a bullet into them that'll give you a real pain. You—you low scum!"

She looked at the now shrinking girl with a hard contempt, as being the base product of a social order beneath her own, in which she was wrong, her conduct being of herself rather than of her class or race. Indeed, relatively to their numbers, there may have been more of the half-barren women of Perdita's own leisured, cultured class without a tithe of Sarah Parfitt's excuse, whose baseness would become apparent under the bitter test of war, a war of a starkness that would strip off the concealing sheath to lay bare tinsel or steel.

Even she herself—had such words left her lips before? Or anything more lethal than a tennis-racket engaged her hand? But it had become suddenly natural that the blow should follow, or even precede, the word. And such words as she had not been accustomed to use! Different, cruder emotions than she had known before had struggled for self-expression, and found her half inarticulate, whose vocabulary—till the last week—had been ample for all her needs.

But, for this moment, those she had found had sufficed. Sarah worked without further demur, and, surprisingly—to Perdita—she worked well and soon showed a recovered cheerfulness, as though that which had occurred was of no moment to her.

Perdita drove herself and the girl hard, resolved to snatch the last ounce she could from the hands of the coming foe, and when the lorry was loaded high, as was soon done, she told Sarah to get up beside her. "They may be glad," she said, "for us to help unload, and if you sit down you'll go to sleep more likely than not."

An hour later they returned in a state of weariness from which even Perdita must admit that exhausted muscles could do no more. There was no lack of beds in these deserted houses—mostly in a state of disorder, for it had been early morning when the order for instant flight had been broadcast with the news of the approach of the bombers—and Perdita, who did not approve the idea of Sarah as a sleeping-companion, said that they would rest in adjoining rooms. She was too weary even to resent, and was barely conscious of the half-sneering, half-jesting remark which this arrangement drew from the girl—that she supposed she would have been an even worse substitute during the night for the man whose place she had taken than she had been in the day. What did it matter, one way or another, that between Eustace Ashfield and herself there had been no thought of familiarities, either by night or day? Or that she and Sarah had different languages, different ideals, different habits of life? It was a time when many feet would slip on the edge of the pit of change, and who could tell what—or who—would endure in a rocking world? All she knew was that she must have a few hours of sleep—three or four should be enough now; it was no more than that to the dawn—and return to the work of urgent salvage again.

So she lay down in her clothes, drawing a quilt round her for warmth, and found that the sleep she needed refused to come.

She was weary. Her muscles ached. But her brain was alive. And it was useless to tell herself that she *must* sleep; that it was a plain duty, that she might wake the sooner again.

She heard Sarah, whose day of toil had been much shorter than hers, and her effort less, moving about in the next room. Probably she was again rummaging in the deserted drawers, attracted half by curiosity, half by greed. And then her voice rose clearly. As she searched, she sang.

"Glory for me.
Glory for me.
That will be glory for me,
When by His grace I shall look on His face,
That will be glory for me."

It proved to be a refrain capable of endless repetitions. It went on and on. Sarah Parfitt's singing voice was clearer, less coarse in tone, than that with which she addressed the world. The simple, appropriate, unpretentious tune was not unmoving in the immediate stillness of night, with its dreadful, distant clamour of fatal sound. Had Perdita not met the singer, it might have seemed the spiritual challenge of humanity to the devils that were surely loose in the night.

"If I get up," she thought, "and pace the room, tired as I am, it may bring me the sleep I need."

So she did, but sleep was not so easily to be won. The song in the next room, which had been still for a time, broke out again. Her mind seemed clearer, more vividly conscious of outer things, for the physical exhaustion her muscles owned. She became curiously, surprisingly aware that the singer in the next room was an individual like herself. One to whom she herself was something alien and remote. One like herself among millions, and like herself, one alone. Born without understanding or will of hers into a strange, bewildering, dreadful world, and, like her, doomed, as all men are, to the lonely passage of death. And death was round her now and so near! Though perhaps less dreadful in its crude violences than when it came to each one separately, in its leisured, selective way. The girl might mean what she sang. It might be consolation to her. She might even see nothing inconsistent between her normal course of conduct and the expectation that she repeated so many times. His little children stumbling in the dark. Where had she read that line? Oh, Fitzgerald, of course. Not exactly a Christian poet. Yet it was a line that held the very pity of God. This was not the way to find sleep. Was there no means of controlling thought? She looked out on the night. The moon had clouded. There were flashes that were not stars in the southern sky. High flashes frequent among the clouds. She knew what must be the meaning of them. Now there was a falling flame in the sky, a leap of intenser flare as the wreck struck earth, a flame that was soon done.

It was no more than a frequent incident of the night, not in England alone but along a war-front of ten thousand miles. The allied air forces might have become too weak to possess the skies, but their fighters could still lurk and hunt, could gather or scatter among the clouds, as they were called to a likely prey, or warned of foes that they would be unequal to meet. They could still shoot the slow bombers down, could deal death to the transport planes, even daring or evading their escorts when storm blackened the air.

It was these constant, continually fatal conflicts which were making it increasingly evident with every day that the air-arm, dreadful in its consequences as it might be, would be less than decisive to end the war. The air forces, if freely employed, as they first had been, were mutually destructive, beyond any possible rate of replacement; they were vulnerable from the ground. Their casualties were a list of few wounded but many dead.

Perdita knew that there were now many English fighters, varying from the huge, three-engined, cannon-mounted battleships of the skies to the swift, light, one- or two-seaters that might carry no more than a single cannon or machine guns fore and aft, which would cruise solitary through the night, signalling at times to their fellows by secret codes, betrayed at times to death by a false lure, but still taking a heavy toll of those who boasted that they had won the skies.

They would set out today—tomorrow—and return victorious to their hidden lairs—and perhaps the next night also. For a week? It was likely to be shorter than that. Life in these days would not be long for those who fought in the air.

It must be such a conflict that she had seen. Oh, pray God, she thought, pray God that it was not ours that fell in that flaming wreck! Did God heed such prayers? She would know much if she knew the answer to that. Anyway, it was over now. The vanquished dead and the victor gone. *A shadow down the sickened wave, long since the slayer fled.* Who—what was that? Kipling, of course. But not airplanes. Destroyers. The lean sharks of the sea. Written before airplanes were made. *Good luck to those who win the day: goodbye to those who drown.* This was not the way to woo sleep. Was she to waste the night in fears, or a selfish prayer? It was work that was needed now. Suppose she took off her clothes? It might be that sleep would then come in a more natural way. And the sooner it came, the sooner she would be equal to work again. Stripping herself of all but a single garment, she lay between blankets, and in a moment was sleeping well.

CHAPTER XVII.

THE dawn came, but Perdita slept. It widened, with a windy brightness presaging storm. There were noises around her much louder, much nearer now, than those that had vexed the night. But she had become accustomed to noise. There could be little sleep in these days for one who would lift her head at a bursting shell.

In the early dawn, while the German advance-guard, having occupied Droitwich during the night, commenced to move forward again on the Bromsgrove road, there had come a fleet of transports high overhead. They had dropped no bombs this time on a land they had silenced before, but had scattered more active seed. By a mode which had been first publicly demonstrated by the Russian air forces two years before, they had released a whole mechanized unit, complete with guns and other equipment, out of the clouds. These settled down on fields which, being already desolate, were not likely to be defended in force, and which reconnaissance had reported to be outside the defensive lines which Birmingham had dug in desperate haste on its southwestern side. Their mission was to discover how, and in what force, the ground between Bromsgrove and Northfield was held to the south of the Lickey Hills, and either signal to their comrades that they need use no caution in their advance or warn them of what they must be ready to overcome, while themselves seizing some defensible post, and holding it, for which they were well equipped, until relief should arrive.

Perdita waked at last, reluctantly, heavily, at a sound of shots in the next room. One. And then two that were almost one.

She half rose, blaming herself that she had slept so long, and half fearful, half uncertain, of what she heard. In the passage outside there were heavy steps, at the sound of which her fear waked alert, and she became aware of an unguarded door, which she had not thought, in the weariness of last night—which it might, indeed, have seemed futile—to lock.

She rose quickly, and, as she did so, stretched a hand for the pistol which should have been at her side, only to observe that it was not there. What could be the meaning of that? Well, first of all, she must secure the door and then dress, and find what was happening without. It was all instantaneous—her throwing the bedclothes back, and springing out to the floor in the single garment she had retained, as the steps she had heard the previous second stopped, and the door opened, for a German officer to enter, with an automatic raised in his hand. She owed her life to the facts that she was unclothed and that the pistol was gone. For it is certain that he would have fired had he seen her armed—and with some excuse, after an experience which he had just had—and that he would have been far quicker than she.

"Who are you?" he asked curtly. "Is that your lorry below?"

"I don't know what's below," she answered, speaking from a mind divided between bewilderment, anger, and fear. "But you've no right to come in like that. Will you go out while I dress?"

He took no notice of that request. "Are you armed?" he asked, in the same tone as before. "You'll be wise if you tell the truth." As he spoke, his eyes glanced rapidly over dressing-table and chairs. He prodded the little heap of her clothes. He threw back the pillows. The automatic, as he did so, was still directed upon her.

"I don't know," she answered, with a literal truthfulness he was unlikely to understand. "It doesn't seem so, does it?"

"Then it's the better for you," he said, in a slightly less hostile voice. And then, more curtly again, as he lifted up the soiled overall she had worn: "What were you doing with this?"

"Wearing it," she answered, with the same literality as before. And then, with the first conscious obliquity she had used: "Trying to clear things up." He may have concluded that she had returned to an abandoned home to find that it had been entered and disordered in her absence. More probably, he did not greatly care what she had done, his question having been sufficiently turned aside.

He looked at her with an admiration she did not like, as he added: "Anyway, you'll come along with me now. You're just the sort that we're glad to have. Put them on sharp, if you don't want to catch cold. You'll come without if you don't. I'm not waiting here."

But that, she saw, was exactly what he intended to do. He would not withdraw till she should go with him, whether clothed or not. With which choice, she made haste to put on her clothes, except the overall, which she had the sense to leave. And it was a simple guess that its use was done.

She said, trying to preserve her poise, to talk to him in a personal manner, as he watched her dress: "You speak English well."

"I was in one of your cursed camps in the last war."

She thought: "And we were fools ever to let you loose, and set you on your feet again as we did." But it would have been foolish to say.

"Walk ahead," he said. "And no tricks. I suppose you know the way down."

"Yes. I suppose I do." If he thought it to be her own house, should she correct him in that? She had become widely awake now, and alert to her environment. She would escape, if she could, even at a great risk.

The door of the next bedroom was open. Immediately opposite, sideways to it, was a bed on which Sarah Parfitt lay. She was still dressed, and lay half across it, with her arms hanging forward and her head touching the floor. Her hair was thrown forward upon the carpet, and around it was a red patch that had spread from her face or throat. On the floor, as it had slipped from the hand of the dying girl, lay Perdita's pistol.

It was no more than an instantaneous glance, but one that she would not forget in the years to come, be they few or more. It was a sure guess that Sarah had stolen that pistol during the night, but with what object was less simple to tell. Probably with no further thought than to secure herself against a repetition of the threat of the night before.

For a moment indignation, pity, and horror caused her to forget her own peril. She said, with contempt clear in her eyes and her lifted lip: "You kill girls like that, and you didn't like it when you were called Huns in the last war!"

"She fired first," he answered, in an unexpectedly reasoning tone. "What else could I have done?"

Justice prompted her to reply: "Of course, I didn't know that." But her mind asked silently, was it true? Yes, she thought it was; though it was not easy to understand. It was a point on which he would scarcely have troubled to lie, and his words had had a genuine sound. But under what impulse of anger or fear had Sarah acted in that improbable manner? Had she meant no more than to wave the weapon in a way that should keep him back, and it had gone off in her unpractised hand? Had there been a gulf of difference between her actual character and the way in which she had talked? Well, give her the best of the doubt there was! She was dead now, and no one would ever know. Perdita still lived, and saw that she had enough to do for herself, if her own honour and her own life were to remain.

Outside, the Germans had found no organized resistance to their unexpected descent. But they had surprised, and more or less cut off, many of those who had been engaged in the work of clearing the deserted houses, and these were being shot down—the men relentlessly, and the women unless they yielded without demur—as they could be cornered and caught. Many lorries had made a successful dash for still-open roads, and had escaped with no more damage than splintered wood and pierced metal where bullets struck. One, too hardly driven, had been overturned at a sharp curve. Another, its driver falling under the wheel as his senses failed from the shock of a shattered arm, had run on unguided for a surprising distance, swaying from side to side of a road that it did not leave, until it struck a vehicle that moved at a slower pace with a crashing havoc that went far to block the whole breadth of the way.

But Perdita saw nothing of this; she heard no more than a confusion of shots and cries. She knew that the Germans were swarming on every side, but she did not know how they had come, and blamed herself more than the fact required that she had slept to so late an hour. Well, if she had done wrong, it seemed that it was the right one who would have to pay! For the moment, she was in a room with two other women, her hands tied tightly behind her back, as were theirs also, and an armed sentry guarding the door. There was nothing hopeful in that.

Of her two companions, the younger was a short, shapeless girl with a fixed, vacuous smile on her lips, which her eyes denied. She did not look as though she would be very intelligent, under the least exacting conditions, and her aspect now was that of one too scared for any process of thought.

The other, a small, thin, elderly woman, with a lined face that looked as though its owner had seen more of the severities than the pleasures of life, was weeping silently, oblivious, it seemed, of her surroundings, or of the bleeding of a bruised jaw.

The officer who had captured Perdita entered the room, followed shortly by another of higher rank.

"This is the woman, Colonel," the first said. "Franz reports that she had a gun in her hand when they shot the man. It was unloaded, but still hot."

Colonel Sieber looked at the woman, who gave no attention to him, being more concerned with her own grief than what he would be likely to do. He was a rather corpulent man of the large Prussian type, with small eyes and fleshy features surmounted by a cropped head, and a habit of slow, heavy speech which made him appear far more dense, though not more brutal, than he was. He said: "Taken with arms? What will you say to that?"

The woman roused herself to point to the white-cross armlet which had become the military badge of the un-uniformed civilian army that was now an enlisted nation to fight this war.

Colonel Sieber said: "We don't recognize that." He called two privates into the room. "Take her out," he said. "She's not worth keeping. Get it over. We can't stay here."

His glance went on to Perdita and the other remaining woman. "Nothing against these?" he asked, and his tone might have implied that it was a pity that nothing could be alleged. "Well, bring them along. We shall hold the ridge to southward, over the wood. You must get them behind there."

While he spoke, the soldiers had taken the older woman by her two arms and were leading her out, against which she made no protest, seeming scarcely conscious of what was done.

It was no more than a minute later that two shots came as a single sound immediately outside the house. Perdita might have been less sure of the meaning of that had not the officer by whom she had been captured looked at her in an uneasy, self-conscious way and said: "Well, what else could we do? We can't keep a lot of prisoners here. Could we let her loose, to be up to mischief again?"

She met his glance with far steadier eyes. "Devils," she said deliberately, "will always do after their own kind. I suppose that's why there's a hell. But perhaps cads is a better word."

She felt a fearlessness, curious and exhilarating, as she said this, which she did not comprehend, though its elation was in her blood. It was as though death were so nearly around that its terror went. Here it had ceased to be stealthy in its approach. It did not come as though ashamed of itself among fairer things. And by that change it had lost its mystery and its fear.

"It is not I who decide," he answered. "But when you come before those who do, it will be better that you should talk in a humbler tone, if you value the life you have."

"Oh, they will let me live," she said bitterly. "I am young. I should call devils too good a name."

"Well," he answered, "you may call me what names you will. I wish you no harm for that. But you are warned. I would have you live."

By this time the two privates had re-entered the room, showing no emotion for what they did. The little party must move. Perdita walked with care, having bound hands, and wishing to give no excuse for those to help whose hands she would have farther away. The girl came at her side, still with that vacuous, propitiatory smile.

The short walk gave Perdita time for thought, and for wisdom in place of indignation to take control. "Need I be a fool," she thought, "because I seem to have lost the feeling of fear? I should be useless if I were dead. England needs us all. He may be German, but he spoke sense, and it was meant in a friendly way. I will live, if it be that I have enough wit to contrive it, and it can be cleanly done. But they would kill me if they knew that which my heart holds, which they would be wiser to do."

She did not think of how much she had changed in the last weeks, as she was beaten on the hard anvil of war. They went up between dead hedges, and past the black wood of trees that would not green with the coming spring, many of which had been burst apart to the core by the intense cold of the freezing gas, and over the crest of the rising ground. There was a dip beyond that, opening to a shallow depression which could not be overlooked while the ridge was held.

In the midst a tent had been pitched. It was green, having been fashioned to match the grass of a winter field, and so to be unseen from above, but on that lifeless ground it was a conspicuous thing. There might be no cause for trouble in that, for in daylight hours the invaders had now little reason to fear that death would come from the skies, and the ridge which buttressed the shallow field was higher than any neighbouring rise. Under it a steam-plough had been assembled from separate parts, and was already trenching the ground.

Pick and spade toiled on the ridge, making emplacements for guns that had come down from the clouds. With very orderly haste the little force prepared to resist attack of which there was yet no sign. The lorry drivers were slain by this time, or had slipped away. There was a pause between storm and storm. But the sounds of war were not distant, nor ever still, by which it might be supposed that the pause would be quickly done.

Perdita was led into the tent, and had time to observe that she had been brought to those who were busy upon matters which (to them) were more important than she was ever likely to be.

The Colonel and another officer spoke, and were not careful who heard. The second was of meagre aspect, and coughed at times, as one who was distressed by the cold, wet weather to which he had been brought through the night. But he wore a staff officer's uniform and spoke as an equal, if not something more. He was, in fact, of a higher rank, but he was there to advise rather than directly to command.

Colonel Sieber said, with an anger in his voice which was not free from the note of fear: "If we advise thus, we shall be destroyed. Do you ignore that?"

That, it appeared, was what the coughing officer did. "So we may be," he replied. "But it is sound science of war. It is the small loss for the major gain."

"You might call yourself a small loss," the Colonel replied, "but I value myself at a better bid. I think to go far in this war, if it lasts, as I say it will. Are we to destroy ourselves for something they do not ask or require?"

"Am I to report that you put your own life before the clear duty you have?"

"If I take your advice, I should say you will not report, being dead. So it seems that it must be nothing, or that, unless you will come to a better mind. But I say that it is no clear duty at all. What is clear is that they have no strength of defence that is west or south of the Lickey Hills, and we may advance ourselves on what width and by all the roads that we will."

"And that the hills should be turned, beyond Clent, on their northern side."

"Which could still be done. But you will take note that I have not assented to that. It is what they will expect us to try, which may make it wrong."

The Staff-officer gave an impatient cough, of a more voluntary kind than he had sounded before. "We can link up with Bessel no other way."

Colonel Sieber's wits made the effort which even those of a dull man may when he becomes aware of his skin's risk. "You think," he said, "you judge more wisely than I, being of some repute in the blackboard science of war, but there are other matters which we who are in command must be able to weigh, which chalk and rule do not teach.

"Have you thought how it would hearten these English swine if they could boast they had caught us here? It would be enlarged to a great defeat. It would be noised over the world. It is Wasser would have the blame. It might mean his recall. That is what you would have accomplished for him. It would not matter to us, of course. We should be dead before then, and there is too much stir in the world today for thought to pause on those who are foiled and slain."

"You are wrong," the officer replied, when a fresh bout of coughing allowed speech. "You are wrong about all but our own deaths, on which you place an importance they do not have. If Wasser but do his part, there will be enough to report by night to make our fates a detail that will not count. But you must do as you will. I can advise, and no more."

"I shall report how we are placed and the advice you give, and Bessel must choose what he will do. But that he will leave us without relief I do not think, for I have known him too long."

"Then he is unfit for the place he holds."

"As, by you, I suppose that we all are."

The dispute ended at this. Perdita would have learnt more had she become more expert in the German tongue. She understood little more than that they quarrelled among themselves, which seemed good. The Colonel was instructing a wireless officer now, giving him a further message to supplement those which had already been sent.

For a second his words were drowned by the noise of a shell that burst in the next field. Perdita, hearing it, must observe the double danger in which she stood. If she were spared by her foes, it might be for no better fate than that her friends should blow her apart.

Yet there was some hope in the sound of that bursting shell. She saw that rescue could only come, if at all, in a perilous form which, she told herself, was much better than none.

Having finished his message, the Colonel hurried out, which he had occasion to do. For whether General Bessel would move in earnest to his relief, or prefer to feint only upon his right while throwing his full weight into the advance of his leftward front, it was evident that there would be hard fighting before any rescue could reach him.

The English military command had been warned by the fleeing lorries, if they had not already appreciated what had occurred, and they were about to prove that they had long-range guns that were sighted and handled well, though it would be too much to hope that they would omit approach of a more intimate kind.

CHAPTER XVIII.

NORTHERN Worcestershire has no heights, except the low hills of Lickey and Clent, which were now the front of the English line, but, excepting the Droitwich salt-pan of small extent, it is seldom or nowhere flat. It is all red sandstone hillocks and clefts, which, when they were undrained before Saxon days, were no better than islands amid morass, so that it had been an ill land in which to live, but also hard to invade; and its ancient history is not much, until Ethelfleda used it for centres of refuge when she dodged and doubled (and fought at the right times) to the final loss of the Danes.

Colonel Sieber had chosen the best position he could for his descent, being drawn thereto by a comparative flatness of ground that was not low. But it was still one which was not hard for infantry to approach under cover, using the winding lanes that preferred hollow to height, and that had been deeply worn by the feet and wheels of a thousand years, before the new hardness of concrete maintained their levels, but made them tiring to human tread.

He had four hundred well-trained men who had been carefully picked, making them of more worth than a thousand of random choice. He had a machine gun for every three, and a battery of good range, though the shells it threw were not large. What he needed was more time for the trenching-tools to make his position strong than he was permitted to have.

He had time to fire the houses for some distance around, which he did, and it was in an atmosphere made acrid by driven smoke that Perdita faced the Staff-officer's inquisition, which she endured better than she otherwise might because he did not understand English, and his questions must be interpreted by the officer who was friendly to her, as her replies must be also, some of which would have been surprising to her had she understood what they became in the German tongue.

For it appeared that she could not be retained as a prisoner, even in this crisis of strife, unless a form were filled up in the meticulous German manner. And even in this descent from the clouds, since the capture of women had become an explicit object of the invasion which was now threatening the British Isles from more points than one, and had become a spreading sore in the Midland shires, there had been forms brought on which such arrests could be recorded, numbered, and named, with entry of sufficient legal reason (if such an edict could be dignified by the name of law) for what was done.

Captain Ebert (which was the officer's name) understood the conditions of Perdita's safety as she was not likely to know or guess them to be. He knew that she would not be allowed to go free. Nor was she the sort that would be uselessly shot if pretext could be found for preserving her for another use. Her greatest danger was that she should refuse either to incriminate herself or to admit that she had relatives in arms on the English side.

For if nothing could be set down such as would justify her retention, then a moment might come when the Staff-officer would decide that her own obduracy of denial gave him no pretext for filling up the form in the manner the edict required, which would close the one avenue of life, such as it was, that the position allowed. He would make no order such as might subject him to rebuke for irregularity in the months to come. But he would justify himself by the customs of war, as he held them to be, in ordering that of which no record need be preserved, and which would be instantly done.

Captain Ebert did not go recklessly wrong, but he interpreted Perdita's replies into that which those numbered questions required to justify the order that would be made. He had not scrupled to send two bullets into Sarah Parfitt's head (having some excuse in the fact that she had first directed one at him with a worse aim), but he did not therefore desire the death of every Englishwoman he met. Nor did he like Perdita the less because she had said things to him which were not smoothly polite. He would not have let her escape for the most pitiful prayer, and, considering the fate to which she was consigned by his aid, it may be said that there was no mercy in what he did; but, for the moment, he saved her life.

The Staff-officer wrote with rapid brevity, doing no more than an act of routine, and one which, under other circumstances, would have been too trivial for his own pen. He consigned Perdita, and then the girl beside her, against whom the evidence and her own admissions were clear, to be taken by air to the Nürnberg receiving-station, from which they would pass to the control of the civil power of the land which was to become theirs, and the Army would be concerned with them no more.

He wrote without regarding the thickening smoke-haze which had invaded the tent. He gave the papers to Captain Ebert, neatly folded and sealed. He said: "You will be responsible for them until they can be handed over to the transport officer, to whom you will give these. But I should say that one man will be a sufficient guard, they being tied as they are, and men are needed for better use. He should have them where they will not be in the way, and in no more danger than the position requires. Tell them that they will be shot if they run."

He ended with a bout of coughing, which was made worse by the acrid fumes that the wind blew into the tent, and which now had a resinous smell. He exclaimed: "What, in the fiend's name must he be at that he chokes us thus?"

"He gave orders," Ebert replied, "that the houses should be fired, lest they be cover for the English approach."

"But the road is some distance below the ridge! There are few houses around except there. They would not smoke us thus, nor would their heat reach us, from so far away."

He went out as he spoke, and it seemed that he was met by a burning world. For Colonel Sieber had done something he had not meant.

It was true that he had ordered the firing of the houses, and also of the little wood that half covered the slope between road and ridge. The wood was nearer than the road, and a greater menace to his position, unless he should occupy it himself, which he had been reluctant to do. He had thought that, being dead, it would burn well.

He was right in that. It rose in almost instant flame to the sky. Those who started the fires must run hard, the wind being at their backs, that they should not be caught by the chasing flames. But the fire, having won the wood, did not stop there, as it had been expected to do. The fields had been surrounded by hedges, dense and high, which had not been trimmed back from their last year's growth. And at intervals trees, perhaps a mere bush of holly, or else a wide oak or a lofty elm, had been allowed to rise from the haw-thorn hedge. These hedges and trees, being frozen dead as they were, had become fuel to burn.

It was a point which the Colonel would have been less likely to overlook had the habit of dividing field from field by a wooded hedge been as common in his own as it was in this foreign land. But he found too late that he had started that which he could not stay.

The Staff-officer stared. He coughed. He exclaimed, as well as the state of his throat allowed: "What crazed folly is this? They can attack under this cover of smoke, and we will not see them till they are here."

The Colonel stood near. He said, with the irritation of one who, knowing he has blundered, does not love to be told: "Do you think me blind? Will you tell me how this can be stayed by the sound sci-ence of war?"

It was not only the Colonel who stood near. The tent was be-coming the crowded centre upon which four hundred men were re-tiring from every side. On three sides of the field the black hedges flared to the sky.

"Yes," the Staff-officer sourly replied. "I can tell you what you can do by the sound science of war, though to tell you how to undo what you have done wrong may be past my power. You can order that this tent be taken down before it ignite from the driven sparks, and you may have the ammunition removed to where it will be least likely to feel the fire. Beyond that, you must change the wind, if you can, or provide rain."

Colonel Sieber was too efficient an officer to allow himself to be ruffled by his companion's sarcasm at such a time. The advice he had received was good, but did not touch the major problem he must decide. The fourth side of the field was still unlit, and there was a gate in the hedge wide enough for a farm-cart to pass. Should he stand his ground, or attempt flight through that gap from the circling fire?

"I suppose," he said, "that hedge and gate would be up in flames before we were all through?"

"So they would. And for those who passed it might prove that the fire would be more active than they, and they would do worse to be trapped in a smaller field. We must remain here."

So they found that there was one point on which they agreed. The tent came down, and a red patch must be trodden out, showing that the next minute would have been too late. Men were set to re-move the gate, and cut down the hedge, right and left, as far as time would permit, to provide a gap, wide and cool to tread, for a forced retreat, or when the time for movement should come. They had not done much to this end before they were driven back, for the fire was on them from either side.

Perdita, being now clear of the tent, could gaze round on a scene of terror and flame-lit gloom which could have been better admired from a secure point, and with less discomfort from the cord that was round her wrists. Was a confusion coming amidst which she might still hope to escape? That was, if any there would escape alive. The chance was not improved by the act of the one man who was now her own and her companion's guard. His thoughts clearly moved in the same direction as hers, but with a contrary will. His prisoners might have bound hands, but what should he do if they should start off in separate ways, even though their pace might be less than his? He knew the answer to be that he must shoot. But he was a humane man, who had not killed so much as a caught rat till he had been conscripted for war, and he was loath to begin on a woman's back. He said, in a fatherly way, though in words that they did not know: "You will both be safer for this." He tied together the cords that bound their hands, so that they must keep side by side or pull different ways. He thought that he had done a good deed, and one that his priest (for he was a Catholic, as some in Germany still secretly were) would approve, in which we must hope he was right, for his death was near. But Perdita regarded it in a different spirit.

It was little pleasure to be tied thus, as she looked upon rolling billows of smoke, yellow and dense, that swept on from the wood, the tree-tops of which were about level with where she stood. The trees crackled and blazed, making a glow, lurid or red, under the dense canopy of the smoke. The hedges now blazed on all sides, raising walls of flame which the smoke roofed, as though a temple had been built to the demon of fire. They were in a heat hard to endure, and the dry, burnt air tortured the lungs.

Yet it was already evident that there would be discomfort rather than peril from the direct action of the fire. The heat was unpleasant but not dangerous to sustain, and could not greatly increase.

But the English artillery, which had obtained its range before the smoke rose, did not cease to drop shells into the obscure inferno which it knew to contain its foes. Fortunately for themselves, none fell directly upon those who were now constrained to crowd into the midst of the field, with the miscellaneous equipment which had been assembled there. But one burst sufficiently near to account for three deaths and a dozen wounds, and another, coming to earth in the midst of the blazing hedge where a holly stood, had scattered fragments of burning wood which had done more harm than its own shards.

Some of the guns had been withdrawn from the positions which had been in course of preparation for them. Others, with their ammunitions, had been abandoned as the gun-crews were driven back by the swiftly encroaching fire. This ammunition burst now, more than once, with deafening reports, and with a shedding of steel and fire more destructive than that which came from the English shells.

When the fire in the immediate vicinity began to subside, as, being consumed by its own fierceness, it quickly did, there was some veering of wind to the east, and a cold rain came down through the smoky air, which was very welcome to those upon whom it fell, from a double cause. For the dead grass, though it did not burn at first like the wood, became more inflammable as it was dried by surrounding heat, and had begun to smoulder in wide patches that spread out from the burning sides of the field, and could only be stayed by cutting away a broad band with shovel and pick, for which men must be driven to work in a place of heat that would be hard to endure, and even this might not long have availed.

Perdita thought of herself at this time less than she might, being occupied with the girl to whom she was so closely attached. She had seen her reduced to a kind of vacuous imbecility by the fact that she was in hostile hands, but she reacted to physical danger in a more positive way. She moaned as she hid her face from the cage of fire in which she may have thought that they would come to a roasting death. She screamed and shook when the shells burst. She kept muttering, "Oh, Mother, Mother, we shall be killed," in a monotonous manner hard for any sympathy to endure.

Perdita judged that the girl's wits must be near to go, but could she help that? War is for the healthy, not for the weak. She told unregarding ears that if some die at such times, there are more who live. She meant to be one of these, if the fates were kind, but she saw that she was tied, in a literal way, to one who might hinder, but from whom she could look for no help at any chance that the moment brought.

When a high tree crashed inwards across the field, its highest boughs, still hotly aflame, being at no great distance from the packing-case upon which they had been kindly directed to sit (they did not know that it contained machine gun ammunition, and that its protection was supposed to be slightly increased by their position upon it), the girl jumped up, and would have run blindly about but for the restraining pull of the cord, and Perdita's refusal to stir.

So they endured or quailed, as their natures were, till they were cooled by the welcome rain, and might watch, if they would, the stir of men who had become active again with the knowledge that the fire fell, and that they must prepare for more conscious foes.

At first the hot lines of the smouldering hedgerows were manned, and there were bursts of machine-gun fire at the sighting of real or imagined foes. But after a short time it was resolved, for reasons bad or good, which were not likely to come to Perdita's ears, that it would be vain to attempt to hold the position in which they were, and that they must endeavour to retire, more or less in the path that the fire had taken, and where it still raged on through the dead land, until they should distance pursuit or reach their advancing friends.

So there was movement now in which Perdita was disposed at first to be slack, and to make the most of the condition of her to whom she was tied, which would have been good excuse at a better time; but their guard acted with a brutality which came in part from nervousness as to what he might be required to do if they could not move at a quicker pace, and in part from his own desire not to be last in a retreat which might be disturbed at any moment by a burst of shrapnel upon its rear.

He chose Perdita, as the one it would be of the more use to impress, for a sharp prick with his bayonet. Even apart from the pain of a wound which she may have thought to be more than it was, it was an indignity which she did not wish to tempt for a second time, nor could she find relief in words addressed to one who could only speak in the German tongue. She pulled her companion on, deferring thought of escape to a more possible time which she soon supposed to have come.

For after they had, as it seemed, eluded pursuit, and even the nuisance had ceased of shells which had not often come very near since they had commenced to move in the smoky track of the failing fire (for the English guns, being few enough for the need they had, were diverted to face the advancing foe), there came the sound of an airplane that circled above their heads, though whether it were friend or foe was not easy to see.

The little force moved in close order now, having abandoned such of its equipment as could not be lightly moved, even apart from that which the fire had consumed or spoiled. It had no fear of a fronting foe, and machine gun units took positions upon its rear where the ground was kind, and fell back, one behind the other, as their occasion was done. Even the Staff-officer could not say that the retreat was not being conducted according to the sound science of war. They were in the midst of a large ploughed field that had missed most of the fire, having a wire fence on its longer sides, and in front a ditch in which there was now some water from recent rain, and beyond that there had been no more than some wooden palings, the burning of which had been quickly done.

They would not have chosen this ploughed field, where the walking was heavy, had there not been some rough land above, that, having been overgrown with furze, had caught fire, and was smouldering still. It was dense with smoke, grey and black under the rain, but that was no trouble to them, for what wind there was blew it away. Had it blown it upon them, there would have been more alive on the next day.

The noise of the plane grew louder over their heads. It was now flying low, but there might be no menace in that, for it was likely that its business was not with them, and it was ten to one that it would carry the German symbol beneath its wings.

Consternation came when it was directly above their heads, and the English colours were caught by the glow of the burning field. The clouds were low, but it came much lower than they. It dropped no bombs on those who looked apprehensively up, for it was not the kind which is pregnant with eggs of death. It was a light two-seater fighter of an old pattern that had been called swift when it was built, but could now only live in the air by the leave or absence of those of a later date. It carried two machine guns, operated by one who sat at the pilot's side.

It passed overhead, doing no harm, and receiving none from those who looked up and were only anxious to see it go, indifferent to themselves. But having passed, it came back. It came lower now. Recklessly low, it swerved over the charred stumps of the hedgerow trees, curved across the field which they approached, skimmed the wire fence, and then, as it swooped upon them, its machine guns opened upon men who replied with a splutter of futile shots, as they crouched between furrows too shallow for any safety, into which they had flung themselves as it came.

Those who could rise when it had passed had no better hope than to run forward to find such shelter as the ditch could give, which few of them would have time to reach before, twice again, the swift plane had returned to mow through them a swathe of death.

Perdita and her companion lay or ran with the rest, as they were likely to do, a friend's bullet being no better than that which comes from a foe, and their guard urged them on with a natural zeal. But it is slow running on heavy, unlevel ground when the hands are tied and two must keep at one pace. They were soon behind, with no more company than the litters of some who had been wounded before, and these, as the airplane swept over them a second time, the roar of its engine deadening the incessant sound of the deadly guns, their bearers had dropped with no more excuse than a coward has, and left their charges to that which chance or mercy might deal.

But after the second rush had passed noisily overhead, Perdita's running was done. She was not conscious of any wound, but she knew that she was tied to a dead girl, and that her guard was too badly hurt to give further notice to her.

She thought at first that she might be safe if she should lie still, while those around her rose for a fresh spurt to the sheltering ditch. She raised her head, and saw that the dead and injured lay thickly around. She heard cries and saw sights which would have been hard to sustain at a different time, but she was too concerned now for her own life to be over-conscious of pains which were not hers. She thought: "Surely I shall be safe if I lie still. There are many around; but they will observe them to be hurt, if not dead. They will waste no bullets on them."

So it might have been, but for the rearguard, of whom she had not thought, but who had had some thought for themselves. Where they had been, there was no more cover than a burnt hedge, so that they would have had little reason to hope for life if the English plane should give attention to them. But they saw those who had crossed the field disappear into a ditch, which they may have thought to be of a better depth than it was. At which sight they had thrown away all that they could, keeping, indeed, little except their legs, and now came over the field with a burst of speed such as might be expected of those who ran for the greatest prize that a man may.

They did it nearly—not quite. They dropped like partridges around the spot where Perdita lay, as the whir of the engine sounded close behind them again. The spot where she had thought that she might be safe had now become thickest with living crop for the guns to reap. For a second she raised herself in the wild hope that she might be noticed for what she was. With a rush like that of a monstrous condor out of the clouds, the warplane came down, almost skimming the barren ground as it swept past. There was a second or less during which she saw the gunner directing his fire upon them, as a reaper's sickle will take the corn. She saw the masked face of the pilot, a slighter figure on his farther side. The foolish impulse died as she saw the soil spurt where the bullets struck. She crouched to the coming death, and, as she did so, the plane lurched wildly. The air whistled to a stream of bullets that passed harmlessly overhead.

The plane, which had swayed like a shot bird, recovered itself, and rose into the clouds. The drone of its engine became distant, and died away.

Perdita, who had thought death or escape to be her most likely choice, or rather that which had been chosen for her, found that she was twice wrong. Captain Ebert rose from a near furrow. He walked over to where she sat up as well as she might for the straining cord. He asked: "You are unhurt? You are fortunate. So are we. That pilot ought to be shot. But I suppose you have few left who are fit to handle a fighter. For the time, you will come with me."

He cut the cord, which he twisted round his own wrist. She saw that, if she were to escape, the time was not now.

In the plane, the gunner asked: "What was wrong?" He did not suppose that that sudden lurch had occurred through Imogen Lister's inability to handle the plane, knowing the reputation she had had before the war, which had not been lessened by that which had happened since, though allowance had to be made for the fact that she had crashed less than a fortnight before, and had come from hospital now, saying that she could sit in a plane, though walking, with the hurt she had, would have been harder to do. While the Germans closed from two sides on the Midland city was not a time to lie in a hospital bed, for which there would soon be occupants with more urgent needs.

She answered: "I saw a girl that I know. I suppose that we had hurt her before, but she was not dead. I do not know whether I stopped you in time."

"Oh," he said, "you did that! There must be twenty Germans living to bless that swerve. Alive to kill us tomorrow."

He did not believe that she had seen one she had known or any woman at all. He thought it showed that the best of her sex are unfit for the pitiless test of war, as perhaps it did. Yet he allowed that she had handled the plane up to that point with a skill that few could equal and none surpass. He said no more, and she thought: "It was Perdita Wyatt I saw. I am sure of that, though how she came to be there is not easy to guess. But I suppose she had been wounded by us, if not killed. I would rather the scouting work that I did till I crashed, however perilous it might be, than this killing out of the air."

Yet it did not enter her mind that she should refuse that which she did not like. It was a moment when death was king. To those who fought in the air, he was a comrade whom within a day—or they might hope for a week if they were of a sanguine sort—they would be most likely to meet. They did not slay from a secure place, as did the chemists who devised fresh horrors in laboratories, beside which hell was a decent abode for the society which it must contain. And she fought in a great cause, as men had fought twenty years before, though the issues then had been less clearly defined, and those who died had been betrayed by the folly of those who were left alive.

They went to earth at the Northfield aerodrome, being one of the two aircraft that were still stationed there and in form to fly, the other being a German fighter which had come down on the Lickey Hills, and in an hour they rose again to the perils of air. Battle was raging now along fifty miles of a crescent front, and they must give the slight help that was in their power in an atmosphere which was becoming murky with storm. During that hour of rest she had made what effort was in her power to secure that Red Cross aid should be sent to the wounded, among whom there might be a girl she knew, but she had found it vain to propose. The Germans were pressing now along all their front, and using every weapon of terrestrial war, except only their super-tanks, which they had not been able to transport through the air or across seas which were still so largely in British hands. It was their troops which would be the first to advance over the charred hedges of that lifeless land.

General Briggs's army drew back to prepared lines of defence, which shortened as it retired. From a wide arc in the north, and from south and west, the armies of Generals Bessel and Wasser converged upon him. If their plans should go well, Birmingham would be isolated by the next day, and its defending army cut off from support. Its surrender should be a matter of no more than a few hours after that, even without the argument of fresh terrors descending out of the air. For as to that, the order was that the city should be captured without the destruction of its manufacturing plants— indeed, any mercy shown to its inhabitants was to be conditional upon these being surrendered in working order.

But this order did not require the preservation of smaller towns that were in the path of the German advance. As the day waned, Kidderminster, strewn with an avalanche of incendiary bombs, rose in one huge pillar of heavenward flame that could be seen, a reflected light on the evening sky as far off as London or even Leeds. Its inhabitants had died in numbers that there would be none living to ever count. But the hours passed, and the thunder of guns did not cease from end to end of the long, incurving advance. North of Wolverhampton, where the two German armies succeeded in uniting their lines, the fighting was of particular and prolonged intensity, as though that centre of coal and steel were to be defended at whatever cost might be required, but meanwhile its evacuation had been ordered, and its inhabitants poured southward by congested railways and roads, until it seemed that men fought to protect that which had become no more than an empty shell.

CHAPTER XIX.

STEELE went back from the Council Chamber to the solitude of his own room and his own thoughts, which were not easy to bring to their usual subordination.

The luxury which had become his in a few hours—the anxious, obsequious attendants who only accepted dismissal with the assurance that they would wait his slightest need during the night—the talk of world dominion from which he came—all combined to emphasize the colossal opportunity either for evil or good, for service to the cause of Christian civilization or self-aggrandizement, which had become his, and on his use of which so much of the world's fate—even to the issue of the war—might ultimately depend.

Or did he, in the intoxication of the event, exaggerate its importance and the possibilities which it would give? Was it not more probable that he could do no more than to wreck himself by throwing aside the dazzling opportunities that shone before him on the ultimate heights of power? To be exchanged for some shameful and useless death, when he should be discovered for what he was?

Temptation came to him in the night such as he could not have supposed that he would have felt, whose purpose until then had been single and strong. He saw that he had von Teufel's confidence, which, if he should continue loyal to him, he would be unlikely to lose. To von Teufel he was Adolph Zweiss, a German of exceptional courage and patriotism, and, beyond that, one whose loyalty had been bought at the most stupendous price that is possible in terms of the world's wealth or of worldly power. It had been cynically said that every man had his price. Was von Teufel likely to think that his would be higher than that?

He knew that those who stand close to a tyrant's throne are not free from danger, either from above or below. They will be brought down by intrigue, or cast down by caprice, or die suddenly from a knife-thrust or a bullet no power would turn. But he thought himself to be of some capacity to control events to his own safety, if he should make that his single aim. He would be in no more peril than that which he had known almost hourly in his spy's life, and how much less than that which must be his if he should continue here while betraying von Teufel's trust! No, if he would regard his own life, the path of comparative safety was clear.

Beyond that, he was subtly tempted by the thought that wisdom and even honour might have much to say on the same side. Must he never cease to betray? Might not the obligation of loyalty really be at its maximum when it had been bought at the highest price? Was it not the world's verdict on his profession that he was dishonoured in all he did? He had long persuaded himself of the falsehood of that, but had it not been by the specious reasoning of one who was partial to his own case? What could be the dishonour of abandoning a career so basely esteemed?

And suppose that, let him do as he might, von Teufel should prove equal to the conquest that he designed? That he would really possess the world, as he had already gone far to do? If that were so, to attempt his betrayal would be to sacrifice himself to no final gain, or even much less than that. For—and this was the subtlest argument of all—if he should become von Teufel's counsellor, how much good might he not do, to restrain, to protect, to divert attention, or perhaps vengeance from those of his own blood? Even now a word might be potent to divert armies to foreign soil which would have trampled on British lands. And might it not even be said that it was that which he had been explicitly instructed to do—to gain German confidence, even to the extent of betraying some English secrets of war, that he might be there for a larger use on a later day?

Was he now to reject such potentialities for the sake of informing England of the date at which the German submarines would crowd through Gibraltar's straits?

It might be impossible to do in sufficient time, even though he should risk—and perhaps lose everything in the attempt. Even his success might not avail. The submarines might still escape. Did not policy, prudence, his instructions alike combine to advise that he should first make his position secure, and wait the hour when he could use it with most effect?

Certainly, should he do that, he would be left with no more honour than spies can claim. He must become intimate with von Teufel—trusted—giving subtly Judas-like advice—waiting the hour when he could most surely betray. *And it was an hour that might never come.*

He imagined himself as one of six who controlled the earth, with the memory of how that place came to be his eating his soul, and it was a conception he did not like. For the moment temptation failed.

But like a receding tide, it returned, now throwing its highest wave. Suppose, by patience and wisdom, he should come at last to von Teufel's place. What an opportunity for beneficent power—vast, almost beyond human dreams—would become his! Surely those who were conscious of the integrity of their own hearts, of love of their own kind, should not avoid to woo the occasion to such an end. *Not great enough for their own destiny.* Of how many may that not have been true who have deceived themselves into the belief that scruples of conscience, not smallness of soul, have withheld their hands from the waiting plough?

To do nothing: nothing that would jeopardize the power that had come into his hands. That was all that he was proposing. *Get thee behind me, Satan.* The text came to his mind, to be ridiculed for the comparison that it seemed to make. Small things and great! The Founder of Christianity and a perjured spy! Yet he reached, with the thought, for the worn Greek testament that his hip pocket inseparably held. It was the one companion he would not lose, even for the sake of the disguises in which he had learnt to be thorough, to the extent of that grafted mole. He had a score of explanations in readiness of how he had come upon it and why he bore it, suited to each disguise, and any form of inquisition that he might meet, but it had not left him through the chances of thirty years.

Now he opened it to read of the temptations that came to one who had the conviction of a power that he had not proved. He read of the three temptations that shook the mind of the greatest Teacher the world has known on the threshold of his career, and could not see that they had application to himself.

They implied much. He who could feel confident that stones would become bread at his word must have thought himself to be more than man. He who was tempted by the lure of temporal power, even of the Roman purple itself, must have thought himself to be much less than an ultimate God. Well, there need be no contradiction in that. Even had he created the visible universe, he might know no more of ultimate Deity than we do ourselves! It was a defect of imagination, an attempt, at the best, to reduce to human language that which transcended its thought, that had framed and phrased the crude dogmas that— But he was too obsessed by his own problem to allow his mind to wander into the speculations its leisure loved. *Man shall not live by bread alone, but by every word that proceedeth out of the mouth of God.* Was there any meaning in that? To the mind of Christ it had seemed a conclusive answer to the devil that plagued his mind. Perhaps to that devil it had been equally clear. But it was less so to Richard Steele. Like other of Christ's retorts to those who sought to change logic with him, it was of a baffling quality. They were sayings that silenced by confusion rather than elucidation.

Yet the meaning, the truth, must surely be there. If men could change stones to bread, what were the divine words for which the use would be gone in an altered world? Fortitude. Courage. Generosity. And a hundred more. It was a strange thing to observe how all noble words must die from the tongues of men who could supply their needs by a mere word of another kind.

But what to himself, to his own dilemma, was the application of this? He could not say. But he knew that without logical process of thought, his difficulty was overcome and temptation had lost its power. His course had become simple and clear.

After that he slept well, and waked with a mind resolute, wary, alert, and feeling equal to that which he had to do. Before all, he must make sure that the German submarines should not slip through Gibraltar's straits to scatter death in Atlantic seas.

CHAPTER XX.

VON TEUFEL spoke with an anger he did not rein, as he would be increasingly disposed to do in the coming days, whenever the course of events hindered his will. "It is against all the laws of war," he said, "that they should not yield! That they should thwart our arms, after all that the last fortnight has seen! It was a knife through their very heart when we set London afire. They have no currency, no trade. Their railway centres are gone. They have lost the air. When a nation is prostrate thus, it is mere sense that they should ask for what terms they can still bargain to get. You shall tell Wasser that he will be recalled in a week, if there is by then so much as a village that does not cower. Let it be known that I will desolate the whole land, till not an English worm shall be left alive, if they are impudent that they will not bend. By all the practice of war, old or new, their lives are forfeit who do not yield when their chance is gone. Zweiss, you know this people better than I: how can they be brought to ground in the shortest way?"

This outburst was at the second Council to which Steele came, after the secretary had reported much of the new advances and consolidations at which the most exacting of military tyrants might have been content for a day, had it not been for the last item of all. It appeared that the two German armies which had been based upon Bridgnorth and Sheffield had half encircled Birmingham to the south, west, and north, their orders being to capture the city with as little destruction as they could contrive, so that it might be put to work for its new lords on the next day; and this had been regarded as no more than a detail of the subjugation of a defeated land.

After a day of fierce fighting along a battle-front gradually contracting from a crescent of fifty miles, which had continued during the afternoon in spite of an increasing deluge of rain that had hindered the handling of the German mechanized batteries more than that of the obsolescent gun-teams which had been frequently observed on the English side, the two German armies had united before Wolverhampton, where they had met with a most stubborn defence. But it had become evident, as darkness fell, that this resistance was intended to delay the occupation of the town rather than permanently to defend it, when it had been learned that the civilian population was being rapidly and completely evacuated.

Anticipating, not unreasonably, that it was the English intention to destroy the town rather than to allow its ten-score foundries and factories to fall into enemy hands, General Wasser had intensified his efforts to capture it too speedily for such a plan to succeed. Attacking the hurriedly fortified English positions during the night with a recklessness which took no count of the price it paid, he had the satisfaction of forcing his way into the town even as the last train, heavy with its human freight, steamed out of the lower station, a futile volley following into the tunnel through which it passed.

Before morning the whole town was so completely occupied, and had been so thoroughly searched, that the fear of incendiarism had ceased to disturb the minds of its new owners. The population had gone, as had much of the town's portable wealth, but an enormous amount remained.

The exhausted troops were quartered in the deserted houses of the town their valour had won, where they were allowed to take their sleep in the day that the operations of the night had denied, while fresh forces were hurried forward to form a spearhead of assault against the English positions that had now been disclosed about three miles to the south.

It was about noon, during an intensive artillery preparation for this further attack, to which the English batteries had made no more than a feeble reply, that a series of terrible explosions, following closely upon one another, had almost completely destroyed the town and started a general conflagration, which demonstrated that fire can be generated from below as efficiently as it can be rained from the sky.

The sleeping troops had been almost annihilated, and at the moment of maximum confusion concealed English batteries, silent before, had opened with devastating effect, and provided a barrage behind which a counterattack had been launched with a sudden fury that had thrown back the whole German line at that section for a distance of two or three miles, leaving an enormous quantity of material in the victors' hands, with the plunder of which they had withdrawn to the protection of their previous lines, before new troops, hurriedly closing in from right and left, could be arrayed in sufficient strength to avenge the blow.

The loss of life had been large, but that of heavy equipment had been even more serious to an army that must depend upon such munitions as could be borne through the skies or wrested from its foes. The gain and loss of confidence on each side was a reversal perhaps most serious of all. The English armies had been contemned in their enemies' mouths, not for lack of personal valour, but as being amateur, improvised, and therefore inadequate to resist the trained professional ranks by which they were being systematically forced backward and herded in. Now the German armies had united "according to plan." Wolverhampton, at their point of junction, was theirs. And it had become a monument of disaster, smoking above the charred bones of their thousands dead. Was it strange that von Teufel's anger should burn fiercely at this rebuff from what he had regarded as no more than a prostrate foe? Or that he should turn to the man who had made England his home for so many years to ask: how can they be brought to ground in the shortest way?

Steele answered boldly, feeling confidence that came from the fact that there was a sufficient measure of truth in that which inclination urged him to say. And he was fortified by the memory of how Admiral Klein had held successfully to his own opinion, even against that which von Teufel had previously expressed.

"I would have been silent," he said, "deferring to the views of those who have more knowledge of the science of war, but if you instruct me to speak, I must say that I think the methods of terrorism to be wrong. I should say that they have already failed, that they have made resistance more bitter and more prolonged."

Von Teufel gloomed upon him, as he said this, with hard, considering eyes and a set jaw. "But," he said, "it is a matter which will not wait. We must have their factories active for us."

"Which, if you sow the land with salt, they will scarcely be."

"Do you say how it can not be done, and no more than that?"

"I do not say it cannot be done, if there be no counting of cost, nor care as to what will remain to the next day. But if I know the English character, as you say I do, I know that methods of terrorism will have the opposite effect from that which we aim to reach.

"If we resolve to subdue that land with all the strength that we have, which is most of Europe, and I suppose more than half Asia now, it should be a small matter enough; but if for that purpose we divert disproportionate strength from the main front of the war, we may be doing that which our foes would choose.

"I should say beyond that, that General Wasser has met with no more than a minor reverse, which we magnify if it be observed that it has caused us to change our plans. He is a good man, I suppose, or he would not have been appointed to such a post. His next report may be of a better kind. Otherwise, he should give place to one who is abler than he.

"For the moment, we should do no more than to replace what he has lost, and give our minds to larger affairs.

"That is how it appears to me, the more especially because of the policy adopted at our last Council, the effect of which there has been no time to observe. But it is an opinion I do not press, and which may well be put aside to hear those of better judgment than mine."

The grimness of von Teufel's expression did not change as he heard this, nor did he invite other opinions when it was done. He said shortly, "We will hear no more on that matter now," leaving his thoughts for each to guess as he would.

Steele was left unsure of how his advice had been taken, and though he thought that he might have delayed, if not permanently prevented, some further frightfulness, yet even so, if he should regard the broad welfare of the Christian allies rather than that of his own country alone, there might be little value in what he had done. Might it not even be a deliberate policy of the allies that England's resistance should distract the maximum of attention from that which must be the decisive front of the war?

This doubt emphasized the soundness of the decision to which he had already come, that he could not content himself with the part of Ahithophel—the giving of bad counsel for the confusion of those who might be persuaded to think it good. Even if he could be sure that he would be heard, he was too uncertain of his own judgment— and with the partial knowledge he had—to be sure of what counsel would be bad or good. He must adventure to aid his cause in more active ways, of which the stopping of those submarines— His thoughts checked at the knowledge that von Teufel was speaking of that which he must not miss, and with some use of his own name.

"It is that," he was saying, "on which we must be most fully and surely informed, and in regard to which, at the right time, Marshal Zweiss may be able to give us a great and singular aid.

"For whether they think to attack us or to wait our assault, they will have a most vexing problem with which to deal. They flee now that they might escape pursuit by the width of the middle sea, as it may be prudent for them to do. But having done that, they must think to raise their heads upon the North African coast, to which they will gather armies from the New World, and from the British Dominions beyond the seas. But their line will be narrow and long, with much desert upon its rear. When Gibraltar falls, we may fling a great host upon their left, rolling them up from that end, or we may leave them there, and may make advance by Sinai and Suez. It must be their doubt which we shall do, as we (if they should become strong enough to invade) might have the same doubt of them; but they would have the less choice, and what they planned would be harder to hide."

This statement led to a discussion which ranged over the broad field of the war, excepting as it moved on the Asian front, with which Moscow was more concerned, but even that must come into it at the last.

The strength and weakness of the North African position was recognized as depending primarily upon the control of the Mediterranean. Without that it would be extremely difficult for the allies to move troops rapidly and in decisive numbers from one flank to another of a position which had the Libyan and Saharan Deserts so widely and closely upon its rear. This consideration raised again the expediency of retaining the submarines in the Mediterranean, to which Steele must listen in a watchful silence, resolving not to intrude any word which might not be needed to tip the scale. He could approve his own caution when Admiral Klein's stubborn argument that they would, in any case, be of more immediate utility in the wider oceans, and that they could be returned (the fall of Gibraltar being assumed) at a later day if it should then appear desirable, secured adherence to the existing plan. And the discussion developed on a different line when von Teufel expressed his anticipation that the allies, if they should retain sufficient command of the sea, would elect to attack rather by the western than the eastern extremity of their lengthened front.

He had some sound arguments for this. He pointed out that American armies, if they should be successfully transported across the Atlantic, would be most naturally assembled in Morocco and Algiers, and that the sea from those parts of the African coast was not wide to cross, and would give some latitude as to the point of attack which might be selected, whereas to advance by way of Palestine and Asia Minor would involve adherence to a narrow, evident route; and while, he allowed, it would avoid some maritime problems, it would be to approach its foes by a long and difficult march, unless they should themselves resolve to give forward battle, when the invaders would already have the Sinai Desert upon their rear.

"It is true enough," von Hoffmann agreed, "but there is another thing which may be potent to guide their choice. There is Armageddon. They may be eager to meet us there."

Von Teufel stared blankly: "There is what?"

"There is the valley of Armageddon, where they may think to prevail."

"Will you say where it is, and why they should look for that?"

"There is a ridge of high ground," von Hoffmann replied, "which runs across Northern Palestine from Mount Carmel to Jordan ford, and there is an old prophecy that North and South will meet in a great battle there, when the followers of the Jewish god will prevail."

Von Teufel stared incredulously. "You think," he asked, "that their strategists would be influenced by such nonsense as that?"

"I cannot tell. But I should say it is an argument some will urge."

The Minister of Propaganda interposed: "It is true so far that it is a frequent talk in the Christian lands. American newspapers are giving some prominence to the idea."

Von Teufel heard this in a frowning doubt. He turned to von Hoffmann again. "You think, if we should give them time, they might make dispositions to meet us there?"

"That is more than I said, and far more than I would propose that we let them do. I would have us press them too hard for that. When Gibraltar is down, I say we should be instant to go to them, and they will have occupation enough. It is in Africa they should bleed."

"Yes," von Teufel allowed. "It is thus that our plans are made." But he spoke absently, as though other visions engaged his mind. He rose and walked over to where the world map nearly covered the longer wall. He said: "You tell me Cyprus is strong. And the English are holding on to Haifa, though the oil wells are gone, and its use is not much to them."

"I suppose," von Hoffmann answered, "we can turn them out when we will. It is one of the places which we are now planning to bomb."

"Yes," von Teufel said, not as one who replied, but as though thinking aloud. "When we will—when we will. But for the time we may let them be. You must turn the bombers another way."

Von Hoffmann saw no difficulty in that. The front of war was so vast that, huge as the air forces which were now under Russo-German control might be, there were more demands upon them than they could promptly fulfil. The order which saved Haifa on the next day would be Malta's increase of pain.

Von Teufel continued to gaze at the map in a long silence which none would venture to interrupt. "It would be to have them all," he muttered, "in a full net! There is desert behind. And right and left there is the desert, or else the sea. But it is a monstrous folly to think.... Was it not by this way," he asked, "that the old caravans came, both for the land route to Africa and for that of the sea?"

"Yes," von Hoffmann, whose knowledge of military history was thorough enough to go back to its most ancient records, replied. "The caravans came through the higher Jordan ford, and then either down the valley to the sea or turned south through a pass in the hills. Egypt used to pay the Philistines to maintain a chain of forts to pro-tect the route. It was to keep it open that the battle of Mount Gilboa was fought, in which Saul was killed."

Von Teufel listened to this with the frowning intentness which was his frequent attitude when receiving information upon a subject which filled his mind. But when it was done, he put it aside with a gesture of impatience, as at an irrelevant prolixity. "So it may have been," he said. "But its use is done. It is nothing now. Can we think that men of reason would be so mad?"

He turned to the map again, saying as he did so that the Council was done for that day. The room emptied. He understood the power of superstition on ignorant minds. But was it possible that its power could be great enough to control the world issues with which he dealt? That it could be so fatuous, so dense? That it could influence the strategy of great armies led by presumably educated, intelligent men? But if that were so, need he seek those who would come to him, walking into that which could be made a most fatal trap? Well, it was unlikely enough! But if only it could be believed....

Von Hoffmann's mind, as he left the Council, remained on the same subject, but in a different humour. He was familiar with the prophecy which was known to the Christian masses through the writings of John the Divine, and which had its roots in those of a much earlier day, for he had been brought up in the Lutheran Church, which he had only left when the National Government had decreed that Christianity was a religion inferior to the requirements of German culture, and when he had realized that he must either repudiate a faith which he had never very actively professed, or see a career jeopardized for which he had a much greater care.

An hour ago he would have said that such a prophecy, by becoming generally known, must defeat itself, for would not any leader, knowing that it had been foretold that he would be destroyed on a certain site, be particularly careful to fight his battles elsewhere? But now he saw possibility of an opposite issue.

He had heard already that there was much being written and talked in the Christian lands which represented this war as being not merely between races of men, as it clearly was, for the control of the world, but between God and Devil, between the powers of Evil and Good, and suggesting that it would end with a decisive struggle in the prophetic area. He had seen this as an idea which, however absurd, would he naturally fostered by those of superior intelligence, as being calculated to give confidence to men who might otherwise take up arms with a poor heart. But he had thought that the idea would be contradicted by the course of the war, and that the Russo-German armies would overrun Northern Africa before any strength could be mustered there sufficient to throw back their advancing tide.

It had not occurred to him that von Teufel might recognize an opportunity of using the superstition of his enemies for their own destruction. Yet that, if it could be done, was clearly the sane, the "scientific" view. But suppose that by becoming obsessed by that idea, he should allow time for his opponents to assemble forces which they might not otherwise have been able to do? That he should be led to dally to his own final ruin? Where it had seemed obvious before that such a prophecy contained a warning that must defeat itself, he saw now that it might be potent to create its own fulfilment, which, had it not been spoken, would not have been.

Thinking this, he had a moment of cold doubt which he put aside with a resolute will. If reason wrestled with superstition, would he not prefer to be on the saner side? Would not the North conquer the South, as the long records of history told that it ever did? He had a nearer concern in the fact that, high as his present office, great as his trust, might be, he had not yet been presented with one of those badges with which von Teufel was decorating his most trusted followers. He must bend his mind to deserve and to win that.

Otherwise he was not greatly concerned. He saw that speculations had become futile now. For good or evil the war must be fought out, to whatever end. But he resolved that, so far as it lay with him to control the event, the German armies should not be mustered in Palestine, but a long distance away.

CHAPTER XXI.

STEELE left the Council with two contending urgencies warring for consideration within his mind. The discussion had confirmed assurance that the orders already issued for the submarines to evacuate the Mediterranean would not be cancelled, but the five days during which that information must be conveyed to the Christian powers, and their dispositions made, had now shrunk to four. To reach Nürnberg unfollowed and unsuspected was becoming hourly a more imperative need.

And beside this urgent call, there was the broader outlook which made it a mere detail of that which it might be possible for him to do, and the questions of what attitude he should adopt, in what activities he should engage, to sustain the character he claimed and the position which had been thrust upon him. How could he harmonize this character with a disappearance which need not be of more than two or three days, or perhaps less? And by what means of transit should that secret journey be made?

His present position of authority was real but vague. He was surrounded by obsequious officials whose conduct showed that they had no doubt of his power. But nothing had yet been required of him beyond attendance at the War Councils von Teufel called. His position was that of a minister without portfolio. For the moment it must be his business, both in his real and assumed characters, less to direct than to learn. And how long would von Teufel allow this attitude to continue? How long would it be natural for Adolph Zweiss to be content without active exercise of the powers which had been conferred upon him?

These questions, debated during the night, found themselves answered next morning, when he was summoned to von Teufel's presence.

The despot, as he might now fitly be called, was exultant over the news of kindred kinds which the day had brought both from the Old World and the New. Communistic riots had broken out in India, in which Calcutta and Bombay had suffered with almost equal severity. In Bombay the mills had burned. Calcutta, previously denuded of troops, was largely in rebel hands. Delhi had been heavily bombed, and its railway junctions destroyed. He knew this to be preparatory to the landing of a Russian army out of the air, which was intended for its capture, and then to operate on the rear of the Anglo-Indian forces which had been hurriedly advanced to obstruct invasion by the expected Khyber route.

From the New World the news was also of rioting and sabotage in mines and factories, and though these outbreaks were being more or less checked, with much sanguinary fighting, in a land where order was still supreme, his satisfaction was little the less for that. His foes slaughtered one another, and in doing that they wrecked mine and mill from which the munitions that should have been their protection came. It must all hasten the day when he would plant a firm foot on the New World's neck, and by then the Communists would have served their turn. He had no doubt that he would be equal to deal with them!

His manner was cordial, though he spoke with the abruptness which had become habitual during the past week: "Zweiss, I must know beyond doubt how the air forces fare, and of the morale of men who have become aware that they are so largely destined to die. I must know more than these figures tell." His hand made a contemptuous gesture towards a pile of papers upon his desk. "I must know from one who has seen, and who is neither fearing censure nor seeking praise. Bloch is a good man, but he is too quickly content. We must drive—drive.... You could inspect much in three days."

He went on to talk of wastage both of pilots and planes, of some defects of co-ordination by which he thought that that wastage had been increased with no adequate gain, and of a plan he had by which pilots might earn a week's furlough, with a substantial monetary bonus, for a specified length of dangerous, successful flight. It was not a plan he liked. He wanted to use every man to the full while his life remained. It must not be considered unless it were consistent with maintaining pressure on every front. But the fact was that the airmen were reported to be talking among themselves of being hopelessly doomed. The heavy casualties, even of victorious fleets, the fact that there were so few wounded for many dead, and the monotony with which those who survived were ordered back to the air, were producing a reckless valour in some, but more generally a feeling of fatalistic depression, which must be overcome if they were to be equal to face their foes. Some hope, some prospect, even if it were to be of nothing more than a week of riotous physical self-indulgence, must be offered as a spur to urge them to the utter risks of the air, He spoke also of a reserve fleet which he wished to assemble for the decisive hour of the war. He mentioned 5,000 planes.

"I can do that," Steele answered, feeling a satisfaction the source of which must not be admitted at this moment, even to the recesses of his own mind. "Is there full information reported there, may I ask, of the rate at which new airplanes are being built, and of the trained pilots who are still in reserve?"

"There is enough here, and too much. It is lost in detail it should not have. I will have the whole file sent to your rooms. But it is that which you can see with your own eyes that I am anxious to learn."

"I shall go with authority to give any orders that may be wise?

"I told you that at the first. I need not say that you will not interpose without cause enough?"

"You can trust me for that."

"So I believe. Where do you go first?"

"By your leave, I will not decide till the last moment, and even then I will not let it be known more than it must."

"It is well. I could give more trust if all were discreet as you."

Steele would have withdrawn without further words, feeling that he had all that he could have hoped, and much more than he could reasonably have expected, to get, and that each extra word had become a peril to shun. But von Teufel spoke again, as he was nearing the door.

"You are still trusted in England?"

"Yes, I suppose I am."

"So I have cause to think, from information which has just reached me from there. If you should let them know that you make an African flight in a plane which you would describe, you would be as safe from them as from us?"

"Yes, I would risk that with sufficient cause. There would have to be a good pretext made and sustained."

"I do not ask it for now. It is to bear in mind for a later day. You could see all from the air, and return with a full report at the vital hour, which our scouts would be less certain to do."

"I must keep their trust, if I am to do that, which will become harder with every day."

"Yes. I leave that to you."

Steele went at this, feeling that there was much gained, with no more than a single shadow, which was as yet too small to obstruct the sun, but which might be the cloud "as small as a man's hand" which would end in such tempest as would sweep him and his dreams away.

He had gained freedom to move at his own will, and a mission which would make Nürnberg a place to which it would be his duty to go. That was doubly good. It would enable him to fulfil his purpose and reduce its risks.

The idea that he might be required to fly over the Christian lines at a later day, and that he must endeavour to maintain his character of an English spy, was good also. It might, at the worst emergency, be used to explain that which would otherwise be impossible to defend. It might even excuse his use of that short wave wireless in Herr Lotz's garret, *so long as nothing should become known of the message that he should send.*

Yes, providing that. For, behind all these causes of satisfaction, there was that small menacing cloud—the information that von Teufel had had from England that he was still trusted there. What was its source? He had been too cautious to ask. Too wary to show any sign of interest. But he had seen from the first that his greatest danger lay in that direction. If, in the inner counsels of the British Intelligence Service, there should be a German spy—as he knew, in spite of all precautions, to be likely enough (look at his own position now!)—he might still be safe enough so long as he sent no further communication through. But the first time he should do that...! Suppose that his betrayal of the submarine plan should be reported back to Berlin, perhaps within a few hours of his message being received? Perhaps even in time enough for the plan to be cancelled, so that he would have sacrificed himself for no certain gain. It was quite a possible—it might even be called a likely—eventuality. So he saw. But his purpose did not deflect for that. It was the kind of risk that his occupation always involved. For the moment, the fates were either kind or ironic in what they did.

With these thoughts, he regained his own rooms, and ordered a fast plane to be ready in an hour's time, well provisioned, and with a pilot who could be trusted both for discretion and skill. He said that it must be fit and furnished for a long flight, but gave no hint of the use to which it would be put beyond that. He ordered a car to be ready to take him to the aerodrome in ten minutes' time.

He had little preparations he needed to make, little packing to have done. The plane would, he did not doubt, be furnished with every comfort without explicit direction from him. He gave some orders regarding clothes, the purpose of which was that those of Wilhelm Lotz should be included. He might not find it easy to wear them in Nürnberg, and go his own way unnoticed, but it was still more certain that he could not go secretly in an air marshal's uniform up Herr Lotz's stairs.

CHAPTER XXII.

THE plane which Air Marshal Zweiss found prepared for his use was of the latest passenger de luxe pattern—a design the building of which had been announced during the previous winter, but had not been put into commercial use when the war began.

It was very lightly and strongly built to combine comfort and speed. It had two powerful engines. It was designed for one or two passengers, for whom there was a comfortable, even spacious, cabin, and for a crew of two. It was now mounted with a machine gun at the side of the pilot's seat, but its safety lay in its ability to avoid rather than encounter danger. The wing-paintings which it had received during the last hour indicated that it had an air marshal on board, and was to receive protection at need, in priority to all other considerations, from the friendly fleets of the air.

"I have given you," the Port-Master said, "the two best pilots I have, rather than one only and a valet who might be more perfect in his own work, so that, if there should be illness or misadventure to one, you will be no less efficiently flown."

"As to that," Steele answered, "I could pilot myself if the need should come. But," he hastened to add, "you have done well. When I have good service, it is a matter I do not forget." He had become watchful to make himself popular among those who now served him with such diligent zeal. He knew that a moment might arrive when much—perhaps all—would depend upon the goodwill of those who now acted from no personal loyalty to himself, but from fear of the absolute power he held. If, he thought, they should know him for what he was...!

The plane rose in the air like a silver bird, cleft the low clouds, and came out to a windy blue. The waste spaces of air were clear of friends, or less likely foes. Once only they saw, far off, ten squadrons of Russian fighters that were being transferred to the Western front. They trailed in a long line of straight, purposeful flight, like a flock of migrating geese, and were quickly gone.

The pilot who was in cabin-attendance was robust and active, but his lined face and close-cropped, grizzled hair betrayed the fact that youth was some distance away. Steele drew him into conversation, first concerning the mountain-peaks that now showed beneath their flight like arctic islands among the clouds, and then on more personal matters. His memories, like Steele's own, went back to the last war, in which he had seen some service on the Serbian front. The name of Adolph Zweiss was one he had known and admired then, though (which was well) he had not met the more famous airman, the Italian and Serbian fronts being a sufficient distance apart.

In recent years he had been occupied as an instructor of pilots, which was still his office, from which he had been called to his present charge, his age and experience rendering him more fit to teach than to be sent out with the fighters.

He spoke modestly of what he had done, both in the last war and during subsequent years, but Steele judged him to be a man of courage and judgment, and of a probable integrity. It was no slight credential of itself that he should be alive and uninjured after having spent the last twenty years in practising and teaching the unstable ways of the air. Wilhelm Minden, he said, was his name.

"Wilhelm?" Steele said, when he heard this. "It is a good name. It is one I like. I have known two of that name since the war began, and they have both been useful to me."

The man was naturally pleased that one so far above him should talk in this affable manner. Beyond that he was puzzled. Steele had been careful to say nothing outside the character and position which had become his, but Wilhelm Minden instinctively recognized him as being different from the high officials of this war of whom he had seen much as they came and went in the air.

Like many thousands of the Germans of that day, he had private thoughts, thoughts which would not be spoken aloud to his dearest friends. He had disliked Communism. He still did. He had been genuinely enthusiastic at first for the Nazi regime. He had been told, and disposed to believe, that it was the only alternative to the disruption of social order. But he had watched a tyranny as bloody, as ruthless, as Bolshevism established, which had now allied itself with that system, after it had become different in little more than name, to launch an attack on the world, the end of which must be hard to see, but which surely gave no promise of kindly freedom to simple men.

He heard of much that he did not like, about which he kept a shut mouth, though he was a good German, and one who felt that *Deutschland über Alles* was a most natural aspiration of which to sing. Now he was slightly, subtly, more reconciled to the horror of this merciless war through finding one in its highest control to be of a different temper from those he had seen before…

As they approached the great Nürnberg aerodrome, the skies, which had been empty before, became alive with squadrons and single planes that came and went on the deadly errands of war, while, like a swarm of bees, a gathering fleet moved to the south, waiting only for its numbers to be complete that it might take formation and pass swiftly away.

Yet, despite the look of this gathering swarm, it was not a hive from which they had come, but a ground-nest of most deadly wasps. A deep-burrowed, venomous nest, from which they rose continually with their warning hum, which was Nature's verdict of what they were. As a wasps' nest in a meadow-land, such was the size of Nürnberg's subterranean aerodrome, relatively to that of the Europe over which its swarms ranged at their fatal work, and came back from the scatter of spiteful death, or bearing spoil from the lands that their bombs had scourged.

Now there was plunder brought of a living kind. Transport planes came down, gigantic, out of the skies, bearing women seized from the ravaged, half-conquered land that was yet not submissive to own their power. Steele gave no special heed to these alighting planes, which were no more than part of a wide panorama of activity spread before him as he approached. The mission on which he had been sent was one which he proposed to fulfil well. His eyes were open to all. He intended to return with a comprehensive knowledge of the air-power which had already been sufficient to devastate England and beat the nations of Western and Southern Europe to submission, or drive them in headlong flight to the North African coast. How far had it exhausted itself as it had done that? He knew that its losses had been enormous. He could not guess how much of its strength remained. How rapidly were those losses being replaced? It was information which could hardly be of less than vital moment for the Christian allies to have.

In the last hour he had assimilated the broader outlines of the lengthy reports which von Teufel had passed over to him, and then concentrated upon those which related more particularly to the Nürnberg centre. He resolved that he would make a detailed inspection here, which would assist him to deal with others in a more cursory manner and to equal result. He saw that, unless he were to prolong his tour beyond the limit of time von Teufel had set, he would still have to leave the vast Russian resources unsurveyed, as also the aerodromes, in various degrees of demolition, and with more or less denuded hangars, that had been occupied in Southern Europe. But he did not require to see all. A comparison of what was reported and what inspection disclosed should be sufficient, in three days' time, to give him material for an accurate estimate, both of present conditions and the potentialities of the immediate future.

So he thought as, with the sun still some distance above the horizon, the plane curved downward to its allotted landing-place. He had resolved that he would remain here until some time—perhaps noon—on the following day. It was a length of time for which no explanation would be needed, and which would allow the opportunity he required for that which must be done during the night.

He was met by the Port-Master, a most busy man, but one who knew that he must put other matters aside for that which Air Marshal Zweiss required. And Air Marshal Zweiss did not care (as he could not guess) how many matters of importance might go worse for the closeness of attendance that he required. He asked to be shown all, and that in an instant manner, as one who implied that any delay would be wrongly read. He said that he would require no accommodation within the town. He would sleep in his own plane. He gave Minden some hours' leave, saying that he would require him to be on duty during the night, when the second pilot would be relieved.

In the course of his inspection he came to where the transport planes were being unloaded. He saw long files of young English-women being marched, two abreast, between the menace of bayonets to canteens where they were to be fed after a flight during which they had sat closely on benches meant for transit of troops, with little comfort, though no deliberate hardship, the while they came.

He looked on with a rigid face, knowing that it might be fatal to show the fierce anger, the self-hatred, that rocked the stability of a mind that had been rarely rebellious against his will. Far beyond fact, he blamed himself for that which he now saw. For the edict had been put in force before the meeting of the Council which he advised. What he had done was rather to turn aside a separate and additional horror that had threatened his countrymen and women than to advise that of which he gazed at the first fruits now.

He looked on white, strained, or defiant faces; on some that affected indifference; on some that were stained with tears of terror or uncontrollable grief. He saw—and would not see—a face that he knew. It had passed out of sight before he had decided what best could be done, though his thoughts had been active while he spoke lying words of satisfaction at what he saw.

"I will choose one or two of these women," he said, "for my own service. I will look them over tomorrow before I go."

"Pardon, Excellency. Our orders are that they shall be entrained tonight."

"For where?"

"For various destinations."

"Well, they must be kept here till I shall have leisure to look."

"Excellency, there are two thousand in all! We have no means—"

"That is more than you need detain. How are they tabulated?"

"There is a numbered list of all who come by each plane. There should be two hundred in each."

"You will retain all of those whom I have just seen disembarked. Among two hundred, I should find some who are good enough."

The Port-Master still looked troubled, but said no more. After all, the accommodation of these women, the delay of a train or two, was a small matter beside the importance of pleasing Air Marshal Zweiss, and, in any case, it was not his part to argue, but to obey. He gave orders that all the women from Transport XP8 should be detained, pending further instructions on the next day.

CHAPTER XXIII.

STEELE returned to his own plane at a late hour, having two urgent matters with which to deal before Nürnberg could be left, but of importances which could not be seriously compared. That which was of world moment must have first attention, there was no question of that. But his mind was at ease, he having provided for that order of procedure by the detention which he had arranged, and having formed plans by which he thought that he could bring both public and private concerns to a good end.

Now he called Minden, after he had given the second pilot leave for the night, and seen him go off at a pace that had no time for a backward glance.

"Wilhelm," he asked, "should you call yourself a discreet man?"

Wilhelm said expectantly, for the Air Marshal's tone was kind, that he hoped he was.

"I wish to visit the town, and observe how certain matters are handled there, without my presence being observed. Could I do it in this uniform?"

"No, sir, I should say not."

"Could I do it in yours?"

Wilhelm agreed to that, but had a troubled look, which he made no effort to hide.

"I can see that you understand. I shall want your uniform for the night. I shall require nothing further of you, except that it be mentioned to no one, woman or man, either now or at any future time. I shall reward you well, for these are days when discretion has a high price. Tell me why you should appear troubled at that. If you speak the truth, you will have nothing to fear, be it what it may."

"If you should meet with misadventure—if you should not return—"

"I will give you a writing to deal with that. It will state that you have acted under my orders, and that I have already paid you one thousand marks for services with which I am well pleased, as I do now. If I am not back by the dawn, you will report my absence, and a search must be made diligently for me throughout the town. But you need not apprehend that. I go to no danger at all, having the uniform you will lend. Is it clear?"

Wilhelm said it was, but what clothes was he to wear, having resigned his? That he was to clothe himself in the Air Marshal's uniform was more than could be lightly assumed. Steele said that he had a suit with him for the event, which would do well enough while Wilhelm would remain in the plane during the night. Should he have occasion in the morning to make a report, the whole matter would explain itself, including his apparent breach of discipline in wearing civilian clothes. He produced those of Wilhelm Lotz, which were a good enough fit, as (which was more important) were those of Wilhelm Minden for him.

He left the plane in the uniform of a pilot, having a pass in the usual form, and another, signed by himself, giving him freedom and authority such as pilots do not often receive. As a last resort it might be useful to have and could do no harm, but he knew that he would be tightly caught if it should become needful to produce that.

He felt, as he walked quietly away, that he had done better than well. He could pass out of the camp and enter the town with a confidence he could not have felt had he had Wilhelm Lotz's coat on his back. He had good reason to hope that he would be able to reach his goal unfollowed; and even if, at the worst, the attics might have been entered during his absence and their secret discovered, he would have a much better chance of observing this without drawing suspicion upon himself than if he should have come disguised as the tenant for whom the police might be vigilantly waiting. He had given Minden the thousand marks (which was much to the man who received it, but nothing to him who could now draw on the world's wealth as he would), and with it a hint, which might seem to be of far greater worth, that he might have use for a discreet man which would continue after this flight should be done.

So it was with more ease of mind than he was often able to feel that he made an unhurried way towards Wilhelm Lotz's attics, wandering about and visiting a cinema, as was natural for a man on leave for the night. It gave him leisured opportunity to make sure that he was not followed. It was prudent, also, to delay his arrival until an hour when the stairs would be likely to be clear. He would have gone later than he did had he not wished to prepare a message in code that would be ready for transmission at midnight.

CHAPTER XXIV.

THE stairs were vacant; the house was quiet: the door of the garret locked as he had left it: inside everything was dusty and undisturbed.

It was with a feeling of great relief that he locked and bolted the door on the inside, and then proceeded to inspect the condition of the transmission set.

There was nothing out of order there, nothing, at most, that a few minutes would not adjust. He was soon absorbed in preparation of the message which might have such momentous consequences, even to the fate of the civilized world—which might enable the troopships of the Christian allies to cross the Atlantic without constant fear of a periscope lifting above the waves, to be followed by the deadly torpedo which would send them to a swift death in the mile-deep waters below—when he was disturbed by a gentle knocking upon the door.

He became very silent, waiting for it to cease, but it became louder and more insistent. Voices outside became sufficiently loud for him to hear what was being said.

"Someone came up, I am sure of that."

"But you may be wrong. He would answer if he were here."

A third voice—that of a woman—said: "Anyway, he hasn't been seen for three days, if not more. I'm sure of that. You'll break in the door, if you ask me."

The first speaker replied doubtfully: "I don't think we can do that. It's no crime not to answer people who bang on your door when you're in bed or wanting to be alone."

"No," the second voice agreed, with more decision, "it's no business of ours. We're just looking for trouble we haven't got."

The woman said stubbornly: "We can't leave it like this. He may be there dying, for all we know."

"Or he may have got one of your sort under the quilt."

"My sort? I should like to know what you mean by that."

"Nothing you wouldn't like, Gretchen. I meant you're the sort that he'd be extra lucky to have. But I don't say that it isn't queer. There'd be no harm if we let the police know and just leave it to them."

At this point the voices receded down the stairs, so that the final decision could be no more than a guess. Steele could only hasten to code his message, after he had delayed, for a few moments, to make preparation for the worst that he had to fear.

He was not interrupted again until he had completed the coded message and established contact with England, which, to his great relief, he had been quickly able to do. He had shortened and somewhat altered what he had intended to say, since he had heard that ominous conversation outside the door. Now it read:

> This may be the last message that I shall be able to send by this means. Do not inquire who or where I am until I have found some means of communicating again. Do not, above everything, let it be known that the information which follows has come from me. There is a spy among you, and if he knows, it will end everything I can do here.
>
> The whole of the submarines now in the Mediterranean will endeavour to pass out to the Atlantic through Gibraltar Straits on Thursday next, during a concentrated attack which will be launched against that fortress both by land and air.

He added a most secret word, known only to himself and two men at the head of the British Intelligence Service, and which was reserved for certification of the authenticity of such a message as he was sending now—one of such a character that it would be disastrous to believe if it were false—and then commenced to transmit it, without waiting to add much else that he had been intending to send. As he did so the noise of knocking recommenced, and now had a more peremptory sound. The voice of authority demanded that the door should be opened at once.

He knew that there was no strength in that door to resist deter-mined attack. It would be down in thirty seconds, and the police, of whom he thought that there were several there, would be swarming into the room. He went to the door. He called out: "Who is there? What do you want?"

"Open the door!"

"Why should I do that? All is well here."

"You can explain that when it is unlocked. Open the door!"

He bent down, drawing back the bolt with a noise that he knew would be heard outside, and would be warrant of his intentions, as he fumbled with the lock, and then called out: "Wait a moment. I've left the key in my other coat."

He turned quickly back into the room. He struck a match, which he applied in two places to a heap of papers and other inflammable litter which he had gathered upon the floor. He went into the farther garret, closing the door between. He sat down again to complete the message for which two minutes should now be enough. He laid his automatic beside his hand. He was resolved that that message should be complete, though his life should pay. But he saw that, if he should engage in a shooting-match with the police there, it might be a matter not easy to be explained away, even if he should not fall to the bullets which would be certain to be returned.

How long would their patience last? How quickly would the fire burn? But till the message was complete he could give no heed to such questions as these.

But completed it quickly was. He even added, in plain words: *Police here. I escape.* He felt that to be a necessary precaution, lest the fire should fail and the transmission set fall into the hands of those who would use it in the wrong way As he did so, in the next room he heard the crash of the falling door. Smoke was coming thickly under the one that shut him off, and through the cracks of a wall that was no more than broken plaster and laths. He did not think that, even now, it would be easy for them to come to him. He had some skill in contriving fires.

But he knew that his own escape could be no more than a des-perate chance, for which each instant might be the one after the last. How soon would there be alarm in the street below? He opened the garret window, through which he must climb, as he had done in the night once before.

In the act of getting out, he looked back. The door which had shut him off from the fire was unopened still. Probably that meant that the flames were already too fierce to pass. He observed how the draught blew. It was imperative that this further garret should be burnt out. He went back and opened the door.

He was met by an outburst of smoke so dense that he found it hard to make a stumbling return, rather by instinct than sight, to the garret window, from which he climbed out to the roof. He had been over those tiles before with a corpse to be dragged along. He made better progress now.

Ten minutes later he had forced another dormer window, and descended to the street by stairs on which he was unobserved. His uniform was now all the disguise or protection that he was likely to need. Confidently, he could mix with the growing crowd, and watch a fire that burst in high flames from the roof under which he had been so short a time before. He felt that his work had been well done, and went back to relieve Wilhelm Minden's rather anxious watch, and to get such sleep as the tail end of the night allowed.

CHAPTER XXV.

NOTHING succeeds like success. It is a proverb capable of diverse interpretations, which are all true. It is true, beyond that, that a success achieved gives illogical confidence in ability to succeed again.

Richard Steele, cool in calculation though he might be, and taught in the hard school of realism that logic can be ignored only at a price that will be bitter to pay, considered the enterprise that he had designed for the coming day in a mood which he might not have felt had he failed to transmit his message during the night, or to control the adventure in such a way that his own part therein remained unsuspected, and its evidences irrevocably destroyed.

Now he intended to rescue Perdita, and perhaps one or two other Englishwomen, though he saw that he must be circumspect if he should go beyond her; for though he was now accepted as being, beyond doubt, the authentic Zweiss, he knew that the roots of suspicion are very difficult to destroy, and its seeds are liable to remain to germinate with the first propitious shower. He saw also that anything he could do by direct action must be trivial in its result. If he would aid his countrywomen to gain release from servitude of the vilest kind, he must work for the overthrow of von Teufel's power; and even that, after what had been done in the night, did not seem a fantastic aim.

It was in this mood that he was introduced to the mess-room which was reserved for officers of senior rank, and overheard Fleet-Commander Aursbach describing Prince von Teufel as a swine-hound of dubious ancestry and uncleanly habits.

There were explanations, if not excuses, for this impiety. Flight-Commander Aursbach's normal conversation consisted mainly of expletives of the baser sort. They had come to mean even less than that his digestion was bad, or his temper ruffled, as it was now, by an order that he had just received.

He supposed himself to be the senior officer there, whom no one would venture to challenge in what he said. He was suffering nervously from the strain of the last fortnight, during which he had been almost constantly employed in the air, with results which had brought him praise; and he was seldom entirely sober while on the ground.

But he became a sobered, astonished man when a cold voice of command behind him said: "Commander, you will consider yourself under arrest. Do you know what high treason means? It is a matter with which I will deal when the meal is done."

After that Steele had the place of honour at a table where conversation became constrained with a propriety which that mess did not often observe. While he ate he considered what he would do. He had power to deal with the matter himself, even to life and death, and von Teufel would not be likely to blame him for zeal in asserting respect for his own name. There was a whimsical humour in the idea of depriving the German Air Force of the services of one of its senior officers, and being thanked for the deed.

But he decided that it would be prudent to proceed to the same end in a more orthodox manner. The words had been heard by many. They were not such as any court-martial would be likely to deliberately condone. When the meal was over, he gave instructions for one to be held immediately for the trial of the delinquent officer. "You will inform me," he said, "of its decision before I leave."

There was nothing in that promptitude to create surprise. At such a time, inquiry must be instant, for the witnesses might be gone on the next day. Commander Aursbach had received orders which, unless he were released from arrest before noon, must be passed into other hands. But release was not a possible issue. Steele saw that. Sympathy there might be—though there was not much of that, for the accused officer was not liked—but who would venture to rule that such words were no more than a venial fault?

Steele heard, as he came back from inspecting the condition of a fleet of bombers which had been sent out to scourge some Macedonian obstinacy, and been damaged in the course of that operation by an ambush of anti-aircraft guns, that the court-martial had sentenced a profanely indignant officer to be dismissed the Service, and to undergo two years' rigorous imprisonment, against which he had announced his intention of appealing to von Teufel himself. Steele felt it to be an excellent verdict, which an appeal should not be allowed to disturb, either for better or worse.

"I will have a word with him," he said. "Bring him here." He added to the Port-Master, whom he had kept at his elbow for the last three hours: "And after that, I will look over the women you have retained."

He heard an order given that they should be paraded for his inspection, and an idea came to his mind. He said it would be well for all airmen within call, of whatever rank, to stand to attention to hear what he had to say to the degraded officer. He received him in the open air, in the midst of an assembly sufficient to assure that what he said would be widely repeated and discussed.

"I have heard the verdict," he said, "that has been passed upon you, and which was of a most merciful kind. I hear that you expressed an intention of appealing against it. So you may do. It is nothing to me. But I will warn you that such a sentence may be varied in more ways than one, and the day you send in such an appeal your head may become less secure on your shoulders than it is now.

"That the court was able to take a lenient view was, I conclude, because they considered it to be such an offence as they would be unlikely to meet again. If another should be heard to speak in the same way—which I will not suppose—he would be likely to come to a quick end.

"Your honour is gone. But your life is something—and all—that you still have. If you are content to be quiet now, you may find that you have gained that which you would otherwise have been most likely to lose. For how many of us who stand here will be alive in a month from now? I suppose few. If you are a wise man, you will remain still."

He dismissed the assembly, including a prisoner who showed no gratitude for that which he heard, feeling that he had done well. If every word he had said should be carried to von Teufel's ears, there would be nothing for him to fear. He had warned those who might take the Dictator's name on profane lips of the vengeance fit for so gross a crime. There was nothing wrong there. He had contrived to forecast that most who heard would be dead in a month's time. There would be no encouragement for them in that! But he could say that he had done it experimentally to test their reaction, which would be consistent with the instructions he had received.

He entered the waiting car with a complacent feeling that he had deprived the German Air Force of the services of one of its fleet-commanders with a neatness that might make a good tale in future days, if peace should ever come to a rescued world. It was astonishing how pliable circumstance became when it was handled in the right way! He came to an inspection of two hundred women, past whom he walked, feigning to observe all, and looking closely for one whom he did not see. He inspected them for a second time, and then a third at a slower pace.

"There is trickery here," he said, with an anger which gave a sound of reality to a threat which he did not literally mean. "There will be men shot if I do not have the truth in a quick word."

Being so urgently summoned, the truth came, and in the end it was hard to see who could be greatly blamed. The order he gave had been correctly conveyed, and exactly followed. The transport planes, which were converted airliners, were not of absolutely identical accommodation. XP8 was exceptionally large, and ten other women, in addition to its own numbered complement, had been loaded upon it.

"I will see the lists," he said. With some unavoidable delay, they were brought. Against the number XO196 the name of Perdita Wyatt appeared.

Where would these women—those of the XO transport—be now? It was hard to say. But, hard or easy, he made it clear that it must be said. A telephone inquiry directed to the Burgomaster obtained the information that the XO contingent had been entrained for Stuttgart on the previous evening. Steele heard this with an expressionless face. There was no complacency in his mind now. Stuttgart had no military aerodrome, large or small. There was no reason—no faintest excuse—for proceeding there.

CHAPTER XXVI.

THE air-transit of Perdita and her captured companions had been without avoidable hardship or greater indignity than must be suffered inevitably by those who are under the physical duress of their hated foes. The manners of the German officers into whose hands they had fallen were no better than would be expected from a race to whom it appears equally natural to cringe or bully, but discipline was strict to protect, as well as to control.

With characteristic German thoroughness, two thousand Anglo-German phrase books had been distributed among the captive women, so that the brief hours of flight should not be lost, but they could commence at once to learn the language which was to become theirs, and their children's, in future years. The sight of these brochures gave a sense of finality to many, emphasizing the permanence of the exile to which they came. The human spirit will adapt itself to much, if it have the aspect of unescapable doom. But the most slender hope will be fuel for a rebellion which will not cease. There were those on whom the phrase books had the effect that the life-prisoner knows when the door of his cell is first shut and the key turns. Some even began to study them, seriously, listlessly, or as being avid for whatever would serve to distract them from memories intolerable to endure.

But in Perdita they roused a fierce hostility, as a first challenge to a duel which she had not yet admitted that she must lose, however desperate the odds might appear to be. There had been a time but a few weeks before, when she had made efforts to improve her knowledge of the German tongue. But now she resolved that there should be none more foolish, none more obtuse, than she. That must be the first difficulty they would have. They could not compel her to become expert in a language which she was resolved that she would be unable to learn!

Having no appetite for the study of German verbs, she had the more leisure for other things. She had the window seat of a crowded bench, so that she could observe the moving landscape below, and judge with some accuracy the destination to which they flew. It was a bitter thought that she should be returning thus, and to a more ominous captivity, to the place from which she had fled by the same route at such peril when war began. The voice of a young woman on the bench before her had interrupted her thoughts: "George always said that he wouldn't fight, and he kept his word. It wasn't sense that I should start fighting for him. I said: 'Gentlemen, you'd better come in, and I'll give you tea.' I don't know that they understood, but it wasn't George, it was my old father, who planked me here."

Her companion's reply was inaudible, but she went on: "Anyhow, I say make the best of what comes. It's no use meeting trouble halfway. Germans aren't so bad. I dare say they're as good as those who have come my way, and a bit better than some."

"And I say," a harsh, confident voice broke in from a seat farther forward, "we're well out of a bloody mess."

The woman next to Perdita touched her arm. She was quite young. Probably she had not come to her thirtieth year. But the shadow of grief had fallen upon her face, giving it the bleakness of age. She asked quietly: "You intend to live?"

The question was the more startling for the gentleness with which it was spoken. "Yes," Perdita replied instinctively, "if I can." She added: "I suppose nothing's very sure now."

"You would get a message home for me, if you could?"

"Yes, of course. But I don't know what chance I shall have better than you."

"You may." She gave a name, and a Lichfield address. "It may be better not to write it down, if you can remember it. If you are sure...." Yes, Perdita said, there should be no doubt about that.

"Tell him that I am dead. He will be so glad."

"But—it isn't true. I don't think I could do that."

The woman made no direct reply. She questioned Perdita in her gentle, toneless voice, having already learnt that she had been in Germany before, as to what their immediate experiences were likely to be. Perdita had the hopeful spirit of healthy youth, but it was not easy to be optimistic concerning that. Inopportunely, she remembered what she had heard before of the Nürnberg Edict of 1935, dealing with the examination of candidates for a marriage licence. If such indignities were considered suitable for German women, what was likely to be the treatment of such alien importations as themselves, in anticipation of the concubinage which was the intended destiny to which they came?

The woman said, as though she dealt with something she had no lack of power to control: "I don't think I should risk that." She went on to tell of her child who had been killed last week by an airplane bomb. Her husband also, she had good reason to think, was dead. It was a brother's name she had given.

She spoke without emotion, as one might who regarded a play that was nearly done. Little anecdotes of the child, hard to hear after being told of its frightful end, were spoken so tonelessly that Perdita concluded that sorrow had numbed her mind.

The short hours of rapid flight were done, and the giant liners planed downward to their landing-place, as geese settle upon a pond. Curt voices, calling in strange, guttural English speech, ordered the women to disembark.

It was now, as they were being lined up to be marched to the canteen, that Perdita, with a pause of startled pulses, saw the face that she had met in Nürnberg before and had found to be an unlikely friend.

It was, with one exception, the only face of a friend that she could have hoped to see, and it had been too improbable to entertain, even had she known that Richard Steele had ventured again into the midst of his country's foes. It was natural that she saw him first. She had been looking round with curious eyes that missed little of what they saw. But she did not doubt that he would see her, and she had some reason for the quick hope that he would not be indifferent, nor powerless to save. He was coming almost directly upon her. She did not expect that he would accost her there. But a momentary recognition of meeting eyes—that would have been sufficient to let her know.

She looked for something she did not get. His eyes were blankly upon her. Unseeing or unregarding, they passed her by. Did it matter greatly which it had been?

As he moved away, she found any hope she had to be a frail flower. She was not familiar with the uniform of a German air marshal, but she saw that he masqueraded as an officer of high rank, having the confidence of those against whom he worked. Well, he might do much! She was glad of that. But had he seen her at all? She was unsure. Would he move to rescue her if he had? After that absolute disregard, she felt less confidence than would have been hers before, had she foreseen that he might be there. She remembered that he had once told her that he would have cast her life away without scruple, to save himself one hour in his vital haste to be home with the news he bore. Might he not be engaged upon matters of equal moment now?

She told herself that she did not expect—did not even wish—that he should forget England to think of her. And, indeed, what claim had she for his regard, beyond the fact of their common blood, on which point she was surrounded by those who could make equal appeal, and the fact that he had done her dangerous and unrequited service before? Reason fought against the bitter protest that instinct made.

In this mood, she had ceased to take much notice of outward things, until she was seated at one of the long tables of the canteen, among companions most of whom were disposed to take full advantage of the opportunity of a good meal. It is a frequent female caprice to refuse food in the minor emergencies or vexations of life, but to meet its real crises in a more practical mood. There were plates that were neglected now. But, with the assistance of hunger and the encouragement that companionship gives, the consumption of food was not low.

And the food was good. For the effect of the dislocation of commerce was not yet felt to the extent of restricting supplies, and the rationing was no more than had existed before the commencement of war, and was now somewhat less rigorously enforced. It was not the intention of the Government that German people should suffer privations of war. Rather, it would have them feel that those which they had endured for the policy of "guns for butter" were justified by immediate affluence when those guns had opened upon the world. And they had already a prostrate Europe on which to draw.

But the captives were not allowed to eat in a peace that might tend to forget the bondage to which they came. While the meal progressed, an officer in the uniform of a Colonel of Military Police mounted a rostrum at the end of the hall and delivered a homily for the benefit of the prisoners.

It was not long, for there were nine other canteens requiring performance of the same office during the course of the meal. It was spoken in excellent English. The orator's tone was not unfriendly, though there may have been some obtuseness in what he said.

He warned them first of the certain consequences of disobedience, treachery, or, above all, spying of any kind. "You must not think," he said, "that your sex will protect you, should you be disloyal to the land which is now yours, for it is one in which the axe is never far from a traitor's neck. And you will bear in mind that you are German citizens from this day."

A voice interrupted, "Never!" from the farther end of the hall.

"That," he went on, "was a word which, in mercy, I did not hear. You are German citizens from this day, and it is a high privilege, which may, if you are wise, be of great advantage to you. For you have come to the dawn of a day in which Germans will be supreme, and it is your honour that your children will be of the dominant race, and that you will have the protection of German men.

"You will show the sense which your countrywomen are reputed to have if you put the past out of your minds and address yourselves to the better life which is now to be. Be industrious and docile, fruitful and chaste, and you may find that you have come to the control of those who will treat you well. But I must warn you to be obedient to the instructions you will receive, and to be prudent both in what you avoid and in what you do."

He paused a moment, and added in a more conversational tone: "I have one thing to tell you which will be welcome to you to hear. By the clement wisdom of Prince von Teufel, by whom the order is signed, you are not to be distributed promiscuously, but will be allocated to the charge of men of exceptional honour or ability in serving the State, to whom you will be reward. Nor, even among them, will you be allotted in a blind way, but they will make their own choices, after they have inspected you in the order that their permits provide."

The woman who had been at Perdita's side on the liner was still seated at her left hand. She had listened with a quiet intentness, eating as one who neither avoided nor regarded that which she did. Now she looked at Perdita, and said, with a grave intensity of request hard to refuse: "You will do me a favour if you will turn your attention another way."

Perdita was never afterwards certain how far she had understood the meaning of that request, and had thereby become a consenting party to what occurred. But as she looked away Rose Wilmot took up a table-knife and turned it towards herself. She pressed the haft against the edge of the board and the point between her own ribs. She leaned forward. The knife was an old black-handled pattern, the blade sharp, though much worn, and having become almost pointed at the end.

Perdita heard a little gasping laugh at her side, a tone of surprised relief: "I didn't know that it would be so easy to do."

CHAPTER XXVII.

HOPE of rescue died from Perdita's heart as the crowded train bore her westward during the night. She passed, as she supposed, beyond Richard Steele's reach or regard, even had he seen her, or had the impulse to aid her entered a mind engaged on other most perilous, and far more momentous, matters.

There was no sleeping-accommodation on the train, and a distribution of small hard pillows did little for the comfort of those who were packed eight to a compartment. There was no lack of time or subjects for thought between spells of uneasy sleep.

The girls who happened to share her compartment, and who had been gathered in a wide-flung net, did not chance to be of sufficiently congenial types to tempt her to share the freedoms of their speculative or apprehensive discussions, though she appreciated the ready kindnesses that shared the resources of insufficient luggage, in which her own deficiency was extreme.

Puzzled and self-critical, she was disposed to wonder that she did not feel the emotions she would have considered appropriate to such catastrophe, had she been asked to define them a month ago.

At need—at sufficient need—would she have courage to equal that which Rose Wilmot had done? It was a question she could not answer. She must wait the event. The courage of women is most often that which will meet and endure rather than self-inflict. Now it had come to a time when it must wake to more active ways. But life is dear. It is not lightly to be cast aside. And that, paradoxically, becomes more evident at a time when the lives of others are falling on every hand. There were great forests in Germany, wild mountainous districts where population was scarce. Would it be possible to hide, to endure till the war—it could not surely last at the pace at which it was fought today!—would be done, and, perhaps, Germany beaten again? The spring was not far. The need for such escape might not be so urgent that it could not wait till the trees were green. But would the war end with Germany down?

Present indications were of an opposite kind. Her dominant feeling was that of a wild animal caught. Wary, watchful for opportunities of escape, suspicious of every movement its captors make, yet not without willingness to adapt itself to the inevitable, if it be offered tolerable conditions in which to live.

They detrained at Stuttgart too early to attract much attention, as they were paraded and marched through the clean straight streets of a city the size of which is a recent growth around the Gothic dignity of its three mediaeval churches. They walked the most part of a mile to a hostel, where they were offered a good meal, and beds which were even more welcome, and were told that they would have a day and night for rest, and to prepare themselves for the ordeal of distribution, which was to take place in the city hall on the following day.

Most of human life is built of frustrated hopes, or fears which prove to have no substance in the event. There are few who die of the disease they most greatly dread. So it was, at least with Perdita, now. What she anticipated, or planned, or feared, of this ordeal of selection by those who would be slave-masters to whom they took, restrained by little but such sense of decency as might be in their own souls, may be put aside, for it was an experience she was not destined to have. She was one of two hundred young women of widely differing characters, ideals, and social orders, though united in a common hatred of those in whose hands they were, who were assembled at noon in the city hall and given seats, somewhat broadly distributed, with instructions that they could occupy them for a ceremony which some might find to be of considerable length, on condition that they should be obedient to rise whenever they should be required to do so.

Perdita looked at a chair which she would have no occasion to use, and at a sheet of printed directions which, being in English, she saw that it would be vain for her to profess that she could not read, but found that that would not be her present concern when a voice became audible in the hall, calling, in a voice of authority, for XO196 to step out of the rank.

There was a moment during which she did not recognize herself by that description, not having given much attention to the number which had been placed upon her, and another during which she hesitated to move. To one of her antecedents and experiences, the voice of brusque authority was not easily to be obeyed, especially when it came out of an enemy's mouth. But she told herself that it was plain folly to expose a reluctance she could not hope to assert, and then there came a sudden guess of what such a summons would be most likely to mean, and as three helmeted police made an unceremonious passage to where her number should be, she met them with an eager movement which she must remind herself that she should not show.

She was no less content when there was a pause at the entrance-desk for the formal discharge of the number she bore, and she watched the name of Professor Bernstein Sturm entered against it on the ledger which had been prepared already to record the allocations of the first two hundred women who had become available to reward Stuttgart's more conspicuous patriots. The Professor's name meant nothing to her; but it was an easy guess that Richard Steele's hand had pulled some subterranean string, and that pretext had been found for her to be claimed by those who danced to a tune that they might not know.

She remembered with sharp regret the lack of trust she had felt before. He had declined to look at her when they had been sur-rounded with hostile eyes. What other attitude had she anticipated that he would take? He would have had little chance of succeeding in the monstrous imposition he had contrived had he had no more wisdom than that! It was no reason for her confidence to abate that she was guarded by a policeman on either side as she was led out to a limousine of American origin, and a size and luxury not common in the Germany of that day; nor that one of them entered the vehicle, and seated himself beside her. She did not suppose, whatever Steele's contrivance for her safety might be, that she would be turned loose on the Stuttgart streets.

Smooth and swift the car passed through the commercial quarter of the city, crossed the river bridge, and traversed the once-separate residential district that is now joined in a common name. It was no more than a few minutes before it entered through gates of wrought iron, wide and high, which closed promptly behind it, and ran on through grounds that might be private to one man of exceptional wealth, but had more the aspect and extent of a public park. Was it a palace? No, she could not think that, even when she reminded herself that she was in a land which she did not know. The great house they approached had something sinister, repellent, in its dark, flat-fronted modernity. Was it a public institution, perhaps an asylum, to which they came?

The last idea was not rendered less probable by sight of windows that were closely barred, but it was confused by the view of an open hallway furnished with affluent luxury, such as either public or private asylums are unlikely to exhibit, and still more by a group of armed guards, and a machine gun on either side of the porch, which led to the thickly carpeted hall.

Stolid, expressionless servants met her, with a manner in which rudeness or reverence might have been equally easy to imagine or difficult to detect, by one of whom she was addressed in words of which only "Frau Sturm" had any meaning for her, and led up a broad sweep of twice-curving stairs, and by passages long enough to give her time for some hopeful anticipation of the haven to which she came.

The head of this vast establishment, as she supposed Herr Sturm to be, was likely to have power for her protection, if he were of that disposition, and it was surely a good omen that she was being led to Frau Sturm rather than him. The Frau's boudoir was small but furnished with a rich simplicity, to which Perdita must give a moment of appreciation, even as her eyes were drawn to a woman, not five years older than herself, but of a tired, sad beauty more suited to the twilight of life, who rose to receive her.

The outstretched hand was not intended for her to take. It pointed to a chair. But the eyes that met Perdita's were kind. They had a sympathy beyond what she could have expected to see in those of a woman of enemy race, even, she might have thought, somewhat more than the occasion required. It made her suddenly conscious of the blackness of the near shadow from which she was rescued now. It seemed that, as it receded, and in this atmosphere of sympathy, she became more conscious of how sinister it had been. That which she had accepted with a stunned mind while its thunders were overhead appeared intolerable as it withdrew.

Frau Sturm spoke to her quickly at first, and then with a slower enunciation, as she endeavoured to break through the barrier of their alien speech. Perdita, listening intently, understood something, but not much. She endeavoured to answer, but their capacity for conversing in German was obviously unequal to that which the occasion required.

Her hostess—if such a gracious word were applicable to the position—endeavoured to speak in English, but here, though some little progress was made, her own knowledge was too slight for interchange of more than the most elementary ideas. In the end, Perdita understood no more than that Herr Sturm might wish to see her at any time, when she must be ready to go to him; and that she would be wise to conform without hesitation to whatever he might require. And meanwhile she would be provided with a room, and a maid "who talk English can," by whom her requirements would be supplied.

She felt that there was much more that Frau Sturm would have said, and that she had been troubled by her inability to do so. Yet, if that were so, and she had a maid who could speak English, why did she not use her as an interpreter?

Well, there might be an easy answer to that. There might be private information to be given as to why she had been brought there, or what was designed for her, which it might not be expedient for servants to know. She saw that, if Richard Steele were really responsible for her being there, he could not have revealed himself—unless, indeed, this great house were controlled by those, like himself, who were secretly on the English side. It was unlikely enough, but after what she already knew—after her experiences of the last month—there was not much that she would have been astonished to hear.

The thought made her circumspect in what she said to the maid who led her to a room which was high and small, and, she judged, of the sort allotted to upper servants rather than honoured guests. She found that the girl could speak English well. She explained that she had been, for two years, a chambermaid at a Southampton hotel. But she was clearly indisposed to talk. She gave even that information with brevity, not mentioning the hotel's name. Perdita thought that she was nervous lest she might say more than she should, and became as cautiously reticent as herself. But the fact that the girl had been in England, and could speak the language, gave some slight vague support to the idea that this might be a harbour of English spies.

Well, she had been brought clear of that hateful hall, where, as she left, prosperous German citizens had already been arriving to choose their slaves! She must be thankful for that, and wary of all besides.

CHAPTER XVIII.

FOR the next two hours Perdita was left alone, except that a silent, elderly manservant brought a meal on a tray, which, though its details were not what she would have selected at a free choice, was ample in quantity, excellently cooked, and most daintily served. Here, at least, were no privations of war; and it was evident that the service was consistent with the dignity of Herr Sturm's palatial abode.

When the same man came again to say, in words that were partly understood, and that were assisted by the gesture of a door held wide open for her to pass out, that Herr Sturm would see her now, she rose with a cheerful willingness to discover the adventure to which she came.

The man led her down a flight of back stairs to a lower floor, past doors through one of which there came the merry voice of a child at play, and beyond that to a long corridor, at the end of which they encountered a door of sheet steel, at which a man was stationed who wore the same uniform as those who had surrounded the porch. It might be military, or no more than a private livery, but the fact that he was placed there, and the two heavy pistols that balanced each side of his belt, were evidences that Herr Sturm either feared violent intrusion against himself or held possessions that must be protected with a great care.

The man who had conducted Perdita to this point said: "The Fraulein for whom Herr Sturm has sent." He turned back, as one whose mission was done. The soldier touched a bell, and a grid opened in the door. The grid closed, and the steel door opened to let her through.

Now another soldier took her in charge, by whom she was led between bare stone walls, treading a cold concrete floor. She passed closed doors, and was aware of a faint scent that she did not like. She was led into a large, high, cold-looking room with the aspect of half of a laboratory and half of a commercial office, occupied by one man who sat at a wide desk, and whom she soon realized to be Herr Sturm himself.

He pointed the pen he held towards a chair at the other side of his desk, and said curtly in English: "Sit down"; and then in German to her guide: "Herman, you can go. You will be at call."

Perdita looked at a man who was tall, lean, with a long, colourless face and a fringe of straight black hair round a bald cranium, which was narrow and very high. He wore spectacles, but the way he stretched a long neck towards her suggested that he was too myopic for them to give more than partial relief.

As Perdita looked at him, the idea that she had come into the care of one who would protect her, if not at his own will, yet under orders he had received, became less confident than before. With the insight that comes to those whose senses are stimulated by peril, she thought: "His wife fears him. She probably hates him. She would have given me some warning words if she could. But they were such as would not safely pass through a servant's ears." Perhaps it was not a very difficult guess. Certainly Herr Sturm did not appear to be one whom it would be easy for youth and beauty to love.

Perdita recollected her hope that ignorance of the German language would delay her danger, though it could scarcely be a permanent shield, but she saw the futility of the idea when she remembered that English "Sit down," and it finally died as Herr Sturm went on to address her, with stiff precision, in her native tongue.

"You are English," he said, as one who enjoys a joke. He added: "And you are here!"

She was silent, these being propositions she could not deny.

"Do you know why I have chosen you?"

"No."

"Nor do I. In fact, I did not choose you at all. Why should I do that? You are all alike. You are cattle from the same pen. You are no attraction to me. Do you know why I should waste time on you at all?"

"No, I don't see why you should. I am sure you must have more important matters upon your mind." Perhaps the interview would not end so badly after all! If he had no time to be wasted on her, she would not quarrel with that. It might be that she would come to nothing worse than a place among the many servants Herr Sturm's establishment must require, and with the hope of ultimate rescue to brace her mind.

"You don't see why I should! I will tell you that. *It is because it is I who have won the war, and I will have the honour that is my due.*

"I said, I will take a number at random, for they are all alike for any purpose of mine. Should I squander time to inspect files of such sleek young heifers as you, of a fallen race? But I said, she shall be taken first, before the choosing of lesser men. I will have the number I pick. Would Colonel Beck have number XO196, he will find she is not or him."

It appeared, as he said this, that he had become oblivious of whom he addressed, or at whom he peered with his jealousy that diseased his mind. It was an exhibition of the same feeling that Steele had observed at the War Council, when von Hoffmann had withstood Herr Geibel's desire for the use of the powder that ate the eyes: the mutual jealousy that divided soldier and chemist in bitter controversy as to which were the more potent to bring misery to the world. And it appeared, as Herr Sturm went on, that he had another, more domestic grievance against a fellow-chemist—in fact, against Herr Geibel himself—over that same powder, which he claimed to have invented at a time when he had been Herr Geibel's head assistant, before he had himself become chief of the gigantic experimental laboratories which he now controlled. Today his own position might be high and his wealth great, but Herr Geibel sat in a higher place and took more ample rewards. He had ploughed his assistant's brains, and put the crop in his own barn.

Herr Sturm may not have intended to say all this when he began. He may have meant no more than to gloat over an Englishwoman who had come into his pitiless power, and to humiliate her with the knowledge that she was despised even below the degradation her captivity implied. Beyond this, he may have meant to say no more than to inform her of the occupation to which she was to be put, and to warn her of the penalty of refusal; but, when he began, from the heart's fullness the mouth spoke, and he went on to expose the bitter jealousies of a mind which was, perhaps, no viler than those of his occupation must necessarily be.

"It was we German chemists," he made a boast which no other nation is likely to envy, "who first gave poison gas to the world. It is we who will prove that it has more power than powder or steel, and far more than your Christian God. And we will have at last the honour which is our due."

His voice had risen shrilly upon these words, and sank abruptly as he added, while his short-sighted eyes endeavoured to focus upon his sole auditor again: "I will show you now what you have to do. And you will see what you have escaped when they brought you here."

He picked up a telephone from his desk, and spoke in German she could not follow, but when Herman appeared again and Herr Sturm rose, while the man held the door open for them to pass through, it was sufficiently evident that she was to go by the same way.

So far she had understood vaguely that he was a chemist who magnified the horrors which his inventions had inflicted upon the world of his fellow-men, and who had jealous complaints both against military authorities and those of his own kind. She understood also that he had claimed her with no other primary motive, better or worse, than assertion of his own importance, but that, having her in his power, he would use her without mercy, as she was sure, and without malice, she could but hope, for a caprice that she could not guess.

By this time she had lost the expectation that she had come to a place of rescue, or that Richard Steele had concerned himself for her relief. Far from that, it impressed her with a sick antipathy, for which, fighting a fear she could not subdue, she told herself that there was no adequate cause.

"I might," she thought, "have fallen into much worse—that is into less indifferent—hands. The man has his mind upon other things, which is how I wish it to be. It is the revulsion from the great hope I had which has made courage so hard to call."

So she struggled to persuade herself, but the fear remained. It was not only personal for herself. It was as though the fiendish purposes with which Herr Sturm's laboratories were busied divorced it from the guarding mercy of God, so that there was no limit to, no restraint upon, the horrors it might contain. It explained the look in Frau Sturm's eyes which the palatial luxury in which she lived could not subdue, and which Perdita had interpreted in too simple terms, as being mere sympathy for herself, a sister-woman who had almost fallen beside the way.

Only one sound, that of the merry childish voice that she had heard through a closed door, gave humanity to the place, as a child's laughter must ever do.

They had passed two doors now—doors that were fastened with locks, and with heavy chains, but were yet covered with noise-proof padding, giving them the incongruous appearance at once of softness and strength. The horror was in that faint scent that she had noticed before, but could not define. It was stronger now. They passed through a laboratory in which men moved as in some weird operating-theatre, white-sheeted, goggled, and gloved. They left it for a place of cages and bars, where attendants passed them with the aspect of warders in a convict prison, such men as must inevitably be found in such a place as she would find that to be, differing from Herr Sturm only in that they had the brutality without the brains. There were now cages separated from them by a solid plate glass partition, on the farther side of which men moved in gas masks of a pattern larger and more grotesque than those which she had seen worn to such futile purpose when Prague perished in fire and snow.

Professor Sturm paused. Through the thick, transparent, air-proof partition Perdita saw a chimpanzee that writhed and hurled itself blindly from side to side of a narrow cage. Its eye sockets were red, sightless pits. Its agony was too great to regard that it struck against bars and walls as it flung or twisted itself at the lash of its tortured nerves. Perdita scarcely heard Herr Sturm's lucid explanations in the blank horror of what she saw.

"This," he said, "is proof of that which is known to scores who have no courage to speak, but which shall come to Prince von Teufel's ears, though it must be by a channel that Herr Geibel has not been careful to block. Who but its inventor should have the wit to improve the powder that eats the eyes? That which is acting there is three times more deadly than the poor dust that Herr Geibel makes. Nor does it stop when the eyes are done: it goes inward to eat the brain.

"You may think that you hear no outcry because this glass is proof against the passage of sound. So it may be, but there is a better reason than that. There is paralysis of the vocal chords, which is another novelty that I have introduced. When a stubborn burgomaster—I should say mayor, should I not, to you?—feels the first specks of that dust tickle his eyes, he will not be able to leave his savings to me! He will find it hard to dictate his will!"

He chuckled at his own joke, which might have put him, for the moment, in better humour than he had been before, had not a recollection of another grievance disturbed his mind. Why had he been forced to prove these things upon dogs and apes, when human beings would have been so much superior for the many tests that his experiments had required?

"They would not give me one," he exclaimed bitterly, "not so much as a mangy babe! Not even one from their imbecile wards. Not *one* from the millions of human trash that the earth contains! Well, it was a time of peace, and they had little wit to foresee. I suppose, if I should ask when the need is done, they would find some they could give me now!"

He appeared to become unconscious of Perdita's existence during such outbursts as these, but he directed his attention to her again as he went on. "When you consider this, you may perceive that, as our peasants say, you are a *Mädchen* born under a fortunate star. For you see that which will be let loose on the winds of your own land, and it is thus that your folk will die, while you are here helping to prepare it for them, which will be more pleasant to do.

"For it is in the preparation of this powder that your occupation will be. There is fine work to be done, such as is most fit for a woman's hands. And I will give you a reward if your work be rapid and true. I did not take you for the purpose that brought you here. As for that, I have a mind that is busy with greater things, and a wife who is all I need. But I do not say but that, when the humour is mine...." He became gross in explanation of what he would do, by which he fell back to the German tongue, so that she understood little, though still more than enough. She made no answer. She felt unable to speak, which may have been no disadvantage to her. She was resolved that she would not toil to prepare the means of that dreadful death, but of what might not Herr Sturm be capable should she decline?

As to that she was soon to learn. He bent his head towards her, peering to see how she took the sentence which he had passed upon her. "Ah!" he said, his humour changing again. "You are white now! You will tell me next that you are not pleased to be here. Perhaps that you have a will of your own! You have more than that. You have other things. *You have eyes.* You will do well to remember that."

He turned, leading her back and chuckling as he repeated, rather to himself than to her: "Yes. If your work should be slack—if you should fail to please me in all you do—you will do well—you will do *very* well—to remember that."

CHAPTER XXIX.

HERR STURM led the way back to his own office, and as he entered and closed the door behind him, Perdita, watching all with the wary alertness of a trapped beast in whom the hope of escape would not lightly die, observed that its heavy locks were so controlled upon the inner side that they would be shot at once by throwing over a little lever upon the latch. To enter the office from the laboratories would require possession and turning of heavy keys, but if the Herr Professor should desire to go out, an obedient mechanism would render it easy for him to do.

The grim joke with which he had concluded the monologue of which she had been the silent auditor appeared to have restored him to the good humour which came and went so quickly, and which may seldom have come from a better source. His manner, though still that of one who regarded her with contempt, if no more active malignity, became almost genial as he told her to sit down while he cleared his desk, for it appeared that, however much longer the work of the laboratories might go on, his own was done for the day.

After giving some telephone instructions, he rose and opened a door behind his desk which was so set into the wall that Perdita had not previously noticed its existence, and which was his private way of retreat to the residential part of the house. He opened it with a small but intricate key, and Perdita, watchful still, observed how short-sighted he was, as they passed into a passage less brightly lighted than had been the electric brilliance of the office—an interior, unwindowed room into which no daylight came. When he relocked the door, she was almost certain that it had not been fully closed, and that the tongue of the lock had been shot outside the socket, but it was not a matter on which she was likely to interfere, nor could she see how it would be of any advantage to her.

The thought came that it might be a deliberate trick, intended to lure her to some attempt which would be excuse for punishment—perhaps for the infliction of some experimental torture upon her, such as would be likely to please his mind. She never knew whether this were not the true explanation, but, if it were so, it worked out to a most different end. Would she have intervened if she had foreseen what that end would be? She might ask herself that at another time, but it was a test she did not have to endure.

As they came to one of the wider corridors of the house, Herr Sturm stopped. He touched a gong. He said: "I am calling a servant, who will find you a room. You have one? He will lead you to that. I shall require you tomorrow. You will be told when."

His tone was indifferent. Rather that of one who postponed useless trouble than as having genuine work for her to do. She saw that she had been brought there by no more than a cruel whim born of jealousy and pride, and which had now become a subject of the satanic humour that diseased a mind, the monstrous criminality of which had found that it could be securely practised—that it was even rewarded, praised.

Perhaps, if she were unobtrusive, discreet, she might still find that honour and life would walk on a common road. But against that was the dreadful threat that she would be employed upon production of the poisons which were intended for the destruction of her own friends—and the alternative of that, dreadful death! At any moment of anger—if she should thwart him, if she should be clumsy in what she did, or perhaps through mere curiosity, or the spontaneous cruelty of his changing moods, or what he would call "scientific" interest in her reactions to such a fate—might he not take pleasure in goading her to her own destruction?

But there was another aspect of her position to which she could not be blind. Must she not, being here, have opportunities of damaging, perhaps of destroying, these foul laboratories, and all the devilries they contained? Perhaps of burning them down? Suppose she should appear subservient, timid, obedient, and watch her chance? Such an object might justify her even in becoming diligent in the hateful service that he proposed.

But would she have the courage, she asked herself, if the opportunity should be hers? Courage against the thought of the ghastly price which, for such an outrage, she would so probably have to pay? It was a question to which she could find no confident answer. A month ago, she had been aware of no darker threat to the sunny threshold of life than lay in a cancelled dance, or the sudden rain that ruins an Ascot frock. She supposed that Richard Steele would have faced the position—the opportunity, it would have been to him—in a bolder mood.

But when he came into her thoughts, it was to turn them to another channel: one not of heroic resolve, but the pain of a dead hope. If he could only know the peril in which she lay, would he have sufficient power—or inclination—to save her now? It was a vain question. He did not know. That of her own conduct—by his standards—remained uncertain.

The private door of Herr Sturm's office was, she believed, unlocked at the present hour, and was likely to remain so till the morning. From there she knew that it would be easy to pass into the laboratories. They might, for all she knew, be left vacant during the night. How much wreckage, how much destruction of irreplaceable data, might she not work? She might even regain her own room without anything more than proofless suspicion being directed upon her! Had she courage—inclination—for that? She told herself that she could not be sure till the night-hours should arrive. In the issue, it was another thing she would never know.

She was interrupted in the barren misery of such doubts as these by the service of a dinner more elaborate than the meal that she had had at midday. She understood the sombre reticence of the unresponsive servants now. It was not that they hated her, as a captive of alien blood. It was less simple than that. The place was tainted. It was too good a name to call it a barracks: it was a gilded gaol. It was pestilent with the occupation it had.

After the meal came the English-speaking maid. Madame said, would she go to the drawing room when her dinner was done? She would show the way. It was not an invitation to be refused. The room to which Perdita was shown was not large, but richly furnished—over-furnished, she would have said—in an ornate style. Only Herr Sturm and his wife were there.

Frau Sturm was at the piano as she went in. The Professor did not rise nor regard her entrance at all. She supposed the surprising invitation to be some tribute to what she was in herself, as distinct from the position to which she had come. Or Frau Sturm may have been conscious only of her own need. That was a third thing she would never know. The whole experience would always have a nightmare quality in recollection, rather than that of the waking day.

The music went on. Perdita had no grievance for that. Conversation would have been difficult with Frau Sturm, and would have had no attraction with her husband, unless it could have established a friendliness for which she was not foolish enough to hope, and which, on her side, in spite of all that she had at stake, would not have been easy to simulate or sustain. And Helena Sturm played well. Under different circumstances the music, which was from the older German masters, would have been a pleasure to hear.

It was interrupted by the entrance of a nurse bringing in the child whose laughing voice Perdita had heard before—a boy of about five years—to say good night to his parents, at an hour at which, by English standards, he should have been long asleep.

He was an alert, curious child, less stolid of demeanour than the youthful Teuton will often be, instant to observe Perdita and approaching her without shyness, disregarding his parents at first for the newer face. He had his mother's eyes, and there might be hope that he would unite the inventive quality of his father's brain with a character of another kind. However that might be, the presence of any child must be like a breath of Heaven there at the very portals of Hell. It seemed to Perdita that even Herr Sturm showed evidence of some kindly humanity as he kissed his son, and that some trace of that feeling remained while he conversed with his wife for some minutes afterwards, though she was unable to understand the subject on which they spoke.

Sitting disregarded thus, she had an impulse to withdraw—a thought that she might even have been expected to do so more promptly. (What could she know of the etiquette of such an establishment? What, indeed, could any precedent of etiquette avail to guide one in a position as unprecedented as hers?) But while she hesitated as to how this movement would be regarded, the nurse who had brought the boy into the room entered again, to ask, with a face which became more anxious as she saw what the answer to her question must be, whether he had returned there.

The question—the news that he had slipped away and could not be found—produced an instant alarm, which Perdita could only partly understand, nor could she know how much occasion it had.

The child was of a curiosity which was never still, even beyond what is usual to his years. It was a curiosity stimulated by the fact that he was forbidden to enter the laboratories, nor would anyone give him the explanation he sought of what their mysteries were. More than once before he had shown persistence in his endeavour to explore them, and ingenuity in contriving opportunity to do so. If Herr Sturm was aware that he had left the door unlocked—if it had been deliberately done—he would have a special cause for alarm which he must not say.

The woman flinched visibly before the fury of anger with which he spoke. "Here?" he echoed. "No! You should know that. What are you for? He is your charge. Go back and find him at once. He will not be far."

The last words were confidently said, and had a probable sound, but his apprehension had been shown by the extent to which his anger had stirred.

His wife, being aware of his moods, and otherwise knowing less than he, may, to this point, have been the less disturbed of the two; but when he rose as the nurse withdrew and said: "I will go myself. I will make sure," she said fearfully: "Then there is doubt? You would never have left the door...?"—and rose to follow him in a more evident perturbation than he.

Perdita understood vaguely what had occurred, and at the sight of Frau Sturm's distress, she asked: "Can I do anything? Can I help?"—and would have followed her from the room. But Herr Sturm turned upon them. "You will stay here. There is nothing wrong. I only go to make sure."

His wife hesitated. But the habit of fear, of obedience, supported by her self-assurance that there was—that there could be—no real cause for alarm, was powerful enough to turn her back to the room.

Herr Sturm went on. He came to the private door of the office that he had left ajar. It was wide open now. He could not think that

Perdita had been there, for he had told his wife to have her fetched down to the drawing room so that he should be assured that she was attempting nothing during that hour of his own ease. He entered the office, and saw that the farther door, which led to the laboratories, was also wide. It was evident that the lever had been pressed and the locks shot. Could a child do that? Yes, with a chair's help, and a chair had been moved near to the door.

He knew that Fritz, who observed everything, who forgot nothing, had seen him turn that lever over when he had been with him in the office, to which he had been allowed at times when his father was there, until the danger of his persistent curiosity had been observed.

He could not doubt now where the child must be. But there need be no great evil to apprehend. He went on.

CHAPTER XXX.

HERR STURM came back to the drawing room. In his arms was a whimpering child, who rubbed his eyes with impatient knuckles. "My eyes itch," he complained. "My eyes have a funny itch." His voice rose suddenly to a scream. *"My eyes hurt."*

Perdita looked on at a tragedy which had become simple to understand. She saw Herr Sturm's face humanized by anguish, impotently aware that there was nothing his boasted science could do to save. She saw the face of his wife, stone-white, not humanized at all, but turned rather to that of a chained wolf that must endure the sight of a tortured cub.

The boy screamed again, and then the cry died in a silent paroxysm as he writhed against the strength of his father's arm. Perdita remembered the vaunt that Herr Sturm had made. But he had claimed no more than he had been able to do. Here was the paralysis of the vocal chords.

Herr Sturm turned to the door.

His wife sprang towards him, catching his arm. "What are you going to do?"

"The lethal chamber."

"There is no other way?"

"None."

She loosed his arm. *"How I hate you!"* she said. But she made no protest at what he did. She followed him from the room, and Perdita, as one who watches a play too dreadful to leave till the curtain fall, followed a few paces behind…

Herr Sturm opened the door of the lethal chamber. It had to accommodate many miserable creatures, large and small, in the year's course, and sometimes there would be many at once, dogs or monkeys, rabbits or rats, when comparative results were to be obtained. But—Herr Sturm would have said because the Government so obtusely obstructed the advance of science—it had had no human victim till now.

It was high enough for Herr Sturm to enter without stooping, and innocuous until it should be closed, and the deadly vapour let loose within it.

It was a ponderous door, fitting into its deep socket with airtight closeness. It was not easy to swing it open with one hand, and the boy, now writhing as in the paroxysms of tetanus, dangled awkwardly from the single grip. But Frau Sturm, following closely behind, gave neither hindrance nor help.

It may have been a natural impulse of pity for the tortured child, of haste to end sufferings he could not cure that led him to step in to lay the boy down, rather than delay to put him into one of the sliding cages which were the means of introduction commonly used.

Though his sight was bad, his hearing had no equal defect. The door made little noise as it closed into its padded socket, but he turned sharply. He sprang back with a sudden realization of what it meant, and with an agility which denied his years. But as his hand came to the jamb, the bolts shot.

He saw his wife's hand upon the lever which would let loose the vapour of painless death. It was a better end than he had designed for his fellow-men, but he was not grateful for that. Fear and frenzy convulsed his face as he screamed a most futile prayer to the woman who had borne his son for so vain a fate. He could only see her lips move as she turned to Perdita to ask, in a wondering way: "Did he think I would let him live?"

As she spoke, her eyes, which had been vague at first, focused upon Perdita in a puzzled manner, as though recovering a difficult recollection of who she was. She changed from German to English words, as she added: "That you go, it is—it is the much better be." And Perdita recognized in a numbed mind that there might be wisdom in that.

Walking blindly, she found her way back to her own room, as she might have done less surely had she been alert to the conscious doubt. She did not commence to undress, seeing, as her mind cleared like a mirror from which vapour retires, that the tragedy was one that must be discovered in a short time, and anticipating that she would not be left quiet when the stir began.

Yet half an hour passed and no one came, and whatever movements there may have been in the great house did not penetrate to the upper floor Was it possible that Frau Sturm had had discretion and self-control sufficient, after she had watched the end of her only child, and her husband's more vocal death, to go back to her drawing room and cause the household to retire, with quiet, plausible words? It was hard to think. Herr Sturm's absence might be unobserved, except by his wife, and his movements would not be for others to question or control, but what could she say to the nurse which would cause her to abandon search for the missing child? Nothing. Or, at the least, nothing which would not make her position more surely damned when the truth should become known on the next day. No, there must be discovery now. There must be confusion stirring or soon to stir.

Yet as the time passed, she saw that to remain dressed and alert might be regarded as evidence of increasing strength that she was aware of, even if she were not implicated in the tragedy that had occurred. Her door had a good lock. It was strongly made. With the key inserted on her side, it could not be opened quickly against her will. She began to undress, and as she did so she heard steps in the passage. There was a sharp knock on the door. A man's voice said: "Open, Fräulein!"

She replied in English: "What is it? Wait a moment." She heard the man's voice in conversation with Gerta, the English-speaking maid who had waited upon her earlier in the day. Doubtless he asked what she had said.

Then Gerta called, and agitation was evident in her words. "There is a dreadful thing! The Captain says you must open at once."

Perdita's mind had become wary and cool. She thought: "The girl was told not to say that Herr Sturm is dead. They will try to trap me with questions to find out what I know." She said: "I was undressed. Tell him he must wait a moment. After that, I will open the door."

The officer did not take this in a patient mood. He knocked sharply again. But she had the wit not to open too quickly, and when she did so to have some minor adjustment of dress with which to busy her hands in an evident manner.

He pushed in as the key turned, taking little notice of what she did. He addressed her in German in a curt, peremptory tone, the effect of which was inevitably weakened by the necessity of interpreting what he said. With Gerta as an agitated medium, the conversation proceeded. "The Captain asks that you will tell him all that you know."

"About what?"

"He says do not—how do you say?—do not avoid…. You must tell him all you know of that which has happened in the last hour."

Perdita's position was one in which she might have excuse if she thought more of herself than of those who were captors and foes, and perhaps she did. But she could not feel indifferent to the fate of the tortured woman by whose act Herr Sturm had come to a better end than inventors of poison gases may fairly deserve. A cold justice might say that he had gone to death by too smooth a road. She saw that, if Frau Sturm had gone back to the drawing room unobserved before raising alarm, it might be hard to convict her of complicity in his death, though the fact of the lethal chamber being closed from the outside—if she had left it so—might be proof that he had not died by his own act.

Apart from that, if she thought of herself, it was far from clear that she would do well to admit that she had stood by while Frau Sturm shot the bolts, and had then walked quietly away.

Thought being swift, and having had time to debate these questions before, she answered without evident pause: "I have been here most of the last hour. What is it that he is asking about?"

"He says you are not to question, but to reply. You knew that the child was lost?"

"Yes, I understood something of that. I was in the drawing room when the nurse came in to inquire. But I did not comprehend very well what the trouble was. I could not understand what was said."

"What did Herr Sturm do after the nurse came to the room?"

"Do? He did nothing. He talked. I think he was going somewhere. But Frau Sturm told me it would be better I did not stay."

"The Captain says he believes you know more which you would be much wiser to say."

"Perhaps I could answer better if you would say what he wants to know."

"He says you may come to be sorry you do not speak."

"I have answered everything he has asked. What can I do more?"

"He says you must not lock your door again. You must not leave the room unless you are told; but if you are called, you must be ready to come."

When he had gone, Perdita controlled an impulse to turn the key. She saw that it could be no more than a futile defence. It would be foolish to show defiance on such a point. She lay down without pretence of undressing again. In the silence, she heard the steps of a soldier who had been stationed outside her door, and who walked at times for warmth, or that he might not doze on his chair. She saw that there might be enough trouble for her when the daylight should come, but it was not of the kind which had been her most imminent fear. It is the likelihood of life that the unexpected will come with another day, and it is a probability which must be immeasurably increased when the routines of civilization are broken through.

CHAPTER XXXI.

PERDITA was undisturbed, except by her own thoughts, till the morning came, and, thinking she would be unable to sleep, after a short time she slept well. When her door opened, it was for the entrance of nothing worse than a breakfast for which she found that her appetite had not failed. Only the occasional steps of the soldier outside the door warned her of the ordeal which was to come.

It came at last in the form of an officer, whose few English words were sufficient for the order he had to give. She followed him with two soldiers upon her heels, in evidence that it was rather as a prisoner than a free witness that she was led to the court of inquiry that was now being held in a room below.

It was a larger room than she had yet entered, and its amenities had been rudely disturbed to fit it for the use to which it was now put. She was led to a chair, spacious and soft, it having been designed for a better time, and was told that she could sit. She faced a row of officers, the President of whom, wearing a General's uniform, began to interrogate her at once, without requiring the formality of an oath.

There was no need for an interpreter here. His English, though sometimes slow, was correctly phrased. He spoke with civility, and though she could not think him a friend, she felt that he was genuinely searching for truth, which gave her some hope, and would have given more had the truth been somewhat other than what it was.

She was questioned to the same point as the night before, and answered in the same way, but when she had done this, he said:

"That is what I hear you have told before, but we believe it to be untrue. If you have a chance—and I would not have you think it is much—it is by telling the truth. You know whether you can afford to do that. But we give you another chance."

"I can only say that Frau Sturm told me to go. I am sure that, if you ask her, she will confirm that."

The reply, which she gave with a confident tone, it being a scrap of truth, where truth was being used with some frugality, seemed to puzzle him beyond what she could understand, so that she felt for a moment that she had won more credence than before. He discussed it with his colleagues in rapid German. But having done this, he said to her: "That is what it is quite certain she will not do."

He paused a moment. He said with a slow, ominous deliberation: "Miss Wyatt, listen to this. According to your account, you left the drawing room at the same time as Herr Sturm went in search of the child. We know that to be untrue. When he returned with the child, you were still there. Will you tell the truth now, or are we to suppose it to be such that you cannot do so, except you condemn yourself?"

As she heard this, she had the first vague intimation of the depth of the peril which lay before her. But what could she say now? How could she guess how much of conjecture there might be in the statement that she had heard? How strong or weak the evidence against her might be? And she must never for an instant forget that, if her tale were true, she could have no knowledge of the deaths either of Herr Sturm or the boy.

She showed some wit, of the kind that the cornered have, when she replied: "I don't see what more you can expect me to say while you don't tell me what the trouble is. I went down to the drawing room when I was told, and when I was told, I went back upstairs. I've done nothing but what I was told since I was brought here yesterday morning."

The President heard this as though it moved him to a second measure of doubt, but, having considered it, he said: "You are lying. There may be things that we do not know. But we know that. But I will tell you what the charge against you will be.

"The court will adjourn now, and will reassemble at 3:00 P.M., when you will be charged with the murders of Herr Sturm and his wife and child."

With a natural surprise, but doubtful wisdom, she exclaimed: "Do you mean that Frau Sturm is dead?"

"They are all dead. The accusation against you is that you followed them when they either found the child in a lethal chamber in the laboratories or took him there for a purpose into which it would be irrelevant to inquire; and that, while they were there, you closed the door upon them and turned on the lethal gas, afterwards unbolting the door again when they were too overcome to make their escape. That is the precise charge which you have to meet, and you have four hours to consider what you will say."

She replied, in a voice which she found hard to control to the steadiness which she felt that the position required: "I can only say that I am absolutely innocent. If you knew me, you would know that I am incapable of such an action. I suppose I shall have some assistance for my defence?"

"No, there will be no occasion for that. This is a court-martial in time of war. You have only to speak the truth, and you will have careful justice from us. You can be certain of that."

Giving her no time for further reply, Major-General Wolfe made the signal for her to be returned to her own room. She had four hours in which to think, to decide. What had happened had now become easy to see. After she had gone, Frau Sturm must have stood watching her husband's frantic gestures of appeal, and his gradual subjection to the anaesthetizing gas to the point of incapacity, if not of unconsciousness, and must then have unbarred and entered the lethal chamber. Obviously, having done so, she could not have secured it again on the outside.

Perdita saw that she must endeavour to approach the matter, as it were, with the detachment of another mind. How far was suspicion legitimately and reasonably directed against herself? How far did her present attitude of entire denial strengthen it or else hold it at bay? If the whole truth were told and believed, how far could she be judged to have acted wrongly?

She knew little of the procedure of courts-martial, but had a vague, well-founded fear both of the drastic powers they possess and the swift severity with which these are put in force. After an hour of worrying thought she decided that it would be safest, as it would certainly be simplest, to tell the truth without qualifications or reserves. If the President had said nothing beyond the fact in warning her that she was known to have been in the drawing room when Herr Sturm returned with the child (and if there had been no observation of the entrances and exits from the room, how should they know that he had gone back with the child at all?), then there might be a better prospect of acquittal if she should be frank than if she should prefer the desperate expedient of an altered lie.

Besides that, she preferred truth, which it was natural to her to speak; and her first reason for evasion had lost its force now that she knew that Frau Sturm was dead.

She found some mental relief when she had resolved this, and some appetite for a lunch which was as well served as before. Evidently, she was not to be treated with any criminal severities in anticipation of an adverse judgment.

Finding some slender consolation in that, she addressed her mind to recollection of the events of the last evening, so that her narrative should be clear and exact, and found that the hour came quickly enough at which she was summoned to descend again to the trial room.

"You will have decided, I hope, Miss Wyatt, to tell us better truth than you did this morning."

General Wolfe's tone had a cold severity of which she had not been conscious before, and which might have been sufficient to shake a resolution less firmly made, but she answered: "I am prepared to tell you all I know, and more completely than I did before. But, until you told me this morning, I did not know that Frau Sturm was dead, which I was sorry to hear."

It was apparent at once, as she said this, that the informal trial was to be conducted with patience and an aspect of judicial care. The President translated her reply to a sergeant, who wrote it down in longhand, as was done with the whole narrative that followed. General Wolfe's fellow judges listened, and would ask elucidatory questions at times, which she understood only if they led to a query being addressed to her.

When this first statement had been recorded the President asked: "Then you knew that Herr Sturm and the child were dead?"

"I supposed they were, though I could not have actually said that it was so, as they were not dead when I left. But may I tell you what happened in my own way, and you will allow for the fact that I do not understand German, and for that reason some things were less clear than they might otherwise have been?"

"That is what we wish you to do."

With that permission, she gave a brief account of what happened up to the time when she had been fetched to the drawing room, and a fuller one of the fatal events that followed; and this, though the President may have shortened what he considered to be non-essential detail at times, was substantially and fairly recorded.

At its conclusion there was whispered discussion among the officers from whom the verdict of acquittal or condemnation must come, and then the President said: "Miss Wyatt, I have to tell you that your tale is only partly believed; but there are some questions I am about to put which I will warn you to answer with care."

"I have told you absolute truth. But I will answer any further questions the best I can."

"So you would be certain to say. But if you saw Herr Sturm confined in the lethal chamber while there would have been time to save him, and Frau Sturm allowed you to leave, why did you not give the alarm?"

"Had I any obligation to do that, being a prisoner here?"

"On the contrary, you were brought here to become a German citizen."

"From first to last, I obeyed orders in all I did."

"There is no living witness to that. It is no more than your word, which has been changed already. If your tale be true, why did you not tell it at first?"

"Because I did not know that Frau Sturm was dead. I did not wish to bring trouble on her."

"Why should you be concerned for that?"

"She had shown some kindness to me, and I thought there was provocation for what she did."

The :President paused over this reply. He began: "There was *what*?" and then he checked himself with: "It is your reply." He translated it to be written down, after which the court consulted again.

The next question showed Perdita the full peril which confronted her now. "You have told a tale that has a wild sound, and which has no confirmation at all. Is it not more probable that you yourself shut both Herr Sturm and his wife in, and unbarred the door afterwards in an endeavour to confuse what had occurred? Can you give me any reason whatever why we should not prefer to believe that?"

"Only that it is not true. Why should I do such a dreadful thing? I thought such a charge had to be proved. I mean that it isn't fair to ask me to prove that it didn't happen."

"That is the best you can say?"

"Yes, I think it should be enough."

There was consultation again. Perdita thought that the President was being overruled by the unanimity of his colleagues to something which he was reluctant to approve, and she saw cause for apprehension rather than satisfaction in that, feeling that, though he might be hard, he would prefer to be just.

When he spoke again, it was to show that her anticipation had been correct. "Miss Wyatt, the truth of what happened will never be certainly known, for you were one of four, of whom three are dead. You are of an enemy race, and, on your own account, you could have saved one or more of these people had you given alarm, which you did not do.

"The account which you would have us believe of Her Sturm's death is one which we cannot accept, or allow to be recorded, on your unsupported testimony. The judgement of the court is that you are responsible for the death of Herr Sturm, and its verdict is that you be shot in three hours' time. I am sorry, Miss Wyatt, but it is a time of war. It is a time in which many die."

She sprang up from the chair from which she had not been required to rise while this informal judgment was given, feeling, and disregarding as she did so, a rough grasp on her arm from one of the soldiers who had been stationed on either side. "But you do not believe it!" she said boldly. "You don't believe it yourself! You *know* it is not true!"

"It is the sentence of the court. There is no more to be said. Take her away."

"But in *three hours*! You can make it longer than that? Surely I can appeal."

"There is no appeal. It is time of war. If there were, it would be useless to you. Take her away." The hands of the soldiers were on her arms, while her mind searched desperately for some argument, some plea, which might be potent to save her now, and for which the next five seconds were all she had. Zweiss—Adolph Zweiss—was his German name. He had been in the uniform of the Air Service. She did not know of what rank it was, though, from the group of officers who had been satellites to his central figure, she supposed that it must be high. She made instinctive choice of that which would be most likely to win attention when she exclaimed: "But I do appeal! I appeal to Air Marshal Zweiss! He knows that it is a thing that I should not do."

The President, who may have been the only member of the court who understood what she said, replied coldly: "But that is absurd. The matter is not one that concerns the Air Service at all."

The soldiers understood the tone, if not the words, of this rebuff. The hands on her arms drew her firmly, though without needless violence, towards the door. She saw that she must submit unless she would engage in an unseemly abortive scuffle before hostile and unfriendly eyes. As hope died, dignity came to her aid. She did not notice that the attention of her judges had been drawn to a paper over which their heads bent together. But as she reached the door the voice of the President called for her to be brought back. "Why," he asked, "did you mention the name of Air Marshal Zweiss?"

The tone was not one to revive hope, and she had a sudden terror that the use of his name might draw suspicion, even bring ruin, to him. She might have become the cause of his death, of the loss to England of all he could do for her at this crisis of the world's fate, and all because she could not die with a still tongue! Yet what had been said was beyond recall, and the question she heard must, in some form, be answered now.

Avoiding mention of the assistance he had given her when she escaped from Nürnberg at the outbreak of war, she answered vaguely: "I was of some help to him when he was in England last. He would not deny that."

The members of the court conferred again. The President said: "The sentence must stand. The execution will not take place till tomorrow noon. In the meantime prisoner will be confined in her own room."

He repeated this in English, so that she should understand. It did not sound like much, but she saw that there must be some reason for the delay, and in that there could be no less than a doubtful hope.

CHAPTER XXXII.

PERDITA saw that in some way the mention of Richard Steele by his German name had prevailed to delay execution of the sentence, if nothing more, even as it had seemed to fail. What could be the meaning of that?

She saw a possibility that it might mean harm to him rather than good to her, that she might be kept alive for a few further hours while inquiry was instituted, so that she would be available for further questioning if required.

But though this reflection brought a sharp fear and a torment of self-reproach, it remained one that her reason did not support. She had understood that his English connection was known to the German Intelligence Service, though its significance might be misread, and that even his action in assisting her to escape had been known and approved by them. Then what more natural than that, in her extremity, she should invoke his name? It would be equally natural whether she should believe him to be in actual truth a German or English spy. Nor would her opinion on that point, one way or another, be regarded as of any importance at all. She could not see how she could have done him harm, but the position was obscure enough to leave her sloughed in a double doubt. She must spend the night in the uncertain anticipation of sudden and violent death, and in the recurring fear that she might have done useless and cowardly harm to one who had aided her, and from whom she had not found it easy afterwards to restrain her thoughts, telling herself that the chances had become a million to one against their meeting again.

Actually, though the shadow of death had not moved widely away, her exclamation had done more for herself than she could expect, having no key to the enigma of what occurred.

When Richard Steele learnt that she had gone by a way that he could not follow, he had put what may have been an excessive caution aside. Having seen one among the captive women with whom he had had some acquaintance before, why should he not desire to claim her for his own disposal? It was what Air Marshal Zweiss might be as likely as Richard Steele to desire. Prince von Teufel had told him, when he had been raised to the high place he held, that marriage would not be for him. Bur he had not said or implied that he might not woo or commandeer what women he would on less onerous, more flexible, terms. And that, as opportunity crossed his path, was what he was proceeding to do.

He put his finger on the number XO196, and said sharply: "That is the one I will have for my own use. There has been clumsiness in interpretation of what I said, which I will not blame. But it must be put right in the next hour. You will wire at once that she shall be sent to my apartment at the Lustgarten Palace, to be at my disposition when I return, and in such honour as is fitting for one who is selected by me."

The telegram which was dispatched to Stuttgart upon that order being given would have been sufficient to secure any one of the 199 women, or indeed that number in bulk, even had they been allocated already to lesser men. The trouble was that when it arrived the 199 were still there, but the one it concerned had just been taken away, and that by the one man in all Württemberg who was utterly beyond the Burgomaster of Stuttgart's control. He saw it to be a matter which might mean trouble from either side, which he was unwilling to have. He referred it back to Nürnberg, reporting what the position was, and suggesting that an order should be sent to Herr Sturm by someone having more authority than his own.

The officials of Nürnberg were more sharply perturbed. They had heard the Air Marshal's voice as he gave the order. They knew that he held them responsible, and that they might be said to have blundered before. They could not report to him, for he had gone by the pathless ways of the air, telling no one where he would alight next.

They did not merely refer the matter to Berlin, feeling it to be one that could not be shrugged so easily from their own shoulders. They asked for a specific order to be issued in support of the verbal direction that Air Marshal Zweiss had given.

This was not refused, but it was not instantly done. It was a moment at which Herr Sturm was not lightly to be offended. Had it been no more than a question of who should have first claim on one who was equally free for both, there is no doubt that the Air Marshal would have had the prize. But Perdita having already passed into Herr Sturm's hands, the matter had become less simple than that. Should he refuse to give her up, the incident, trivial in itself, might bring the friction between soldier and chemist to an open breach at a most inopportune time. It was a development over so small a cause which even Air Marshal Zweiss himself might not approve! The order he had given had been without possible foresight of the position which would result. Might it not be best that it should be left till there could be further reference to himself?

In the end, and not till the next day, a telegram was dispatched to Herr Sturm, explaining the position, and asking as a favour for that which might have been required in another tone. Beyond that, it suggested, if Herr Sturm did not wish to part with what was understood to be no more than a random choice, that he should keep the woman *virgo intacta* until the Air Marshal could be informed.

It was this telegram that had been passed along the row of Perdita's judges, just as she invoked the name with which it was so largely concerned. Her cry gave it a significance it might not have had otherwise, while it showed that she had not mentioned a name that she had no business to do. And after that, her explanation that she had done a service to the Air Marshal when in England did her more avail than would one which might have held a larger leaven of truth.

It was a position which all the judges would not have met in the same way. The President said: "Send her to Zweiss with a report of what has occurred, and let him deal as he will." Others objected: "He would not claim her against the law. With a world's choice at his feet, would he give two thoughts to an alien woman who had been convicted on such a charge? He would say that the sentence should take its course." In saying this, they were influenced by consideration of the jealousy already mentioned, having a fear that, if she should go unpunished, it would be said that they, being military officers, were little moved by a chemist's death, even though his services to the Reich were far greater than theirs were ever likely to be. Beside such questions, what was the life of one woman—and she English!—at a time when thousands were slaughtered with the passing of every hour?

Between conflicting views, there was ready agreement with General Wolfe's proposal that reference should be made to Prince von Teufel himself, and the execution postponed until the next noon.

CHAPTER XXXIII.

AIR-MARSHAL ZWEISS came back to Berlin on the fourth day. He had flown far and seen much. He had found that the German preparations for aerial war had been even greater than he had believed, and though both they and their Russian allies had suffered heavily in the gigantic operations of the last three weeks, they were still of an immense and constantly recruited strength, as opposed to that of the Christian nations, which, for the moment at least, had been largely shattered and beaten down.

But he had formed certain conclusions which he had resolved to report to von Teufel as honestly as though he were, indeed, the German that he professed. He was unsure whether the policy he would recommend would be considered preferable by his own friends, but he saw clearly that he would not remain secure in his present position of confidence and power if he should make a practice of giving von Teufel false information or bad advice, while even a sound policy would be maimed if he could succeed in betraying it before it could be put into operation.

On his arrival at the Lustgarten Palace, he made immediate inquiry concerning Perdita, but was told that she had not arrived. Beyond that nothing was known. This was not information likely to cause acute alarm, even had he heard it with an unoccupied mind. There had been no public talk of Herr Sturm's death; no word of it had reached him by the wireless news which had been almost his only source of information during the last three days. It was not a time when such news would be freely published. He knew nothing to raise a doubt of any worse event than that she had not been transferred from Stuttgart to Berlin with the celerity which his order should have secured.

He said: "She should have arrived. She must be brought here with no further delay. Let it be known that I am not pleased, and that there may be much trouble for those who are slack to observe my will. Report to me when I return."

He had already been informed that von Teufel waited to see him, and it was not a matter to be longer delayed.

He found the Dictator of half the world pacing his room as one who had found it hard to remain still. It was as though a growing fever were in his blood, which he could not rule. He greeted Steele as one he was glad to see, but resumed pacing again.

"You are one I trust," he said, "of whom there are few. I can call you friend. And you can be cool when the hour requires. I am surrounded by lying lips, or by those which speak the language of fools, who are more hard to endure. It is the hour, I suppose, when Gibraltar falls. And it is even now that our submarines will be slipping out to the deeper seas. I do not say Klein was wrong. The liners come from the New World like a string of geese, and they are heavy with munitions and men. They should be lanced like a school of whales in the reddened seas. Yes, we will say he was right in that. I will have men who are right, even though they shall call me wrong.

"You are one I am glad to see. You shall tell me what our strength is in the air. Would you believe that Boroff has left Vinski alive? And that he is now out of control, with his corps moving southward towards Siam? Well, he is one with whom I shall be equal to deal on a later day! But could not Boroff remember the lesson that Stalin taught? When he purged, it was not done in a niggard way. He did not palter for proof. A doubted man was a man dead. Well, tell me where you have been! We shall not be disturbed, unless it be to hear we have our flag on Gibraltar rock. Have you seen how they clear the site where our great palace shall rise? Now I have an idea! I have an idea, by the gates of hell! I will have Vinski here with his whole corps! They shall bear the bricks. He will have less courage to plot than when he camps on the shore of the China Sea."

There came a pause here, sufficient to require reply. Steele said that he had seen the demolition which was now desolating the very centre of Germany's capital city. He said they worked fast. Leaving aside the question of Vinski's loyalty (though it was a doubt of which it had been pleasant to hear), he went on to make report of his own tour.

As he talked, von Teufel appeared to resume self-control. He sat down. He spoke soberly and shrewdly of what the air forces could do, and how far their work must be supplemented by terrestrial arms. He heard Steele's advice that there should be a settled policy of confining their activities to purely military objectives, not, of course, on grounds of humanity, but from more practical considerations.

He said: "It is soundly put. We will talk of it at the Council tonight. We should have news of Gibraltar then, and we can plan what we will do beyond that. We will teach those who swarm on the North African coast to wish that they were farther away."

He broke off suddenly to say: "Oh!—there was a matter of yours. A small thing. But I would not appear to countermand an order that you had given, though it had to be done. You had ordered that an English girl should be sent from Stuttgart to your own rooms?"

"Yes." Steele controlled himself with the word to an expressionless face, wondering what was to come.

"Well, she had been taken by Herr Sturm before your order was there."

"Herr Sturm?"

"Sturm. You must know of him. He was the gasman Herr Geibel hated."

"And you have retained her for me? I am most grateful for that. She is a girl I have met before, and I had a whim that I would have her now."

"So I would have done, but she had cooked her goose before it came to my ears. She had murdered Sturm and his wife and child. It is not clear how. The court that found her guilty referred to me, as you had given an order they could not ignore."

"And you wish me to deal justly with her?"

"Oh, it is done! But I would not sign an order countermanding that which had been issued by you. Men must learn that your orders are to be as final as mine. It is the place I insist that you have. I sent the order for her execution under your own name, that your prestige should not be smirched for a little thing."

Air Marshal Zweiss heard this with an impassive face, giving no sign of his thoughts. He said: "I must be grateful for that. It was most graciously done. The Council tonight will be, I suppose, at the usual hour?"

Receiving von Teufel's confirmation of this, with no haste, but no loss of time, he withdrew.

He returned to his own apartment with a mind resolved, which, in fact, it had instantly been as the information came from von Teufel's lips. It was an audacious plan, but its audacity might be its security also. And it was a surer way than arguing with von Teufel, which might have failed, and left his present intention more perilous and more precarious than it now was. Besides, there had been the vital question of time, which might already be fatally, irretrievably, gone. But he had a better hope. And no second should be lost now.

"Have a telephone line to Stuttgart," he said, "instantly cleared. *Instantly*. Get me the General who would have charge of court-martial proceedings there, or his representative if he is not about. I must be speaking to someone there within thirty seconds from now. Now send this wire: *Execution of Fräulein Wyatt to be postponed. Imperative. Zweiss.*"

It was more than thirty seconds, but less than two minutes, before he heard General Wolfe's voice. "Yes," he replied. "Adolph Zweiss speaking. You have an order from me for Perdita Wyatt's execution. Cancel that. She is required for examination. *What?* But it must not be too late. Stop it instantly. In fifteen minutes I will call you again. Yes, General. But don't talk now. *It must be stopped.*"

He rang off. He had done all that he could. He saw the danger of such a telephone conversation being tapped and reported to von Teufel himself. But he thought not. The matter was, in itself, so trivial beside the issues to which the Dictator's attention was given. And how should anyone know or suspect that he did not speak with the authority of von Teufel himself? Had he not just come from conferring with him? No, at this stage, at least, its audacity should ensure success. If only it were not too late!

He waited scrupulously until the fifteen minutes had passed, being careful that it should not be apparent to others that the matter agitated his mind, and in the interval he read the reports on the case, both from Nürnberg and Stuttgart, which were waiting upon his table. Then he said: "Get General Wolfe at Stuttgart for me again. That you, General? You were just in time? Good. Miss Wyatt is required here for examination. The matter must be so arranged that her execution will be recorded as having taken place. But you will do nothing more in the matter—nothing at all—till you have written orders from me, which will be dispatched by air in the next hour. In the meantime, discretion and silence cannot be too strictly observed."

After that he wrote:

> The execution of Perdita Wyatt is to be officially recorded as having been carried out in accordance with the verdict of the court and the confirmatory telegram that you had from me. But she will, in fact, be sent by you to me here, under the name of Miss

Amelia Braddon, with an escort on whose silence you can entirely depend, so that she will arrive here precisely at 4:00 A.M.

From the enclosed sum of 20,000 marks, for which you will not be required to account, you will make any disbursements necessary to ensure that these instructions are carried out with exactness and absolute secrecy, and so that no record, except of the execution, will remain.

Well, that was done! For good or evil he had broken a lifetime's rule that no personal interest—in particular, no woman—should intrude into the great purpose for which he lived. Yet to call it a personal interest was, perhaps, less than fair. She was a compatriot whose life, he having the power, it had surely been his duty to save. And she deserved much, if it were true, as he had been told, that she had contrived Herr Sturm's death. And there might be ways in which she would be useful to him!

CHAPTER XXXIV.

PERDITA came to Berlin, leaving behind an experience such as most would have found hard to endure, nor could its torturing uncertainty have been often excelled, even at this time when the powers of evil were loose on a scourged world.

She owed her life (and more than twenty-four hours of acute suspense) to the scrupulosity of General Wolfe. She may have been right when she said boldly that he did not believe that she was guilty of Herr Sturm's death. But he had given way to the opinion of the majority, which there had been strong reasons of policy to support. When he proposed delay of the execution until the following noon, he had assumed reasonably that it would give ample time for a telegram to reach Berlin, and for a reply to arrive.

So it would; had not the routine course of the telegram been obstructed by its own wording. The fact that it was addressed to von Teufel himself would not have occasioned delay, neither would it have come to him. Having the gigantic operations of a world war that moved with unprecedented speed to engage his mind, he did not allow it to be distracted by such details as that. In the orderly course, it would have been dealt with by an official having full power to control such an event, and yet with six others above him before it would have been near to the Prince's ears. The trouble was that it mentioned the name of Air Marshal Zweiss, giving the matter a doubtful importance which could not be resolved safely while the Air Marshal was absent, and his address unknown.

Faced by a doubt of this kind, the prudent official will prefer to pass responsibility on to a higher than he. It became a question of reference and delay, with consultation resulting, and a final device by which it reached von Teufel himself, not by the regular channels, which might have resulted in sharp rebuke, but by the hand of the humbly familiar Lessing, a medium by whose unimaginative discretion matters of exceptional character had on some previous occasions been short-circuited to the Prince's ears.

General Wolfe, finding that a reply did not arrive, and considering that it was not a matter on which silence could be held to imply consent, decided on his own responsibility that the execution should be further delayed. If he guessed well, he would merit thanks, and if he were wrong, the mistake need not endure. A head may be lopped off tomorrow, if not today, but that which was severed yesterday cannot be put back, even at an air marshal's desire. General Wolfe acted with a prudence of which Perdita had no cause to complain, but the procedure gave her a period of prolonged tension, such as no one would wish to have. She watched the hour of noon approach, till the moment arrived at which she listened for the feet of those who would lead her to death, and the clock ticked, and they did not come. She was not executed, neither was she reprieved. Late in the afternoon, she was informed that she would not be shot until the next day. This may have allowed a faint hope to remain, but not much.

Morning came, and the hour of nine, and she again found that she did not die. The next two hours held some excuse for a growing hope, which came to an abrupt end when a telegram was brought for her to see. General Wolfe, wishing, with a possible humanity, to let her know that hope was finally gone, and to inform her at the same time that the appeal for which she asked had been made, sent von Teufel's telegram for her to see, and, lest it should be beyond her knowledge of his own tongue, he wrote below it the English words: *Sentence approved. Adolph Zweiss.*

Could she guess that it had not been written by Steele's own command? Not willingly, of course. He would have done it not for his own but for England's sake, as he had once told her that he would have taken her life without thought of regret if that would have saved him a single hour.

The thought gave her some increase of fortitude in the thought that she would not die in a casual manner, but as by the deliberate decision of one of her own race who had seen it to be the best service to England that it remained for her to do. Nor could it be said that she died to no purpose at all. The event which had come through her, and had snared her thus, had destroyed a malignant foe, not only of her own race but of human kind.

And there was an actual sense of relief that the suspense was done! She had been told that, even now, she would have three hours to live, General Wolfe having allowed the same grace after the telegram came as the sentence had provided. She asked, could she write letters? Yes, if she wished. That they would be delivered to England was an extreme improbability. Even had it not been an enemy country, its conditions were not such that a regular postal service could be maintained. Yet she would not readily abandon the desire that her parents should know her end, which might not be the blackest sorrow to them—for they would know that she had escaped the degradations of the slavery that she had been intended to undergo.

What could not be mailed might be given to some friendly hand, or even orally communicated for transmission as future occasion should allow. But what friend could she hope to find in this hostile land? She remembered that it is common for condemned persons to be visited by a priest of their faith, and she asked for this privilege to be allowed. But she found again that she had asked for more than she would be likely to have. Again, it was not refused. The priest was for her to name, which she could not do. Nor, it appeared, would one of any form of Christian faith be easy to find. Christianity, after four years of persecution, had now been officially banned; though, with the lack of humour which is the bewilderment of the rest of Europe, the German Government still permitted, if it did not actually encourage, the worship of Odin and Thor! If a Catholic or Lutheran priest should come at her call, he might expect to be in trouble on the next day.

They gave her paper on which she could write what she would, and a good meal, which she was welcome to eat or leave.

So the day passed, and a third time came the hour of death, when she must fight to control a feeling of giddy sickness that vexed her as her nerves broke under the long tension they had endured, telling herself she must not shame herself or her race before callous or contemptuous eyes. And for the third time the clock ticked past the hour, and when steps came after further prolonged suspense, they were those of General Wolfe, who had thought it prudent to come himself to explain the instructions that had reached him by the swift way of the air.

She supposed his belated entrance to be signal that her last moments had come, though, when she saw who it was, she would have roused herself to the vanity of a last appeal, had he not been quicker to speak.

"There is something here you should read."

He handed her the letter, adding: "I will translate, if it is not clear."

She looked at it with puzzled, half-comprehending eyes, so that hope came, and then joy, at a slow pace. "It means that I am free?"

"Scarcely that." He translated with care.

She restrained her words. She must not tell him that it was freedom to her.

"You will remember," he said, "that you are now Amelia Braddon, and that you are to say and do nothing to draw attention upon yourself, for I suppose that your life (if it is to be saved, which is more than we know) may depend upon all this being done in a secret way. It is plain that all men must believe that you have been shot here."

"Yes. I will do that."

She must remember that she was Amelia Braddon now. But who was she? Why had he chosen that name? It was not one that she greatly liked. In fact, Steele had made random use of the first that rose to his mind at a time of haste. Well, if she had no worse trouble than that…!

Suddenly she became aware that she was very weary, so that she felt little care even for the life which had survived from so close a risk. "I would sleep now," she said, "if I may. But I will be ready when you require."

"So you must," he replied, "without fail, in the next hour." He thought she took the boon of life in a most casual way.

CHAPTER XXXV.

AN hour later, an English-speaking officer entered Perdita's room. "You will excuse," he said, "that I tie your hands. It is not for long."

She went down between bayonets as one led to death. She faced a cold wind in the outside dusk; sleet beat on her face. Awkwardly, having no use of her hands, she was hustled into a waiting car.

In the darkness, she knew nothing of its direction, which, in any event, could have had little meaning for her, but it had not gone more than three or four miles when it drew up under a black shadow of pines at the side of a narrow lane. Almost immediately another car, coming from the opposite direction, drew up beside it, in such a way that a mere step was necessary to make the transit from car to car. It was so dark that even this would have been difficult without the aid of a torch that was flashed by the occupants of the second car.

In a moment the cars had parted. Perdita heard General Wolfe's voice. He gave an order in German. He said to her: "Miss Braddon, if you will permit, the officer at your side will untie your hands."

Major-General Wolfe had decided that he could best fulfil the order of secrecy that he had received from so high a source by delivering Perdita to the Lustgarten Palace himself. He had engaged the assistance of two officers who were personal friends, one of whom drove the car. It was a procedure which Air Marshal Zweiss could not fail to approve, and had the advantage of leaving the bulk of the 20,000 marks in the hands to which it had come.

Reaching a broader road, the car increased speed. It ran smoothly and fast through the night, of which Perdita knew little, having fallen into a sleep of exhaustion which continued until the car had passed beneath the entrance archway of the Lustgarten Palace, and she must be roused to alight.

She did this alone. If General Wolfe had thought that he would be received—perhaps thanked—by the Air Marshal himself for the discretion that he had shown, he was largely wrong. The waiting official, who came forward as the car stopped, said no more than: "Fräulein Amelia Braddon? Good. You are thanked, and your duty discharged. It is not occasion for a written release."

In three minutes the car was back in Potsdamer Street, heading for the Stuttgart road.

Perdita was led to an apartment of more luxury than she had often seen, though she had been more familiar with the appointments of wealth than poverty during the short years of her sheltered life.

"Anything," the official said obsequiously, "which you do not approve will be changed; anything you require further will be supplied. In a few hours you will have the service of a maid who has been taught in your own tongue. But before that, at the hour of ten, I am to tell you that you will be honoured by a visit from the Air Marshal himself."

He retired, bowing. Perdita could observe that the position of foreign mistress to Air Marshal Zweiss, to which she must suppose that she had been designed, was one of much material comfort, whatever else of honour or shame it might be considered to bear. She would have understood better had she known how bewilderingly high the reputed German aviator had risen in a changing world.

Putting aside the thought of sleep, of which she had still had less than enough, she took the good that the moment gave in a toilet such as she had lacked opportunity to enjoy since she had been employed in retrieving food from the houses of North Worcestershire's frozen roads. It was better to be bathing thus than to have been thrust, a blood-drained corpse, in the narrow grave that is the portion of those who fall to a firing squad. It might be much better also than would be her lot at any moment of the precarious future. For if she could feel relief that she had not become the white slave of a German lord, she was not blind to the different peril of the position as she supposed it to be.

When Richard Steele entered, with no ceremony of delay, at the hour when she had been warned that he would arrive, she thought that she bore little remaining trace of the ordeals through which she had come since they had parted no more than two weeks before; but he recalled her as he had seen her first, as a guest of the British Envoy in Prague, when he had been disguised as a casual servant, and she had taken no heed of him. He saw five years' difference in a face that was still assertive of vital youth. She was symbolic to him. He thought: "This is what the Russo-German outrage has done to the world. Can any weapon be wrong which is needed to lay it low?"

She looked at him, and the words she would have said died, for she was rebuffed by a stranger's eyes. They regarded her with approval but without friendship, or recognition of having seen her before.

"Miss Braddon," he said—and she was acute enough to catch the full significance of the slight stress which he gave to that unfamiliar (and detested) name—"I see that those whom I trusted have chosen well. I am pleased. And, if you are wise, you will find that you are a very fortunate girl, for I have no wife, nor am I likely to wed, having a place which I must not share.

"But there are things you will not forget, or you may find yourself in a worse place. I speak English now, which you see I am well able to do. But you must learn German at once. Have you commenced to do that?"

"I have learnt some. I have been so placed that I had reason to try." She could afford to smile at a peril past as she added: "I had open ears."

He frowned slightly at that. "I do not wish to hear what is past. Those who come here must forget. You are German now. The English, as a nation, will cease to be. They are flat now, though they still kick. You are fortunate that you have come to live in what will be the dominant land."

He said this in so satisfied a tone that it stirred her to a thrill of fear. False to one side, if not both, she knew him to be. She had thought, with some cause, that she knew which. *But if he really were Adolph Zweiss?* Where would she be then?

It was not until afterwards that she was able fully to reassure herself with the realization that an authentic Zweiss would not have rescued her in the way he certainly had. With less than full knowledge of the complications involved, she supposed that he would not have vexed her with a strange name. It was a tribute to the thoroughness with which he maintained his part that while she had not doubted his integrity when she had seen what purported to be his signature for her death, she should be shaken to doubt it now.

But for the moment the doubt remained, and while it did so a servant knocked and entered, bringing a breakfast that Steele had ordered to appear. As the door opened, his hand came upon her shoulder in a familiarly, insultingly possessive manner. He was saying in German: "But you would be no worse for another stone. You must eat well."

The doubt in her mind caused her to shrink from his hand with a more instinctive repugnance than she might otherwise have shown. The servant, spreading for two, heard the Air Marshal say in German: "I shall not be here. I have changed my mind. I have much to do." And then, more directly to Perdita: "Do you understand that? You must be active to learn our tongue."

The words were sharply said, and the man thought: "The girl shrank, which he does not forgive. She will not be long here, unless she become more docile beneath his hand!" But any woman, he thought, would be that for so soft a bed.

Perdita abruptly left, wondered how much was acting, how much she must prepare to accept. She knew Steele to be thorough in all he did, and she had no doubt that he would expect the same standard from her. Having brought her here in the way he had, he must mean more than to save her life. Would he expect her to be his mistress in fact? And would it be with no stronger impulse than that of making as real as might be their most deadly pretence? How would she feel about that? It was a hard question for her inexperienced virginity in a world where all conventional restraints, all precedents, must become fluid as civilization rocked to the earthquake of worldwide war.

But for the moment she had no doubt of what she should do. She must be as thorough as he would wish. Having eaten as good a breakfast as though she were in grave pursuit of that extra stone, she bolted herself in her inner room, and not only removed the "Perdita Wyatt" from the poor, soiled clothes that she could now discard, but was careful to substitute the name that had been so capriciously thrust upon her.

CHAPTER XXXVI.

SUMMER came, and the war slackened on its long front, though it did not pause.

"Slackened" is not a word that would have been used by those who toiled and fought in the tortured lands, for the order of von Teufel was that pressure should be relentless at every point. Yet, as the poisoned bloodstream finds a spot where it will assemble an unendurable evil that breeds within it, so the war drew to a head which gave partial relief to those who must face the foes of remoter fronts.

Von Teufel, still confident that final victory would be his, had found it slower to come than his first expectations had been. He had supposed that, before summer waned, he would have been operating against the New World, if he had not already felt it beneath his feet. But August had found the New World to be still coming to him, though it must be by a hard and at times a most bloody path, even before there was approach to the front of war.

The main reason for this delay was that the Mediterranean had proved a stronger moat than had been forethought, partly because the Northern Eagles were still second upon the sea, and partly because Gibraltar could not be won. Blackened, scourged, scarred, almost silenced at times, it still flaunted the Red Cross flag. Its rock-sheltered batteries still fired at times upon those, more numerous but more exposed, that surrounded its landward side; they still spat upward at the terror that swept upon them out of the skies. In two continents' space, there was no spot where the mortal agony had been more concentrated or more sustained. It lay like a wounded beast, crouching in its unapproachable lair. Mortally wounded, it still would not consent to die.

Now the rock itself, and the low neck of dividing land, were thickly strewn with the wreckage of fallen planes. The corruption of that ceaseless strife must have inflicted the final misery of disease but for the easy burials of the waiting sea.

But now, even at Gibraltar's rock, was relaxation, if not cessation of strife, and Malta's fire-blackened stones lay bare to a clearing sky. Even in England, those who watched by the hidden sky-pointing guns would be less often roused to swift activity at the sight of some deadly high-flying eagle between the clouds. For like Gibraltar, England still endured her foes in a broken way.

Her air forces were gone, or were at most no more than a few scattered, close-hidden planes which would venture perilously abroad in the moonless nights, or when storm blackened the sky, to strike some sudden solitary blow, and flee back to their lairs before pursuit could be dangerous on their rear; or, once and again, to assemble like hunting wolves on a Galway moor to make a swift, unexpected lash at an enemy too confident to watch as the occasion would prove that it had required.

Not that the German air forces could sail secure in the English skies, in which event there would have been no English neck that must not have bent to the German yoke. Their peril came from below. The whole land, except those parts that were entirely in German hands, was now sown thickly with anti-aircraft guns of a range and accuracy of which there had been no experience in the last war. They could not easily be located, largely consisting of mobile batteries which might change positions with every night, or else lurk in some unsuspected cover from week to week, sure that, sooner or later, their chance would come when a fleet of bombers or fighters would cross unsuspectingly within range of the deadly shells, or, it might be, a line of heavy, escorted transports, loaded with recruits or stores for the German camps.

The Germans held Sheffield. They had taken Bradford and Leeds. The patch of central England on which they had come down from the clouds was an ulcer that slowly spread. It threatened Manchester now. It lay on the outskirts of Birmingham, which it could not win, neither had the defenders of that busy arsenal strength to thrust it farther away. At a range of no more than 400 yards the snipers exchanged their tokens of equal death.

Farther south, London slowly cleared its wreckage and even made some effort to build again, but most of what recuperative energy it had was given to provision of more and yet more defence against the dread of a second torment out of the clouds. It had now a score of high-pointing guns for every one it had had when the war began. It had learned late.

In the far north the Germans had failed to establish permanent footholds, though the country round Stirling had been in their hands for some weeks, and they had made a smoking ruin of Glasgow's docks.

It is possible that the conquest of England would have been completed in the early summer had not von Teufel listened to the advice he had received from Air Marshal Zweiss. He had found that the Air Marshal's advice was generally sound, and in this instance Richard Steele himself remained unsure whether he would not have given the same counsel had he honestly desired the success of the German arms. He had said that England might be subdued—though of that he was less than sure—at a price which would draw too much of the German strength away from the more vital centres of war. He had suggested that this was the very purpose that the continued English resistance was intended to have in the plans of the Christian allies. In particular, that it should result in a wastage of the air-arm disproportionate to any effect it could otherwise have upon the final course of the war.

He had known this to have some measure of truth, but he knew also that the value of any counsel he gave was largely reduced when he had communicated the resulting decision to England and her allies. And when he had heard counsel from other lips that he thought bad, he had been careful not to interfere with a better word…

But now, for three weeks past, the German army in England had been content to hold without extending its lines. It had not been further strengthened from the air during this time, the recruits it had received in return for the cargoes of sick and wounded it had sent away being no more than were required to replace the daily wastage of war.

And in far-off Asia, where the progress of conquest had been hindered less by organized resistance than by the inertia of its own mass—though such resistance, mainly under English and Japanese leaderships, had been stubborn and often heroic in deserts and mountain ranges, and at last on the vast, million-teeming Asian plains—there had come the same slackening of forward strife.

Only in Palestine—in that land where the Hebrews had once dwelt in such comfort as a dog may find that lies down in the middle road—and for five hundred miles around on its landward sides, did the hell-brew thicken, though here the heavy fighting was yet to come.

As the weeks passed, and the world gathered its strength for the final test, it might seem that Christian and pagan were too crude descriptions to give to the opposite hosts that were assembling to die on their destined day. Nor might it have been forethought that, while England herself struggled for the breath of life beneath the incubus that had descended upon her, the great armies that gathered upon the Nile were assembled under the English flag. But these were matters that Russia and Germany had united to procure in no other way.

They had cast out Christianity as a faith unfitted alike for their own murderous rules or to incline their populations to the pursuit of aggressive war, and then, by persecution, they had united Christian and Jew, so that they must fight in a common cause and under a common flag.

Mohammedan, Buddhist, Confucian, and Parsee found themselves rallying to the same cry. Christ and Anti-Christ divided the world, and they must decide on which side they would choose to be.

All idealism, all faith in the beneficence of the unseen, all beliefs in anything better than the rule of the brutal heel, were thus impelled by His open foes to enter the fold of Christ, for the Cross had become the one symbol of hope and courage sufficient to lift its head against the black shadow that was moving southward to blight the world.

And the English flag was not the rallying-sign of that gathered host merely because they included so many who came from British Dominions, or had the heritage of a common speech; it was because it bore the sign of the threefold Cross, and stood for the hope of freedom that moved the hearts of all courageous and kindly men.

CHAPTER XXXVII.

IT was on the third day of September 1938 that Prince von Teufel called what was to be the last War Council he would hold before leaving Berlin to make his headquarters at Aleppo, that he might be present at what, from the disposition of the forces on either side, must and was intended to be a decisive battle.

His preparations were complete. The day, he would have said, with literal accuracy, was of his choosing. Yet he was under the constraint of the fact that time had become an adversary, each week of delay now strengthening the ranks of his enemies more than it augmented his own. Besides that, there was the fact that a wild but formidably equipped army of many nations and tongues was advancing over the Euphrates plain, which would be near enough, in less than a week's time, to threaten the communications on which the left wing of his huge force depended for its supplies.

It was elementary strategic wisdom that would plan to destroy the Palestine army before this menace could reach to his own flank. Yet a menace it must remain, harmless if he should win, but deadly in its potentialities if his great army should be in flight for the Caucasus and Anatolia, the two main routes by which it had come. It was this army of the Euphrates which determined that he could not be defeated with less utter ruin than a like failure would mean to the Christian hosts, with the wide desert upon their rear.

But he did not expect to fail. He regarded his army as better disciplined, better equipped, better trained than the heterogeneous host collected from Europe's refugees—Africa, the two Americas, the scattered units of the British Empire, and the far ends of the earth—that he would require it to overcome. It would be a clash of realist and dreamer, of professional and amateur, which could have but one result, even without the decisive argument of the air.

And he had a still further reason for anticipating the confusion of foes who had shown themselves to be infatuate in choice of the region where they would die. It was a secret so closely kept that it was known only to Field Marshal von Hoffmann and himself, even among those who sat on the Council of War.

It was a Council on which but two of those whom Steele had met when he had taken his own seat still held their own places and the Dictator's precarious favour, and even one of these had experienced a period of eclipse.

Field Marshal von Hoffmann was the first of these. Shrewd, reasonable, moderate, and fundamentally ductile, he had heard the worst storms of von Teufel's anger pass over his head, without their lightnings being loosed in his own direction.

Admiral Klein, fat, quiet, stubbornly uncompromising, sat in a place which had been otherwise occupied for several weeks after the arrival of the disastrous news that more than half the German submarine fleet had been destroyed attempting to break out of the Mediterranean.

He had faced the black rage of von Teufel then without admission that he had been wrong. "Will you blame me that we are betrayed, as I say we are?" "Will you recall that I would have had them through a clear ten days before, from a place where, by my will, they had never been?" "Must you storm at me that you took good counsel a day too late?" So he had met the wrath that he would not fear, and to the sentence of degradation that followed he had said no more than: "It is yours to say. I will wish you luck of a better man than I think I am."

But after that, things had gone badly upon the sea, and von Teufel had called him back to his former place, which had been a poor day for the Christian allies. Every light cruiser, every submarine that remained to be collected from the ports of Europe, every one that could be hurriedly completed in the many ship-building yards that Germany now controlled, was let loose upon the sea-routes along which men and supplies were being transported to Africa from Australasia and the New World. Operating from secret bases scattered over the world, so that they might avoid the perils of homeward seas, they had created a sleepless terror from which the remotest ocean was not secure. Few they might be in comparison to the navies they must avoid, but great was the wealth, and many the lives, that they sent to a cold grave. A troopship had been torpedoed with the loss of some thousands of lives when Sydney Harbour had not been fifty miles behind.

Admiral Klein's stubborn assertion that his plan for the submarines to evacuate the Mediterranean had been betrayed had some support during the following months in the fact that other most secret dispositions had apparently become known to the Christian allies, and though no suspicion, either of treason or indiscretion of speech, had fastened firmly upon any member of the War Council, this leakage may have sharpened von Teufel's restless inclination to change his councillors, and explained more than one sudden dismissal on what had seemed to be merely capricious grounds. But Admiral Klein kept his recovered place, and his small eyes had dwelt much of late upon Air Marshal Zweiss, with an intently considering gaze which the Air Marshal did not appear to see.

Now, half an hour before the Council was due to meet, Admiral Klein sought von Hoffmann, to whom he had spoken a blunt suspicion during the previous week.

"Have you thought of it?" he asked, assuming that his auditor would guess the subject on which he spoke. "Yes, but it is an incredible doubt."

"Well, I have ceased to think. I have become sure."

The Field Marshal looked troubled at this, but his opinion did not change. "Zweiss," he said, "is one whom I like and trust. So are you. I should call you the two on whom the Prince most surely relies, and I should say he is wise in that."

"I should say von Teufel is mad. I supposed you knew that."

"I should call that a foolish word, which you do not mean. The Prince is obsessed by a great thought. He would win the world."

"Then he thinks to win more than a man may. We are on a slope where we cannot stop. But we must win the war. We agree there. We must save Germany if we can. I was not talking of that. Have you thought that Zweiss came on the Council on the day when we resolved that the submarines should slip out, and that there was a time when he was known as an English spy?"

"It is those submarines that you will not forget! It was by the way in which he had worked long to gain the confidence of the British Intelligence Service that he was able to help us so well when the war began."

"Well, I am sure. I will say what I think tonight, and see how he replies. He will have a shock. Will you support me in that?"

"Without proof? It would be asking for our disgrace, if no more. No, I will not."

"Is there no proof? We know that leakage exists. There are but three who have been on the Council from then till now. Is it you or I? If it be not Zweiss, I must ask you that."

"That is suspicion, not proof. And, as you justly say, it is not against one but three, as the Prince might not be slow to observe. There may be leakage in other ways."

"Well, there is more than that. There is the English woman he takes about."

"But she was no more than we were all entitled to have. And it is what a spy would have avoided to do. He had been less bold."

"But I have inquired, and I have come upon a most curious thing. There was none of the name she bears on the lists of those who were brought from England, among whom it is said that he made his choice."

"That English doll? Will you tell me next you suspect her? She is not the breed. Can you make much of an altered name? It may be explained in a simple way, and you may have said that which the Prince will not forgive."

"I may have more. I may have it in the next hour."

"Then you will do well to wait till you see what you will have from that."

"So I will, unless we agree in another way."

They parted at this, there being still about fifteen minutes before the hour when the Council was due to meet, and von Hoffmann considered what had been said in a worried and doubtful mind. He told himself again that it was an incredible thing.

He could not doubt that Adolph Zweiss was a German who had shown conspicuous patriotism and valour as an airman in the previous war. He believed that to have been absolutely proved when the question was raised before. He had now gained one of the highest places that ambition could hope to reach. Was it likely that he would risk it all for the rewards that a spy can hope to obtain? The question answered itself.

And in the last months the position of Air Marshal Zweiss had become firm, and he had not scrupled to assert it in ways such as the example of Prince von Teufel would suggest that his favourites should. The marble palace of the Prince rose, immense, portentous of coming power, founded on the destruction of the very heart of Berlin. Some of those who had been dispossessed of factory or home had been compensated by the gift of a Christian church, for which the old use was done, at a time when all men were required to make a sign of worship to their new god, and to say "Heil von Teufel!" when they met, before conversation began. (A draper had been beheaded publicly in Berlin because he had asked a man to discharge an outstanding account before he had remembered his god.) The Air Marshal did not expect that men would make signs of adoration to him, but he had imitated the Prince in a smaller way by seizing one of the best houses in Berlin, and ruthlessly clearing a contiguous space, so that his private plane could be hangared and take off at any hour from his own door. Already all of wealth or luxury that the world could yield had become his, or waited his claim. Why should he risk that?

Von Hoffmann considered also that Zweiss had been diligent and honourable in all that he undertook. He was, perhaps, the only man whose word, on a point of fact, the Prince would always take without verification. And in this von Hoffmann could not think that the Prince was wrong. And the Air Marshal's counsels were known to all to be moderate and sane. Is it of such sort that spies are made? He thought not.

Yet the doubt, being born, was not quick to die. It lingered in his mind like a sickly child who will neither thrive nor expire. He had said truly that Zweiss and the Admiral were the two whom he thought von Teufel was wise to trust. He himself trusted the Air Marshal's honour, with patriotism and self-interest for its supports. But he trusted the Admiral's judgment also, and there was confusion in that.

He turned his thoughts to the girl. Perdita had followed instructions she had not liked, but the wisdom of which had been easy to see. She was to become greedy of clothes, beyond reason, beyond restraint. Blatantly wasteful in all she did, as one whose mind was diseased by the possibilities her position gave. Steele had said: "I like silly women. It is only some who have the wit that a fool requires." She had to guess what he meant, proving that she had wit enough, for his was an acting that never ceased. At least, not while they were in Berlin.

And it had been the same when they had been in the air, till the new plane had been built to his own design. From the first, he had taken her with him wherever he might have occasion to go. He had said: "I must be amused." But there had been the possibility, even then, that the pilot would oversee. He had acted still.

The new plane was very light, very powerful, and very swift. It was meant for no more than two, though it had some comfort for them. It would do 300 miles an hour. It could do more than that, but how much more even Steele himself did not know, for he had never tested its utmost power. He did not wish to demonstrate what it could do in the German skies.

No one but Perdita and he had been aloft in that plane. By the time it had been built, it had become a matter of unobserved routine that he took her wherever he might go. It was a whim not to be criticized or remarked by those who were less than he. He was known to be a most skilful pilot. And his flights in so swift a plane had been mostly short, except only when he had traversed the length of the North African coast, taking photographs that von Teufel had been glad to have.

None could guess what happened when they were alone in the heights of the summer air. Or if they should make a ribald guess they would be nearly right, and far wrong. There were times, when they had soared to heights that were empty and clear, at which the plane could be left safely to its automatic controls. Then they would become themselves, as it was pleasant to do.

There were times when they were even able to put aside the world's travail, by which they were caught in so close a net; for though war may be the unchangeable law of life to the world's end, love is ever stronger than he.

There were other times when Steele would teach her to fly the plane, lest an hour might come when it would be what she must be single to do.

Von Hoffmann remembered Amelia Braddon as he had once talked to her at a reception von Teufel gave to celebrate the occupation of Delhi. He had thought her superficially attractive but rather dense, as he knew that some men will prefer their women to be. Certainly she had not tried to draw from him any secrets of State! And afterwards she had made an unpleasant scene, protesting in bad German that the wife of a minor official had a dress which had been made in imitation of hers, which the woman must retire to remove, as, at last, she had been persuaded to do. And then she had been in a panic fear, which she lacked discretion or self-control to conceal, lest her misconduct should come to the ears of the Air Marshal, of whom she had appeared to be greatly in dread—which was how it should be, but scarcely consonant with the idea that they were a couple of English spies. He concluded, with a limited penetration, that an Englishwoman, discreetly reticent, in the background of an assorted seraglio, would be more shrewdly suspect than this girl whom the Air Marshal paraded so openly as his sole companion, and who lacked balance in what she did.

Still, leakages *did* occur. Suppose, he thought, getting a stage nearer the truth than he had yet done, that Fräulein Braddon were a spy, cleverly disguised even from the Air Marshal's eyes, and who might draw him to indiscretions of speech by the front of folly that she put on?

If that should prove to be the truth, what would von Teufel be likely to do? Would he satisfy himself by crucifying the girl upside-down, which was a form of punishment for spying which he had lately introduced, of which three examples ornamented *Unter den Linden* now? It was hard to say. His vengeance might include the Air Marshal more likely than not, even though indiscretion might be the limit to which he erred. And that vengeance would commonly take fantastic or ghastly forms.

He remembered how Herr Geibel had come to an abrupt and unpleasant end, when examination of Herr Sturm's papers had disclosed that not only his brains, but those of another scientist, had been the steps by which Herr Geibel had climbed to an eminence he had not deserved.

"I believe, Herr Geibel," von Teufel had said smoothly, "you have some expectation that you may receive a signal recognition of your services to the German cause?" At which the scientist had flushed in anticipation of the honour he had expected to have.

"And you have felt at times that the Government—of which I was not then in control—refused you the freedom of experiment which the importance of your researches deserved? As, for instance, in the provision of human criminals on whom you might have tested your brews?" To which Herr Geibel had replied that there were times when a speechless ape must be a poor substitute for a human subject who could be stimulated to discuss the sensations in which he died.

"Well," von Teufel had said, "if you make further complaint, it will be from an opposite cause. Herr Sturm had prepared a memorial before he died, in which he asserts that he had produced a powder which would dress the eyes much better than yours, as to which you will soon know, though (as I understand) you will not be fluent on what you feel."

Slowly, from a bewildered doubt, the meaning of these words had entered Herr Geibel's mind; and it had been rather dreadful to see, even though an inventor of lethal gases may not be classed as a man, and it may be supposed that the devils will wash their hands after they have bound him upon the bars.

Von Hoffmann, thinking these things, came to a general resolve that, as for tonight, he would discourage the Admiral's tongue, except only if von Teufel should disclose the secret which was, as yet, known to themselves only (and those who were concerned with it some thousands of miles away), as, at a previous meeting of the Council, his unmeasured speech had come near to do.

The betrayal of that secret to their opponents would be a disaster of such magnitude that he would run no moment's risk by restraining the Admiral in the course that he was inclining to take. When they met again at the door of the Council Chamber, he said: "You must judge for yourself what you will say, or whether you will be silent tonight, for the risk is yours; but if you see me put my hand to my left ear, it will mean that I will give you support, which you will not otherwise be likely to have."

He thought that Admiral Klein wished to say something in reply which it might have been of moment for him to hear, but Air Marshal Zweiss came up the passage and stood back, rather than push past them into the room, with a courtesy such as he would show even to much lesser men. He was self-possessed, and had not the look of an English spy.

CHAPTER XXXVIII.

THE front of the Christian allies stretched for no more than fifty miles, from Haifa to the Jordan Valley. It occupied the high ground that, with one narrow gap, reaches, northwest to southeast, from Mount Carmel to the river ford, with the valley of Esdraelon—of Armageddon—below it, and beyond that the hills of Galilee and the

Lebanon heights, which von Teufel held. The Jordan gorge protected the Christian right, and its left rested upon the sea.

Transjordania was also in Christian hands, but was held, and faced, by more mobile forces, which would be likely to fall back if they should be heavily engaged, in the event of a turning movement being attempted by either side, against which danger the Christian host, which would have been somewhat narrowly contained, had strongly fortified the whole length of the Jordan Valley to the Dead Sea.

Within these lines there was now the most terrific concentration of the artillery of death that the world had seen, unless it were that of the opposing host, which, with its headquarters at Damascus, had made one gun-bristling fortress of the whole Lebanon range.

The Lebanon hills were hollowed also with subterranean aerodromes, more numerous, and relatively almost as large, as wasps' nests might be in a hedgerow bank. The reserve air forces which von Teufel had prepared for the decisive hour had been transferred gradually to the front as they had been built and their pilots trained, and as these subterranean lairs had been burrowed for them to lie secure.

The Christian air forces had also grown to a great strength, though, having been gathered from many lands, they were of more various types. The main fleets, of British and American origins, and manned entirely by English-speaking pilots, were stationed at Cyprus, which had become a vast aerodrome, from its coast to the wilderness of its interior hills.

With these gigantic potentialities for mutual destruction, the actual fighting in these regions had been less during the last three months than, perhaps, at any other portion of the long front of the war. In the air, particularly, there had been an equal disposition to conserve strength rather than to exhaust it in conflicts that had been abundantly proved on other fronts to entail a wastage beyond proportion to the results obtained, unless a process of attrition were in itself the object at which the operation was aimed.

The hot summer air was black with the flying swarms, but they would avoid crossing each other's lines unless some sudden chance should come of striking at an outnumbered foe, when there would be a loud, brief flurry among the clouds, and the flaming fall of the lost to stony Palestine fields or the hissing sea.

Only in Transjordania, and outward to the Syrian Desert, had there been open fighting, at times heavy and sanguinary, though indecisive in its results. It had only shown, as had been proved already on many fields, that the mechanized army is strong for aggression only when it cannot be met by a defence of its own kind. The stoutest tanks, when met by anti-tank artillery, became no more than prominent marks within which it could be supposed that there would be men waiting to die, and their waiting would not be long. And while the wind piled the desert sand upon the wreckage of shattered tanks, and the vultures tore at their broken dead, the desert horse, the desert camels, burdened with their batteries of Lewis guns, came back to their ancient right.

Such was the position of which von Teufel spoke as the last War Council met in Berlin. He had hoped (as he did not say) that the Christian host would attack, but he had confidently prepared for that which the advance of the Euphrates army rendered it foolish to delay longer. Now he would have von Hoffmann rehearse the great plan by which the Christian front should be held, if not driven in, while a wide turning movement through Transjordania would endeavour to penetrate to the south of the Dead Sea, threatening to cut off the retreat of the doomed host, even by the inadequate though now multiplied railway lines that crossed the Sinai Desert, to the comparative safety that lay on the farther side of the Suez Canal.

Some differences of opinion followed. Technical questions were raised affecting the speed with which the flanking operation could be expected to complete its movement, and even whether it could not itself be cut through and isolated by a sufficiently vigorous and well-timed counterattack. A side issue was introduced as to whether there should be a strong force detached to face and delay the Euphrates army, or whether it should not be allowed to advance as rapidly as it would, that it might be more conveniently placed for its own destruction. "Let them come to us," said one truculent voice, "and when they see that their friends are down they will find it harder to get away, and we shall lose less breath in pursuit."

But other voices were of a more moderate tone. They did not speak a thought that they may have had, that if they should be the ones to fly, the Euphrates army could not be too distant away. They urged that the time which the outflanking movement would take could not be exactly foretold.

Von Teufel listened, speaking little, as his way would be at times, till he had heard all that others could be encouraged to say. He had his plans formed, his decisions made, of which von Hoffmann was aware and approved, and he thought victory sure. But he had the sense to prefer that those on whom he most nearly depended should be of a single mind, and he had two arguments in reserve, which he felt the time had come to expose.

"Gentlemen," he broke in at last, "you have said much with which I largely agree, and it is well to feel that you are as competent for your own parts as are my officers in the field. But there are two things I will tell you now, which should make us absolutely at one, even where we have differed before.

"First, it will be found, when the battle joins, that our air forces will be of so great a force that they will chase their foes out of the skies, as was done when the war began.

"You will say that it was done at a great cost, as it will be again, but it is one we can pay, and it is not loss if a plane fall, having first inflicted an equal wound. "We have talked of a reserve fleet of 5,000 planes. But it is not that; it is 15,000 we have. This is the fruit of the ceaseless work of every factory in Europe that we control, from the first day of the war. This has been known to Air Marshal Zweiss, who has given service in this that I cannot too largely repay, and (except von Hoffmann, who knows all) it has been private from all but him.

"I tell you this now because we have come to an hour when it would do us no harm, nor themselves good, though our foes should know. Rather, it might cause the sinking of heart which is the presage of near defeat. They have great air forces assembled there, as we need not deny to ourselves, which they also have conserved for the day when the battle joins; but they must be much weaker than ours, for they have been allowed to hear our talk of 5,000 planes, and it is that which they have thought it a great effort to equal, if not excel, in addition to all that must be scattered along the distant face of the war.

"And there is a second thing, which may be no less important than that. South of Nasrah (where I am told they say that their god was born!), you will know that we have burrowed a great aerodrome, at which some have cavilled as being too near to the Christian lines, its entrance being under the fire of their longer guns, as it is today.

"So it is, and so it may have been soundly said. It is an aerodrome now in which are harboured no more than 300 planes, for its purpose is more than that. It is the greatest mine that was ever tunnelled by human hands. It is more than we imagined at first, we having come to eight great caves when the miners reached to the hills, by which much labour was saved, and the debris need neither be brought out nor guessed by those who may watch from the air, as we have made it hard for them to do.

"There is now—or there will be completed in two days' time— such store of explosive beneath where their centre lies that we think to send the very mountains aloft, and to make a gap in their line through which an army can force a scarce-hindered way. You will see why this has been kept a most secret thing, which I tell you now, so that you may judge rightly how little we have to fear from a doomed foe. It is from this cause that we have withheld our trenches from too near approach to the Christian lines, lest they be involved in so wide a death as it is likely to be."

Admiral Klein asked abruptly: "It could be fired in less than two days from now? It could be fired in the next hour?"

"No, it is less ready than that. It would do much now, but yet much less than is meant. Beside, it would be abortive of half we plan. We must be ready to advance the instant we rend the gap. And, besides, it must be so timed that when they run we shall be forward upon their flank to cut them off. We must be near to round the Dead Sea on its southern shore."

There was a murmur of assent to this explanation, but the eyes of Admiral Klein were fixed hard on von Hoffmann, whose hand, as though forced by that hypnotic gaze, went slowly to his left ear.

Admiral Klein asked: "Then if it should be betrayed in the next day?"

Von Teufel stared at this. "In the next day? How would you say that that is likely to be?"

"It is Zweiss who should tell you that."

Von Teufel turned his eyes on the Air Marshal, impatient, puzzled, perturbed, but not yet comprehending what was implied.

Air Marshal Zweiss said easily: "I am afraid the Admiral attributes his own wisdom to me. It is a matter of which I know no more than we have all heard."

Von Hoffmann put it into plain words, which he knew must come: "Admiral Klein means that you are an English spy."

The second of astonished silence that followed was broken by Steele's voice, level and quiet: "Admiral Klein is one for whose judgment I have always had great respect. I don't think he would be so foolish as to mean that."

"But I do, and it is what I have become active to prove."

"Which I am sure that you cannot do."

"Will you say that the woman you keep is not in the English pay?"

"Yes, I am sure she is not. And even if she were, I tell her nothing she could betray. I am discreet of speech, as I think you know."

"Will you say she did not murder Sturm?"

"Yes, I will say that."

Von Teufel interrupted sharply: "Murdered Sturm? Why do you talk of him?"

Recollection of what had been a trivial incident at the time recurred to his mind. "Klein," he went on, "you have got something wrong. The woman who did that was shot at the time. I gave the order myself. Will you say it was not obeyed?"

"That it was certainly not."

Steele spoke again, and there was nothing in his voice to betray his sense of the deadly pit which opened before his feet, both for himself and for one who had become dearer still.

"Admiral Klein," he said, "is one with whom I will not quarrel unless I must, for I am sure he is honest in all he says. But he is making much of a small thing."

He turned more directly to von Teufel as he went on, his voice apologetic and yet firm, as one who feels that he has explanation sufficient to meet the case.

"It is a fact that the girl was condemned—wrongly, as there is no question at all—as a matter of policy rather than that an ugly truth should be laid bare, as being responsible for Herr Sturm's death. The matter was referred to me; and you sent an order for the girl's execution. But you did this only because I was absent, and in my own name, so that it clearly rested with me, on the authority your method implied, to take further action if it should be required, as in fact it was. Nor did I trouble you again on so small a matter, as it would have been against our practice for me to do. But I was careful to have such dispositions made that the verdict stands, and the execution is recorded to have taken place, and I had the girl's name changed before she was brought to me."

He paused a moment, giving von Teufel opportunity for reply, which he did not take. The Prince looked to be moved by one of the fits of black anger in which he would be likely to do savage and merciless things, but he had shown before that he might control even these fierce mental tempests when urgent wisdom required.

Now he avoided the Air Marshal's eyes, but he looked at Admiral Klein in a silent anger, dreadful to see. His left hand clenched and spread itself on the table with spasmodic movements he made no effort to still.

Pausing no more than a long second, Steele went on: "As to the girl being a spy, it is what I should not believe without proof, of which we have had none. Certainly she has learnt nothing from me. She was never asked, nor should I talk of State secrets to her. Besides, is it a likely, or barely possible, thing? She was brought here by force, without warning and against her own will."

Admiral Klein interposed. He had heard much of that which had come to him no more than a few minutes before the meeting began turned so adroitly that what he had meant to advance as a damning circumstance had been made to appear evidence of the discretion with which a delicate matter had been controlled. He did not mean that this should happen again, if he could be more prompt to accuse. He said: "She was here before! You befriended her then. She was at the Prague Legation before that, and you knew her then."

The interposition was disconcerting. Steele felt that it weakened his argument at a moment when he had won support by the reasoned moderation of his reply. But he was adroit to turn its point backward from his own breast.

"That is true! That was the strongest reason why I took the course I did, knowing that Prince von Teufel could not fail to approve.

"Had he sent the order in his own name, I should have had no right, and less disposition, to interfere. It could have taken its course. But she had appealed to me! And it had been made to appear that it was I who sent her to death. Do you know that I had helped her before with the approval of our own Secret Police? I suppose, as you know so much, you may know that?

"Had I ordered her execution, I should not have dared afterwards to fly over the African coast, as I was able to do."

Admiral Klein would have made a stubborn reply, instancing the leakages of vital importance which there had been since Air Marshal Zweiss had taken the seat he held; and he had been quick also to see the weakest side of the last argument, for if the girl's rescue had been so secret, and the official record of her execution remained, how had the knowledge of her safety been conveyed, unless she had been in communication with her own country? Well, in the dual part that Adolph Zweiss (if it were he!) had admittedly played, there might be plausible explanation of that. But, as he was about to reply, von Teufel turned on him with a sudden fury: "Will you be still?"—after which the Council sat silent, waiting for him to speak at his own time, which he did not find it easy to do.

Zweiss a traitor? The doubt filled him with a murderous rage. But it was incredible! And on so slender a proof! Yet he had done a most insolent thing in his cool way. Cancelling the death warrant that he himself had sent, and without mention to him. Surely he should be punished for that! And there was more in this matter of the girl than Zweiss was disposed to admit. He was shrewdly certain of that. Yet that might be no more than a carnal infatuation, such as will make thralls of men who are wisest in other ways. Then had she used her power to worm secrets from him? Probably the truth was no more and no less than that, which would be enough. But to lose Zweiss at this moment? It was the worst—it was an almost impossible—time! He had all the threads of the vast air force preparations in his own hands! The control could be changed, but the knowledge could not be so lightly transferred. Of course, if he were a traitor, he could not be relieved of power a single second too soon. But was he? That was the torturing doubt. If he were not, Admiral Klein might be striking a paralysing blow at his own cause at the most vital hour of the war. It was he who should be called traitor for that! And he had been a cause of trouble before.

In the end he asked, in a voice so mild that it was more startling than if he had broken out into the expected tempest of savage rage: "Von Hoffmann, what do you say?"

Von Hoffmann saw the Prince's dilemma plainly enough. Also, he saw his own. He was temperate, and perhaps temporizing, in his reply: "If the matter be no more than the cancellation of an execution order under circumstances that can be somewhat explained, I should say that subsequent services may be held to outweigh any fault there was. And as for the girl (whom I am slow to take for a spy), there can be inquiry held at a better time." He might have ended there, but that his promise to the Admiral came to his mind, which he would have been glad to forget. He would not add more than: "But Admiral Klein will say there is more than that."

Von Teufel spoke with a voice of sharp decision: "The Council will adjourn for an hour. Zweiss, you will not fail to be here then? So I have no doubt that you will. Von Hoffmann—Klein—you will stay with me."

CHAPTER XXXIX.

RICHARD STEELE drove back to his own house. He thought hard. It was a bitter thing that it should have come to this end, when it had seemed that release, and all that life had to give, were no more than a few hours ahead. He would have liked to think that he could still escape, and serve himself and his kind by the same road. But he knew that it must be less simple than that, that it was treason now to the Christian cause, and to many thousands in a dire peril they did not know, even to think of himself—or her.

He judged that von Teufel did not really credit the charge of espionage against himself, or he would hardly have left him free for the next hour. He thought that conviction would not readily be admitted to the mind of one who had lost, in the last few months, a normal capacity to make admission that he could err. And his own place had become so great, he had received so large a measure of trust, that he saw that—and at this crisis of coming battle!—von Teufel would be fiercely reluctant to accept the suggestion that he had been so largely misled, so immensely fooled.

Yet convinced he might be, and that at any moment from now. Admiral Klein might have more to say than had yet been heard. And he had a stubborn honesty of opinion that was likely to make its steady pressure felt on the most obdurate mind. Even now Steele could not suppose that he would be free from observation, or that his plane could take off (as it was very ready to do) without interference or swift pursuit.

Yet that which he had learnt must be conveyed to the Christian camp, and so, if possible, that it would not be guessed that he had been able to get it through.

His car, to which other traffic had given way, had taken four minutes to cover the distance between the Lustgarten Palace and his own home. He had had that time for thought, and he alighted with resolutions made. He said to the chauffeur: "Wait here. You must take me back to the Palace in forty minutes from now." He saw, without turning his head, that a police officer had lounged up to talk to his man as he entered the door. There had been no time lost! But the man would say that which it would be best for the inquirer to hear.

He went straight to Perdita's room, as it had been planned that he should do with a different purpose than he now had. She had a meal served ready for him and her, wishing to be alone when he should arrive, and not knowing when that would be. The outer clothes that she would wear on their soaring flights were laid out on a couch, so that they could be quickly put on.

She saw his face, which told much, for it was a book she had become expert to read, and he had now no secrets from her. She asked: "What is wrong?"

"Listen! There is no time for a wasted word. They have found out who you are. They suspect all. Within an hour the Council will be meeting again, and I must be there."

"You mean that…."

"Listen! There is more than that. You must remember this with a clear mind." He told her of the mine that had been driven under the

Christian line, and of the battle tactics that had been discussed. He did not need to mention the 15,000 planes. He had communicated all that he knew himself of these preparations from week to week, and the surprise would not be for the Christian host, but for their enemies, when the battle forces should be deployed out of the clouds.

"When I have gone," he said, "you will take the plane. You will fly alone to the same place as before. If you get clear of Berlin, as I think you may, you will write what I have said, but not before that. You will pass the letter in the usual way. Afterwards you must wreck the plane. You must wreck it at a place where it will be quickly found, and they will think that you have failed to escape, through attempting to do so in a machine that you could not control. You may escape if you can, so that you do what I have said. You have the parachute. But I must warn you not to be recaptured alive. Almost anything would be better than that."

White-lipped with fear, she said: "I will do that. But what of you?"

"You must not give me another thought. Think of the disaster that only we can avert. There are only two things to regard: that we shall get a message through, and that they shall think we have failed."

"You—you will have time for a meal? It—it is what you like."

"No. You must eat. It is the last thing I ask. But I have no moment to lose. There is much to be done. We have talked too long."

Their hands met, but at the look in her eyes he drew back. "There is no time."

"If I thought you would get away!"

"You must not think. Not of me. I depend upon you. You must think only of that."

He turned abruptly away and went into his own room.

She told herself that she would do what he had said. She would eat, as he had wished. She would not think of him, nor shrink from what she would have to do—if she could, of which she was less than sure. She would think—*think*—of that fearful mine, and of all that now depended on her.

Meanwhile, in his own room, Air Marshal Zweiss sent out orders to many lands, stretching all the authority that he had. He worked hard for the next half-hour to confuse the organization that he controlled. He removed good men from their commands. He transferred them to places where they would not be easy to trace. He consigned supplies to depots where they should not be. He ordered busy factories to cease production and to be dismantled at once, on the pretext that they would be put to another use. He scattered squadrons of bombers in confusion about the skies, or with orders to strafe their own strongholds, as having passed into enemy hands.

He kept no copies of the orders he sent out. They would not be quickly traced, nor their evil stayed. He had planned long for this hour in the wakeful nights, and he lost no second in what he did.

At the last moment he rose. He had done all he could. For England. For Freedom. For the Faith he held. He had done it by methods he was not concerned either to defend or condemn, for his mind was not often upon himself, but on greater things.

He paused at Perdita's door, but, with a gesture of resignation, he went on. Why should he weaken himself or bring grief to her? They had work to do beside which their lives, their loves, were of small account. Would she be equal to what he was relying on her to do? That was all that could matter now. He felt some confidence that she would, though he had known a time when her courage failed. And the seconds passed. He went on to the waiting car.

CHAPTER XL.

PERDITA had the harder part, having leisure for her own thoughts, which—when she let them wander from the great service which she must do, if she could, to the Christian cause—would either be numb with sorrow or cold with fear, or would become sharply, strangely intent upon some trivial thing. She looked back on a life that had been bright with hope before this shadow fell on the world. If death were near, should she not recall once more those days, so recent and so utterly dead? Memories which were hers alone, and would perish with her? Her glance fell on a letter—an invitation addressed to Fräulein Braddon—and she had a thought of relief that she had done not merely with that alien name, but with the hateful personality which she had built upon it. She would be herself for the brief minutes that still remained! And with that came a further thought that she must be worthy of the race and the name she bore. And to be equal to that she must put him out of her thoughts, as he had told her to do.

The hour passed. She saw that she must attempt nothing until he would have had time to return to the Lustgarten Palace—until they would know certainly that he had no intention of flight—and observation, if there were any, might be relaxed. No one would be likely to think of her seeking escape alone by way of the air. No one knew that she had any ability to handle the plane, or that she had access to it, apart from him. As he stayed, was it likely that he would increase suspicion by letting her go?

So she waited, though she knew that it was a later hour than that at which they were accustomed to leave, and that it might be hard to reach the rendezvous at the appointed time. But they had never tried what the plane would do at its utmost speed! She must hope something from that. She had a sharp, immediate anxiety as she entered the passage to the aerodrome which was private to Steele and herself. If she should be hindered, frustrated, now! It would be to lose all with no sense of compensation in what she did. To know that she died in vain. But all was quiet to which she came. The plane had been run out in readiness for them to take off, as the Air Marshal's orders were that it should always be when the attendants retired. When she switched on the lights, which she could not avoid, there was nothing to cause alarm.

There was a full moon, but little light came from that, the sky being covered by clouds that were heavy and low. Well, that was better for her! She knew that she must take off to the right, for there were high buildings she might not otherwise miss, but after that she had no trouble to fear. She had only to soar till she came to a clearer air, which she would soon be likely to find.

She felt inadequate at first, nervous of all she did. It had been different when Steele had been at her side, to advise, to alter anything she did wrong. Overhead, as she rose through the clouds, she heard the droning of many planes that circled above. It was simple to guess that they were hawks that watched for a single prey, and that she was the pigeon they thought to have. Probably they had been advised of her escape by now, and their guns were waiting to bring her down. And she was not to let it be thought that she had any skill in handling the plane! Well—a smile flickered strangely upon her lips—there might be no difficulty in that! Nor, she knew, must she let them guess the direction in which she fled.

She had friends in the partial clouds, and in the flatness of the country around Berlin, which made it less perilous to fly low than it would have been in a rougher land. Besides that, there was the speed of her plane, and the fact that she was able to slip off at last through the clouds in a direction she was not expected to take. But there was a time before that when she must dodge like a mouse among pouncing cats, and the guns were loud in the summer night. After a time, she rose to an empty sky. The moon was full overhead, the clouds a silver carpet below.

She looked down where the silver floor had a black tear. She saw sea. How swiftly she must have come! She had been flying due north. Now she turned some points to the west. After all, she would have time enough! There were still two hours before dawn. And the speedometer showed that in an hour she had traversed nearly 400 miles. She wrote now, as he had told her to do.

It had been the security of Air Marshal Zweiss that his plane was built to a design, and painted with signs that were special to him, and which were known to all who took the ways of the air. He had flown like a wasp whose golden bands make sure that the greediest starling, the swiftest swallow, will pass it by. But that security would be surely gone. It had become the one plane that would be sought in every land where the Eagles preyed and the Cross fled. Its conspicuous design and colouring made its peril more. Its security, apart from its speed, must be that it had come to a lonely sky.

When she had finished writing, the Scandinavian coast lay behind, dark and high beneath the edge of the coming dawn. The Shetlands were dimly seen on the left. The Faroes would be straight ahead. This was where she should be. She flew high, and began to circle widely, as a dove will do when it seeks a sign of its distant home.

Soon, out of the south, a plane came. To a close, interior view it would have been clear that it had been built in another land. It had different engines from hers. But to an outer view, at a distance across the skies, it had the same colours, the same shape. It had, in fact, been built to imitate that of Air Marshal Zweiss to specifications he had supplied. They were the two planes, in a world at war, which, from different causes, could fly safely in any sky: or could have done till today.

From the oncoming plane Imogen Lister looked out at that which she had not expected to see. Eustace, who had been trained to something better than the digging of Wolverhampton's mines, was at her side.

Here they had come, twice a week, to be met about half the times by the two who flew from Berlin, and who would drop a letter to them through the air. But it had been understood that, when Armageddon's battle would be near, Steele would take a last flight with Palestine as his goal, having done all he could by that time at Berlin, and intending to put the knowledge he had gained of the Russo-German forces and dispositions at the service of the Christian allies. But apparently that time had not yet come.

Imogen flew on. She came close. Almost too close; for the plane she met was not handled with the skill that she was accustomed to meet. Seeing that Perdita was in the pilot's cabin alone, she drew somewhat farther away, with watchful eyes, and hands ready on the controls.

By the side of Richard Steele she would have flown as closely, as confidently, as two swallows with brushing wings. But she saw that she must act now with a different care. Falling back, she dipped, and flew well under the German plane. The second time she did this Eustace took the letter that came down on its trailing rope.

Seeing that it had been secured, Perdita lost no time. She knew that she should be far to the south and east while the morning was still young. She turned to make speed on her backward course. She waved a hand, and saw her greeting returned by those who must be the last friends she would ever see.

Eustace had taken the open sheets from the wallet in which they had been enclosed. His eyes ran quickly over the lines of Perdita's somewhat emphatic script. He said to his companion: "You must get the utmost speed that you can. There is a great mine in Palestine under our lines." Imogen nodded in reply. Her hands moved quickly, releasing power.

Eustace looked at the disappearing plane. Flying higher, faster, than they, it was already a mere speck in the cloudless heights. He saw the difference of human fate. For themselves, the doubtful hope of life and happiness, though the world might fall, in a married life which had just commenced. For one who flew on another course, as he had read enough to perceive, a sure death that she must not shun.

It was four hours later that a German patrol sighted Air Marshal Zweiss's plane flying southwest over the Black Forest, which was a foolish direction for it to take. At the wireless call, the chasing planes rose for its destruction, far and near, upon every side. They knew that a reward of 20,000 marks had been broadcast for the crew that should bring it down.

It was handled badly, as by a pilot who did not know the exact consequences of what she did, but for a time its blundering speed enabled it to avoid its foes, dashing now here, now there, as it was headed off from the way that it had foolishly sought to go.

It was over Constance that the end came. As it approached, it descended somewhat from the altitude it had kept, as though it would have sought some refuge between the mountains that surround the lake. There was a fighter on its rear, firing at a long range, and two swift single-seaters coming obliquely across its front.

Perdita looked down. Her speed was over 300 miles an hour. The lake was now not more than half a mile below. She was tired, and became aware that she had lost the fear she had felt before. She thought: "I have heard it said it is instant death. They will say how clumsy I am, which is what he wished. In an instant, if I delay, it will be too late."

Foolishly, she preferred water to land upon which to die.

The plane turned too steeply as it avoided those which were closing upon its course. It dived, but not so that a good pilot might not have straightened it out, which it seemed she was unable to do.

The lake rushed upward...was very near....

CHAPTER XLI.

STEELE came back to the Council Chamber wondering what he would have to meet, and met nothing at all.

Discussion went on, as it was likely to do among those of whom some would remain in Berlin and others fly to Aleppo on the next day, but without reference to the charge that Admiral Klein had made.

It was a development that he could not tell himself that he had foreseen, for he recognized that von Teufel's actions would be incalculable to any human foresight, yet he was not greatly surprised, nor reassured.

Had it been a false move to send Perdita away? He thought not. For what else could he have done? How else, being under the suspicion which, at the best, would not be entirely and instantly lifted away, could he have made sure that the vital information would have been sent? He might have fled with her, of course. But next to the importance of getting it out was that of concealing, or at the least leaving a great doubt of, whether this had been done.

For if it were certainly known that the existence of the great mine were in process of being betrayed, would it not be instantly sprung, even though it might not be as ready as would be preferred, nor the time as good? But if there were nothing more than a little doubt, would it not be allowed to remain, that it might be used to so much greater effect on the later day? So he had thought at first, and he thought still.

But he saw that the course of the event was natural enough. Suspicion against himself might be stirred or stilled, but proof would be more difficult to reach. He could imagine that von Teufel, after probing all that the Admiral had to allege, had definitely put it aside. He could imagine more easily that he would be closely watched while further inquiries were made. He could imagine that von Teufel would discuss it with him alone, still having a will to trust, though with a disturbed mind. Knowing von Teufel, he could more easily imagine worse things.

The Council had not been sitting more than half an hour when it was interrupted by that which it was for von Teufel to know. He read the paper which was laid before him. His voice was harsh with anger as he looked up to say: "Zweiss, here is something more that you will explain! The woman who is not a spy has just escaped in your own plane. Did you know she could handle, and had access to, that? We shall not let her get far!"

Steele heard this with a sharp fear which made it easy to look the part which he had to play. If they had been so watchful, so instant upon her track, would she be equal to getting clear? And, if not, he had lost not only their lives, but all else, something at least of which might have been saved had he gone with her.

"I am sorry to hear that," he said. "She is a scared fool. I should say it will be little difference whether you catch her or not. She will wreck the plane."

Von Teufel was still not sure, but he did not think that Zweiss could have meant her to get away, at which it seemed sure that she would not succeed. (As to which he would have been right had she taken a western or southern course, as she was expected to do.) It did not seem sense that he should have remained and have let her go.

"Why," von Teufel asked again, "will you say she has done that?"

"That is easily said. I questioned her when I got back, as I was likely to do. I thought her innocent, as I still incline. But I must have scared her more than I meant. Anyway, it is done now. It was the act of a fool. You may say that Admiral Klein had his way with her."

Admiral Klein looked up at the challenge. He said: "She was not much. I was not aiming at her."

Steele saw that he was of the same mind, whatever others might have resolved.

"It is possible," von Hoffmann said temperately, "that she may have feared the sentence by which she had been condemned before."

Steele saw that he had a friend here, which was to say one who thought him true to the German cause. He would be none if the truth were shown nor would he go far on a doubtful road, being one who thought first for himself; and last also, more often than not. Still, these remarks made it easier to guess how the discussion had gone.

Von Teufel said no more, letting the talk resume where it had been broken off. He concluded that, let other matters be as they might, the girl (confessing her own guilt in the act) had made a separate effort to get away. It did not increase or reduce his doubt of the Air Marshal's good faith. In fact, it made no difference at all. Had he been sure of his treason to him, he would have suffered no common death.

Steele looked at von Teufel, wondering what was in his mind, but having ceased greatly to care. If she had got away, they had won, and though there might be little to hope, there was surely less to regret. If she had not—well, they had done what they could, and the game was lost. He must leave it at that.

He looked at von Teufel with the prescience of those who are close to death, and he thought that the tyrant's end was not far. He could not foresee how, when the coming battle would be at its height on the seventh day, he would break down from a small physical cause, so that he who would own the earth would be unable to swallow a mouthful of solid food; but he saw the futility, the smallness, of all that von Teufel was set to do, the vanity of supposing that there is another road than that of service to lasting power.

He looked round at those who bickered or boasted of what they were near to do, and they had the faces of ghosts rather than men, being under a doom that they did not guess. The Council was rising now.

He went out with such a quiet and confident mien that some who had watched fearfully for the storm to burst in destruction of either Admiral Klein or him thought that there was one whom even von Teufel could not disturb. Were they to see another revolution, another sudden transfer of power?

Steele entered his waiting car. It ran swiftly and well till it was near to his own gate, when a tyre burst. A man came to the window, saying that there was another car at hand that the Air Marshal could use. He pulled open the door, inviting him to alight.

Steele was already out of the opposite door. He laughed: "I had not thought he would be so crude." Automatic in hand, he sank quickly on to the step. He saw a dozen figures closing upon him. The street became loud with shots, and the darkness was streaked with fire.

ABOUT THE AUTHOR

SYDNEY FOWLER WRIGHT (1874-1965) penned over seventy volumes of science fiction, fantasy, classic mysteries, historical novels, poetry, and non-fiction, many of them being published by the Borgo Press Imprint of Wildside Press. Please visit his website at:

www.sfw.org